ORCHARD BOOKS

First published in Great Britain in 2017 by The Watts Publishing Group

1 3 5 7 9 8 6 4 2

A CIP catalogue record for this book is available from the British Library.

ISBN 978 1 40834 512 2

Typeset in Helvetica Neue by Avon DataSet Ltd, Bidford-on-Avon, Warwickshire

Printed and bound in Great Britain by Clays Ltd, St Ives plc

The paper and board used in this book are made from wood from responsible forests.

MIX
Paper from
responsible sources
FSC® C104740

Orchard Books
An imprint of Hachette Children's Group
Part of The Watts Publishing Group Limited
Carmelite House
50 Victoria Embankment
London EC4Y 0DZ

An Hachette UK Company
www.hachette.co.uk

www.hachettechildrens.co.uk

BOYWATCHING

SEASON THREE

CHLOE
BENNET

ORCHARD

To my friends. Who like me,
even though they know me

Also by Chloe Bennet

Boywatching
Boywatching: Up Close

⇉1⇇

No More Mr Nice Guy?

'Why would you DO that to him?' The voice of Sally, my BFF, rose to a pitch that I never knew it could reach. She looked at me, eyes and mouth all round in perfect Os of astonishment.

'I would DO that,' I said sternly, 'because I am angry, and he is a louse.' I looked across the room at the louse. He was tall, with dark wavy hair and the world's most expressive eyebrows. Even gazing in horror at the mess I'd made of his jeans by accidentally-on-purpose spilling hot chocolate down them, he looked beautiful.

As if it weren't enough for Mark to stand me up on New Year's Eve... To give me more terrible news, today, on New Year's Day, was too much. Especially as New Year's Day is my birthday.

'First he tells me he can't be with me on New Year's

Eve because he has to go and see some family friend,' I said to Sally, 'and now he tells me that the family friend is actually a French girl he's doing an exchange with ALL NEXT TERM. So he's going to be in France, some place near Dijon-or-wherever, staying with this *girl*, for ten weeks. Ten weeks! And he tells me this on my birthday, at my birthday party. So yes. A louse. And he's lucky it was only chocolate.'

Sally was now looking at me with a very worried expression on her face. Ever since I had properly and absolutely got together with the love of my life, one Mark Anderson, she had held me up as the ultimate real-life Elizabeth finding her real-life Mr Darcy. I was, she said, the shining example of How It Could All End Happily, and it gave her hope that she and Rob – the crush of her life – would end up together too. Obviously in Sally World nothing must go wrong between me and Mark, so she clearly wasn't liking the look of us at that moment.

'But—' said Sally.

'There isn't one,' I interrupted her.

'But look at him,' said Sally. I looked. As he used a napkin to de-chocolate himself, Mark was actually looking – cross, I think, might be the word. But being cross made him look even more handsome, and me feel like I needed to go over and say sorry. Even though I was very angry and sad.

Mark frowned as he saw me come over. But then he must have noticed that I had my Abject Apology face on because he seemed to soften a bit.

'It's not *actually* the other side of the world,' Mark said, looking down at me through narrowed eyes. Which would have been a bit scary had he not had the ghost of a grin and the beginnings of a dimple showing. 'And it's not *actually* for ever.' He still sounded cross but the grin was now unmistakeable.

Unmistakeable and also a bit patronising.

I looked up at Mark's crinkly smiling eyes, trying hard not to be distracted by the way his wavy dark hair fell over one side of his face, and how his right eyebrow lifted up in such an interestingly intelligent way. 'It's my birthday,' I said, trying hard to keep the quaver out of my voice. 'You're supposed to be making a fuss of me. But instead you're telling me you're going off to *France* with another *girl*.'

Mark reached out his hand to take mine. I'm ashamed to say that I snatched my hand away from his. 'It's my *birthday*,' I said again, with a trace of petulance.

'I know it is,' said Mark patiently (and still quite

patronisingly). 'Look, I'm only going away for a few weeks. A French exchange is part of the course, and it's not my fault there's a girl in the house I'm staying in.'

The kitchen was full of my family: Mum, Gran and Ghastly Ralph (my stepfather), plus Sally and my other two best friends, Gemma and Amy. Fortunately, everyone except my watchful BFF seemed to be too busy talking to each other and helping themselves to large chunks of my special 'Happy Birthday, Chloe, 15 Today' birthday cake to notice the birthday girl getting on her high horse. (Although even in the heat of the moment I couldn't help noticing that Sally had taken such a large piece of cake that she had most of 'Happy' on her plate.)

'Come on,' Mark said. 'Open the rest of your presents and don't let your mum see you getting cross.'

Oh, but Mr Darcy was so wise for his age. Only seventeen, but still capable of taking me off the high horse and back to being a proper person.

I looked over at Mum. She was smiling and nodding at something Gran was telling her. Genetically speaking and in point of fact Gran was her mother. But it was hard to believe that someone so acid could have given birth to someone as sweet as my mum. Just looking at the scene, and even without the subtitles, it was clear that Gran was finding fault with something (why break the habit of a lifetime?). But Mum looked pale and serene as she carried on smiling. Pale because of the effects of her treatment – Mum had been very ill, actually was still very ill – but she was really brave, and never complained, not even when acid Gran was on the warpath about Mum having bought The Wrong Sort of Toilet Paper.

I went over to the table, where there were still two more wrapped presents sitting among the unwrapped ones.

I'd been (mostly) very spoilt this birthday, and was pleased that everyone had lived up to their own reputations, present-wise. Mum had given me a state-of-the-art alarm clock. I'm sure she meant it in the nicest possible way, and perhaps it would actually be helpful not to oversleep quite as often as I do.

Sally had given me a necklace with a ladybird charm, attached to a card that said 'friendship is a knot that cannot be untied'. Which I thought was incredibly cheesy, so I can't explain why there were tears in my eyes when I undid the wrapping and saw them.

Ghastly Ralph, the ghastly stepfather who never ceased to live up to his name, gave me a card with a crumpled five-pound note in it. The card said 'happy fourteenth birthday', which actually tells you most of what you need to know about Ralph.

And then Gran gave me a *Pride and Prejudice* colouring-in book. Now, my adoration of Jane Austen is famous and knows no bounds. But what I love about Jane Austen – being someone who wants to be an award-winning writer when she grows up – is her way with words, and stories, and characters. Why would I want to fill in a picture of a girl in a Regency dress with a red crayon? Or a blue one, or a green one? I mean, why would I want to do that? At any level? (Is what I didn't dare say to Gran when I unwrapped the parcel.)

Amy, sweet Amy who could never say a mean word about anyone even if she wanted to, which of course she didn't, had given me a handmade photo frame with a picture of the four of us inside it. Not just sweetly but also very cleverly she'd managed to find a photo that didn't just have Gemma looking great (Gemma always looks a bit like a supermodel) but us too. There we all were, clean hair, spot-free, and smiling in the way you do when you've just been told you look like a million dollars. The frame was made of cardboard, which added to its charm. (Amy's parents were good people like she was (this is where genetics had got it right) but they never seemed to have much money, so cardboard had a longer life in their household than in most people's.)

And then Gemma, the supermodelly one. Gemma was an original and a law unto herself. With her amazing looks (cheekbones, hair, figure, everything just like you'd order off the Looks Menu), her rich father, and the long list of boys who would give their eye teeth (whatever an eye tooth is) to go out with her. And even though her mother ran away with someone else, and didn't see Gemma for eight years, she was a great lady and they now had a great relationship.

So Gemma seemed to have it all sorted. And yet, and yet…maybe no fifteen-year-old girl has it all sorted. And if this one did, I don't think she'd be such a good friend of mine.

I approached the present table. I picked up one of the last two parcels, wrapped in thick gold paper. I thought, that would be Gemma. No point in using ordinary paper if you've got gold paper. I think she was such a conspicuous spender because she hated her father, Merv, so much that she never missed an opportunity to spend his money. (See what I mean? You can't be sorted if you actually hate your actual parent quite as much as Gemma did Merv.)

Inside the layers of gold was a box of lip glosses. Take your lips from dull to radiant; achieve that silky trendsetting smile with a unique tip for mistake-free application it said.

I think the news of Mark's trip to France had made me a bit acid and bitter. I should just have loved the luxurious things; instead I thought, 'She thinks I'm dull and can't put make-up on properly'.

So it was only when I opened the other parcel that I started to feel better. Inside was a perfect pair of tiny silver earrings, one of which was a little silver stick boy, and the other a little silver stick girl.

As I looked down at them in my hand, I realised I was starting to have a slightly goofy smile on my face.

I looked up at Mark. 'Thank you, they're lovely.'

Maybe I was going to have a happy birthday after all.

Or maybe not.

The person who irked me was Mr Darcy himself. ('Irk' is a new favourite word. There's something about its shortness, and the things it rhymes with – berk springs to mind – that make it a particularly pithy way of expressing displeasure.) 'Gotta go, Chloe,' he said, pushing his hand through his beautiful wavy hair and making himself look ever more dreamy in the process. 'You know.'

I suppose I did know. Mark had a date with his mother – who was having her birthday dinner that night. Needless to say, when I first discovered that Mark's mother and I shared a birthday, I had got thoroughly over-excited. After all, I had thought, if this wasn't A Sign that Mark and I were meant to be together, I didn't know what was.

But now I was starting to think that, much though I loved his mother – no really, I really do – it was going to be a bit irritato to have to share her son every birthday.

Still, I was grown up enough to smile understandingly and put my face up in a pointedly hopeful kiss-me kind of fashion.

For a split second. I thought that maybe I was going to look very silly with my face pointing upwards and nothing much happening. But then he bent down and gave me a lovely long slow kiss. I half wanted it to be much longer and slower, except I suddenly felt terribly aware of Gran's horrible pink spectacles pointing in my direction.

I knew Gran thought I was Much Too Young to have a boyfriend, and I could feel her disapproval boring into me. It was enough to take the edge off the moment, I can tell you.

I watched Mark pick up his jacket and head over to Mum to give her a goodbye hug. He did both these things beautifully: Mark had a sinewy way of moving (I think I mean 'sinewy') that drew your eye. He had picked up his coat with one perfect movement, smiling over at Mum as he did so.

Mum was devoted to Mark, as well she should have been, and it was lovely to see how kind Mark was to her. I knew it wasn't just that he felt sorry for what she was going through (chemo, for breast cancer, but I tried not to say those words out loud too often) but he was properly fond of her.

I liked that we liked each other's mothers.

What a pity I couldn't like Mum's mother so much. As soon as Mark had gone, Gran came up to me and said, 'Now, young lady. It may be a certain person's birthday, but that doesn't mean you shouldn't help your mother tidy up before you go out.'

I noticed that a biscuit crumb trembled from her lower lip as she spoke. A nice granddaughter would have pointed this out, but I am not that granddaughter.

'Of course I'll tidy up, Gran,' I said through gritted teeth.

My birthday was on a Sunday night, not normally a Going Out day, but it was the last weekend of the Christmas holiday, so we were all going out as much as we could before the horrors of homework and other evils associated with full-time education began again on Thursday.

'Hey, Chloe,' said a voice behind me. Amy – smiling sweetly, and carrying a large pile of dirty plates. 'Where shall I put these?'

Honestly, when they were handing out saintliness genes Amy must have been first in the queue.

'Come on, Chloe,' said Gemma. 'Time to go and see what the boys are up to.' Not so saintly, but still a friend who had our entertainment at heart – she knew that at least three of the boys who'd give their eye teeth to go out with her were down the road at Papa Pietro's Perfect Pizza Palace. (A restaurant that made up in wordage what it lacked in atmosphere.)

Full of cake and the sort of fizzy drink that comes at a price and with a health warning (which sounds like champagne, but is actually lemonade), we left the oldsters to their own brand of fun and headed off to the pizzeria. Because there is of course no such thing as being so full of cake that there isn't room for a pizza.

Papa Pietro had decided to base his perfect pizzas pretty much next door to Sally's house. Which was very handy when it came to moving seamlessly on from the pizzas to the ice cream. Sally's mum, Liv, was very partial to ice cream, and kept a giant stock of chocolate chip mint fudge caramel cookies pistachio – or whatever flavour we fancied – ice cream. Because if cake makes room for pizza, so too does pizza make room for ice cream.

Papa P was also a dab hand when it came to employing handsome waiters. His were definitely the best looking in the world (not that I've actually done the research to prove that), plus they were very good at making us feel grown-up and beautiful. And we liked feeling both of those things very much indeed.

As we opened the door a blast of hot air and the noise of a hundred shouty people hit us in the face. Outside it was a bit of a thick socks and winter coat sort of day; inside it seemed to be more of a beachwear and sandals sort of day.

Before I could start to tell the others something about my theories about Papa P wasting fossil fuel on making us very hot in the middle of a freezing winter, Sally gave a loud yelp. The sort of yelp you might give if someone had trodden on your toe, kissed you and slapped you in the face all in one go.

'Look,' she squawked in the general direction of my ear. 'Look over there, by the window.'

I looked. All I could see was a large group of mostly boys who were a bit older than us, with a few girls who looked anywhere between fifteen and twenty-three. (Which means probably about our age, but with better make-up skills.)

Sally was by now hopping up and down on one foot – not a good look, I thought but didn't say.

The three of us peered more intently at the crowd of people.

Ah. Now I could see the problem. In the middle of the mostly boys side of the table was one Rob – a guy in Year Twelve who played football, the drums and the fool, not always in that order. He was a nice sort of guy who had spent quite a bit of the last year being nice to Sally. Which made Sally think that they were practically engaged. At least that's what she thought some of the time. At other times, she was convinced that he didn't truly appreciate the real Sally and was quite likely to run off with someone else.

This was one of those times. Because Rob was sitting next to a short but lively girl, who was staring into his eyes and talking brightly and excitedly. He seemed to be hanging on her every word.

And this wasn't just any old short but lively girl, it was Maggie. The Queen Beeyatch herself. The only girl in our school who had an honours degree in making your life a misery. The only girl who could tap into your greatest fear, make you feel small and meaningless and then get the whole of the rest of the class to laugh at you. Half the school lived in fear of being on the sharp end of her viperish tongue, and the other half sucked up to, hung out with, trailed along behind the Queen Beeyatch…for fear of being on the sharp end of her viperish tongue.

I'm sure other schools have class act psycho-bullies, but I'd put QB Maggie up against any of them, any time.

'Our table's over here,' said Amy into my other ear, seemingly oblivious to the drama going on. And we followed one of the very, very handsome waiters to the far corner of the restaurant where there was our special birthday table for four.

It took Gemma a while to follow us because on the way she had to say hello to a tall, skinny boy with long greasy blond hair and wristbands all the way up to his elbow. Jezza.

Jezza was the lead singer in a band called Shedz, the band Rob played the drums in. He really fancied himself, possibly even more than he fancied Gemma which was, to be fair, a lot. He was Scottish, had a very short fuse, and thought I was a pedant because I once told him off for confusing 'imply' and 'infer'. (OK, he might have a point there. I knew it was a mistake at the time; some people just don't care as much about language as I do. But I digress…)

Eventually we were sitting at our own table, and able to survey the scene. Sally couldn't take her eyes off the big table by the window.

'Whatever's the matter?' Amy asked her once we'd sat down. Amy was looking particularly pretty and in the pink in every sense. The pink of her tracksuit showed off the pink of her radiant complexion – no need for luxury boxes of make-up for her. And this pinkness, it must be said, is probably entirely due to the amount of time she spends running round a race track – not everyone's idea of fun, but certainly hers because one day (they say) she's going to be running seriously, like seriously in the Olympics.

I'm sure she'll still be friends with us when she's famous.

'What's the *matter*?' said Sally, eyes wide open in disbelief. 'Can't you *see*? Over there by the window? My whole life is falling to bits. It's a sacastrophe.'

'Catastrophe,' I said quietly. Because even though you know it's not good to be a pedant, sometimes you've just got to help people get things right.

'That nightmare COW,' Sally was saying. 'She's just *got* to make everyone's life miserable, hasn't she?' She dug her finger viciously into a bowl of salt as she spoke. 'I mean,' she went on, waving salt all over the table, 'can't she get her teeth into someone her own size?'

'Calm down,' said Gemma, tossing back her long shiny hair with a dramatic gesture that I couldn't help feeling was meant to attract the attention of the entire room. In fact, looking around, it seemed to be working. 'Maggie's just trying to make someone jealous. Bet you anything. She doesn't do that sort of full-body attention thing if she isn't up to something.'

Sally was now in middle of tearing her napkin into tiny pieces with an expression of fury that seemed to be doing a good job of keeping all the waiters away from us.

She looked up from the scene of destruction. 'What do you mean?'

'That boy sitting on her other side,' said Gemma

narrowing her eyes in the direction of the QB. 'That really handsome boy with the thick blond hair and the blue shirt that shows off his tan.' I could tell that Gemma was warming to her subject. 'See? Looks a little bit like Tom Hiddleston.'

We all looked where she was looking. 'Ah,' said Sally, absent-mindedly gathering all the little bits of napkin and piles of salt together. 'I see what you mean.' She wiped the pile of napkin bits carefully and slowly on to the floor, not taking her eyes off the distant table.

'The point is,' said Gemma, 'that he is not taking any notice of Maggie. And Maggie isn't liking it. That's the only reason she's making a fuss of Rob.'

Sally looked confused. I think she was uncertain whether to be relieved, or cross that Gemma seemed to think Rob wasn't fanciable.

This was all getting rather complicated. Plus I was starting to think that Tom Hiddleston was taking all the attention away from me and my birthday. I managed to catch the eye of a handsome waiter, who came over looking charming, and then a bit less charming when he saw Sally's artfully constructed pile of rubbish on the floor.

I tried to distract him by ordering my favourite pizza

very slowly and politely. A mushroom pizza with extra mushrooms. Not hard to make. Not expensive. I am a cheap date.

Sally, her thick red hair hanging down over her face, was now studying the menu as she worked out which pizza represented the best value for money, and the fewest calories. Very rarely do the two coincide, I could have told her.

By the time we'd worked out the perfect Papa Pietro's pizza for each of us, and Handsome Waiter had gone off to make our dreams come true, the big table was standing up and getting ready to go. We were in a dark corner, and I was quite happy about that, since none of them seemed to see us, and I felt I didn't need the drama of the QB, Tom Hiddleston and Rob coming between me and my birthday.

Once the pizzas had arrived there was something very comforting about focusing on trying to cut them up into the right-sized slices. That way we didn't have to dwell on trickier problems like who was chatting up whose boyfriend...

'The thing is,' said Sally, lying on her bed and looking

down at her phone with an expression of concentration I knew only too well. (Sally's relationship with her phone was intimate, unchanging, constant.) 'The thing is that maybe Mark going away is going to be a good thing. You know, like they say about absence being such sweet sorrow and parting making the heart grow.'

Usually I would comment on how interesting it was that Sally's misquotations (and if there was a quote to be misquoted you could usually rely on Sally) often ended up meaning the same as the original. But this time I was too busy wondering what was going on downstairs, where there seemed to be a lot of shouting happening.

Sally lives with her two younger twin brothers, Harris and Jock, and her mother Liv. This in itself would not be so very unusual – people often do live with their mothers and brothers – were it not for the fact that the other member of the household was her brand new father, who had recently replaced the gardener.

Literally. Sally's father had disappeared in mysterious circumstances almost before she could remember, had been temporarily replaced by a handsome gardener called Patrick, and now her real father had mysteriously reappeared. Something about spying, the Middle East and leaving behind an ex-mistress. Liv had seemed on the whole happy to have him back, but judging by the shoutyness downstairs she might have been changing her mind.

'What's going on, Sal?' I said to the one on the bed with the phone. 'It sounds like an episode of that American TV thing where everyone shouts at each other. You know, the one where the more closely related everyone is the more they seem to hate each other and the louder they shout.'

'I don't know,' said Sally, slightly grumpily. We had got back from Pietro's Pizzeria, leaving Amy and Gemma to be driven home by Merv in his shiny new sports car, and we were now full of pistachio caramel ice cream.

Perhaps Sally's grumpiness had something to do with feeling sick after three lots of ice cream (she had plumped – her word – for the 'most thinning' pizza, which seemed to make her think she was entitled to several hundred extra ice-cream calories).

Or perhaps she was just brooding on the fickleness of The Boy, having seen Rob appear to flirt with the most horrible girl in the school.

I didn't have any more time to dwell on the mystery myself, as we heard a loud thump coming from downstairs. And then silence.

'Oh my god,' I said, horrified by the sudden silence and the loudness of the bang. 'She's killed him. Or he's killed her. Or maybe it's the twins. What has happened?'

Sally gave a tiny little burp and carried on looking at her phone. 'The twins are asleep and James' (this was her newly returned dad, who she hadn't yet got used to calling 'Dad') 'isn't shouting any more. So it must be Mum.'

She looked up at me. 'I should think she's probably fallen downstairs.'

This was a difficult new development. I had thought that Mysterious James coming home to Liv was the beginning of a happy ever after, and that it would mean that Liv would break off her close relationship not just with Patrick-the-gardener but also with Mr Pinot Grigio. This was Liv's chosen form of refreshment: an Italian white wine that most people drank by the small glass, while Liv preferred the large bucket.

'Shouldn't we go and see if she's all right?' I said, even though I hadn't the faintest idea what we'd do if she wasn't.

'She'll be fine,' said Sally with her special world-weary voice. And, indeed, at that very moment we heard Liv's voice again – shouting in just the same tone, as if she'd only paused for the commercial break.

A low, grumbling male voice answered from another room. You couldn't make out the words, but it didn't exactly sound loving.

'So what I mean about Mark is this,' Sally said, obviously not going to be distracted from whatever it was that she meant. 'He goes away for ten weeks to live with this girl—'

'He's not actually living with a girl!' I said, sort of outraged at the way Sally made it sound. 'He's doing a French exchange with family friends of his mother's, and the exchange person just happens to be a girl. Plus, last time I heard, apparently the girl, Cecile, is the most incredible tomboy. Like, very short hair and plays rugby. Also, there are two brothers. And he's going to be studying at the *Lycée* most of the time. And she studies different subjects. So he'll hardly ever see her. In fact, they'll be ships that pass in the night. I expect they won't spend more than two days in each other's company. I expect,' I added, my voice trailing away a little.

'Well, that's OK, isn't it?' said Sally. 'You'll be fine then, and you'll FaceTime each other, and it'll be all lovey dovey when you get back. It's all right for some.' There was bitterness in Sally's voice. Also in pretty well everything she had said ever since we'd left the pizzeria.

'I think you've got into a state about Rob,' I said, absent-mindedly drawing a picture of Gran on Sally's Chemistry pad. (There were no other marks on it, Sally having very little time or inclination for Chemistry, so I reckoned I might as well make use of some perfectly good paper.)

'Maybe what we've got to do is make sure that Tom Hiddleston or whoever he is takes a bit of an interest in the QB so that she lays off Rob.' I finished drawing some complicated curlicues on the edges of Gran's Dame Edna Everage spectacles. 'And then Rob will start missing you, and you'll feel like making a plan to see him before we go back to "Queen Misery's" on Thursday.'

Our school, Queen Mary's School for Girls, wasn't actually that full of misery, but at this time of the year, early January, after Christmas, in the cold, nothing much to look forward to apart from some practice exams and long dark nights, well, it didn't seem that cheerful a prospect.

'OK,' said Sally. 'How's all that going to happen?'

As I put a final black mole on Gran's chin, I noticed that everything had gone quiet downstairs again. I wondered if that meant Liv and Sally's new/old dad were kissing and making up, or whether one or the other of them had just passed out.

'We're going to ask Charlie,' I said. 'He knows everyone and everything, and he's bound to know who Tom Hiddleston is, and where he's come from. We'll make him one of our Major Boy Watching Projects for the term.'

Charlie was the boy in our lives who scored every possible point on our 'Boy Watching' (© *Chloe Bennet,* ™ *Pending*) charts. These charts and their system of points and unpoints for boys' good and bad looks, behaviour and interest in us, had been invaluable to us in the last year. We had learned so many lessons about The Boy, and how he thought and behaved, and – most of the time – we'd managed to put this new science to good use.

Well, I thought I had. Sally thought she had. And Amy certainly thought she had, because Charlie was, literally, her darling. They were The Ones for each other, without question. Charlie was tall, fluffy-haired, kind and handsome, and seemed to adore, no, DID adore Amy. So much so that he actually followed her all over the country when she had athletics trials, and training and all those sorts of things. And some of these sorts of things went on and on, and sometimes in the most out-of-the-way places. Being the boyfriend of a near-professional athlete was a real Devotion Tester. The rest of us thought there couldn't possibly be anything more boring than watching someone run round and round an athletics track, but actually Charlie seemed to like it. And that could only be because he liked Amy so much.

Anyway, Charlie, with his fluffy hair and crinkly eyes, knew everyone, and if he didn't he soon could. So, I thought, with his help we could get to know Tom H, point him in the direction of the QB, thus leaving Rob to continue to be the happy object of Sally's adoration. It would be a sort of Advanced Boy Watching; it would teach us some lessons. Plus, it could help our friend.

A text message from Ghastly Ralph arrived as I put the finishing touches to Gran's perm.

'pm esu yjrtr om 3'

Ralph never bothered to put his glasses on before operating his very old-fashioned phone. Luckily I could work out this was a one-letter-to-the-right day, and he was telling me he'd be picking me up in two minutes.

We went downstairs to try to find Liv to say goodbye and thank you. But there was no sign of either of the adults or either of the twins, so I said goodbye to Sally and let myself out of the front door and into the battered estate car that smelt of stale beer and Ralph.

I thought that on the whole it had been a good birthday; all the right people had made a fuss of me, I was full – very full – of all my favourite foods, and at least there were three more days before we had to get back to school and its horrible History...and Physics... and Geography...and Chemistry... There was just time to paint my toenails before bed, and then Monday was going to be a busy day.

⇒ 2 ⇐

The Next Big Thing

I woke up in the morning to the sound of bullets ricocheting through my bedroom door. This made total sense as only seconds before I had been running for my life from dozens of handsome Italian waiters who were waving torn white napkins and guns shaped like lipsticks.

For a second I lay frozen, in the sort of S-shape that I usually form when I'm properly asleep, but wondering if I wouldn't be safer if I ducked down underneath the duvet so the gun-toting waiters couldn't see me.

Half a second after that I woke up properly and heard the rumble of Ghastly Ralph's voice, as he banged on the door to wake me up.

'Eight o'clock, Chloe,' he said gruffly. 'Not your birthday any more. Your turn to do the shopping and get your mother's breakfast. I'm off to work.'

I rolled stiffly over to the other side of the bed, the side that wasn't blocked by the oversize wardrobe with the doors that didn't quite open, and I stood up slowly. (What is it about eating too much that makes your muscles ache the following day?)

'OK,' I shouted through the door. I noticed that the duvet and the sheets were covered in puzzlingly uneven pale pink lines. I wondered vaguely why Mum had chosen sheets that looked as if someone had smeared nail varnish all over them. And then I looked down at my toes and saw that all the carefully applied varnish of the previous night had mysteriously disappeared.

There wasn't time to worry about how I was going to cover up this latest crime, so I threw the duvet back down to cover the incriminating evidence and made my way to the House of Methane, aka the bathroom.

The methane content of the bathroom is probably familiar to those who have the misfortune to share a bathroom with the male of the species. In fact, our bathroom was only Half a House of Methane at the moment because the other male who usually lived with us, my brother Steve, was away learning how to be a soldier – much to Mum's horror.

I guess, like most mums, she naturally assumes that her only son is almost certainly going to be somehow the sole focus of the enemy's displeasure. Even though the chances of Steve actually being in any actual danger are extremely remote – after all, he's still at the marching-with-a-backpack-on-Welsh-mountains stage – mums are generally hard-wired to imagine the worst.

And anyway, it wasn't all bad. Steve's acne was clearing up, he seemed to be learning stuff, and he'd been definitely less irritating when we'd last seen him. Plus he was making some new friends which, if you're his sister, can only be a good thing, because the Boy Watching pool needs to be as wide and varied as possible. In fact, what's the point of having a spotty irritating older brother, if he doesn't bring back some interesting boys in uniform for you to inspect?

Obviously I am spoken for. Mark is definitely The One, even if he *is* going to abandon me for weeks at a time, but it always pays to have plenty of experience of the opposite sex, partly to make sure about 'The One' being the one, and also to provide us with good material for our favourite study: the science of Boy Watching. It is a difficult and imprecise science at the best of times, which is why you have to do so much of it.

But for now Steve wasn't there. That morning, there were no unpleasant odours, and everyone else was up, so I made the most of my fragrance-free time and spent a while inspecting The Eyebrows. Astonishing how often one could get up in the morning, having gone to bed with perfectly matched eyebrows, and suddenly discover that one was infinitely larger than the other and that both were crooked. All very puzzling.

This morning was one of those mornings. But as I reached into the cupboard for my tweezers, I saw some of the paraphernalia of Mum's treatment. Two packets of pills and a small syringe. The pills were neatly positioned side by side next to the syringe.

There was something so organised, so tidy about these medicines, as if they were the most important and central part of Mum's life; literally in every sense a lifeline. As I glanced at them I found myself catching my breath. It was all very well not saying the words 'breast cancer' and 'chemotherapy' out loud, but when you are unexpectedly reminded of something as painful as your mother being so ill the fact that it catches you by surprise makes it even worse.

I was just starting to feel thoroughly miserable – very sorry for Mum and very sorry for myself – when actual Mum knocked on the bathroom door.

'Someone to see you, love,' said Mum, sounding so cheerful and well that I instantly felt cheerful and well too.

'Coming,' I said, putting back the tweezers and shutting the door on the packets of pills.

I felt ready to do battle with the world as I came out of the bathroom, tossing my hair back in a Gemma sort of way. I did this quite a lot, even though my brown wavy hair didn't quite have the straight chestnut sheen that Gemma's had. But I reckoned I could at least practise the moves for when I found the right shampoo and the right hair straighteners.

Mum came out of the kitchen drying up the special Mother's Day mug that Steve had given her last year. ('You Are the Best Mum, Love from Name Here' it said. Steve hadn't realised that there was more than one stage to the creation of a personalised mug.) 'You'll never guess who it is,' she said, smiling. 'It's your favourite admirer.'

I heard a snuffling sound coming from the kitchen. For a minute I thought Gran's cold had come back – Gran's nose wasn't a very discreet organ and had a way of letting you hear exactly how uncomfortable it was feeling – and then I realised who it was.

Albert.

Albert was a rough-haired, rough-mannered little border terrier. He could sometimes fool people into thinking that he was extremely sweet because when he was asleep or begging for food he could bear more than a passing resemblance to a teddy bear.

In fact, he was really naughty, and rarely did what he was told. But I think this was just because he'd been very badly brought up by his owner, our downstairs neighbour Mr Underwood, who I think must have been very badly brought up himself. So no wonder Albert was programmed to disobey. I'd always felt that if Albert and I could just spend enough proper time together I would soon have had him behaving like a little gentleman.

'Mr Underwood has had to go to the police station, so I said he could leave Albert with us for the morning,' said Mum.

I was riveted at the thought of Mr U having to go to the police – what had he done? Offended public decency by going out in the street in his revolting dressing gown? (Mr U never seemed to wear anything else, and it certainly was revolting.) Been drunk in charge of a shopping trolley? Assaulted a traffic warden with a blunt instrument?

But before my imagination could get further carried away, I had to say hello to Albert. I could see he was safely tied up to a knob on the cooker, but he jumped up and down like crazy as I got nearer to him.

'Albert,' I cried, as I put my arms round him. 'You haven't been to see me for ages. How ARE you?' I don't know why it is that we ask dogs so many questions.

'What have you been up to, you bad boy?' I went on, because that's what you do when you're having a conversation with a dog. And then, 'What's that funny smell, Albert?' This time I was asking a question that I genuinely wanted to know the answer to. There was a strange burning smell. I looked round for Mum but she'd obviously decided that we needed to be left alone for our emotional reunion.

Ah. I saw what the problem was. 'Clever Albert,' I said to him. 'You've turned on the grill.' And the strange burning smell from the grill which Albert's twisted lead had somehow switched to 'on' now started to have a distinct whiff of old bacon to it. Which was making Albert even more overexcited.

I turned off the cooker, undid Albert and decided he could come with me for a proper walk when I did the shopping. All that old bacon smell was making him hysterical – much more noise and I knew Gran would be on the warpath.

I went to find Mum.

She was in Steve's old room which was now Gran's

room, and sitting on Steve's old bed that was now Gran's bed. Gran was sitting on Steve's special adjustable desk chair that Mum had bought him to help him pass his exams. (It didn't work.)

There was something surreal about seeing the older generations of Bennet women sitting on branded football products. Steve, being a dyed-in-the-wool fan of a Premier League football team whose name keeps on escaping me, had a room full of scarves and crests and posters. Even after it had been cleared out for Gran, it was still undeniably a shrine to football.

'Have you had breakfast, Mum?' I said. 'I thought I'd take Albert shopping, but if you want me to make you some tea I can do that first.'

'You'd best get that creature out of here before he disgraces himself,' said Gran before Mum could answer. Her pink spectacles were shaking with disgust as she looked at Albert – who for once was sitting quietly at my feet looking as if butter wouldn't melt.

However beautifully Albert behaved with Gran, I don't think she was ever likely to forgive him for the nip he'd once given her left ankle. We had tried to convince her that it was a mark of his affection, but Gran's mind was made up. Albert was a 'pest' and a 'nuisance'.

I exchanged a quick and secret smile with Mum and took the pest out of Gran's room.

Grabbing my phone, the shopping list and Mum's purse, Albert and I headed out of the front door, down the stairs and past Mr Underwood's/Albert's front door. Pausing only to wonder again what the police could possibly want with Mr U, we set off for the supermarket.

There was a coffee shop attached to the supermarket, which I always used to think was for boring old people, or people with babies in buggies, or sad people to sit outside with a cigarette…but I started to think about it completely differently when I suddenly got a text message from Mark that said, 'Hey you. Come to the CoCo-Coffee shop in 20. Someone I want you to meet! Mxxcxxcxxxxx'

Suddenly the world took on a merrier hue. Less boring-old-day-after-my-birthday Monday, and more the-world's-an-interesting-place sort of Monday.

Also, I loved being called 'you'.

And also I loved the huge number of XS, even if some of them *had* got a bit mixed up with the CS. (Of course, I couldn't resist trying to work out what number it would all make in roman numerals. Perhaps I am the geekiest person I know. 1,210, I reckoned.)

It was only five minutes' walk to the supermarket, so

Albert and I had time to go the long way round through the park. Even so, I was on a tight schedule, so I didn't let Albert off his string (Mr U's idea of a dog lead) as I didn't want to spend the morning running after an energetic terrier when I could be sitting in the CoCo-Coffee Shop with Mark.

So by the time I got to the supermarket and tied up my furry friend to the special dog pole outside the entrance, I only had about five minutes to do the actual shopping.

Albert was not impressed at being abandoned like this, and started to vent his fury on a pit bull and a German Shepherd tied to the same pole. For a minute I thought everything was going to go horribly wrong, and Albert would be eaten/flayed/beheaded, and I would be thrown into the police cells for irresponsible dog management.

But after a moment, the three dogs settled down to sniffing each other's bottoms, in the way that dogs do, and I thought it safe to leave them to it.

I rushed round the familiar aisles of the supermarket in minus no time at all. Years – well, two – of practice meant that I knew exactly where the sausages, the butter, the tea and the sliced bread were. And, yes, in case you're wondering, ours is indeed a household fuelled by processed food. I blame Ghastly Ralph, who loves his fry-ups and his instant toasties.

But at least instant food meant instant shopping, so I was heading towards the coffee shop with Albert and my bags of cholesterol within five minutes.

This time the dog pole which was outside CoCo-Coffee was unattached to any species of dog at all, so I tied Albert up in pride of place and decided to try not to worry about him.

On a slow Monday morning in January, CoCo-Coffee didn't seem to be doing much business. In among all seven of their customers it was easy to spot Mark at a table in the corner. He was deep in conversation with someone whose back was towards me. So I could only tell that he was male, fair haired – and would rather be playing ice hockey. At least, that's what it said on the back of his sweatshirt.

I approached with caution. Someone who would rather be playing ice hockey was probably sporty, outgoing and very possibly American. I could identify with none of these things, so I was relieved when Mark looked up, caught my eye and gave me one of his best make-you-melt-at-the-knees smiles.

I smiled back. I hoped it was the sort of smile that melted HIS knees, but had a feeling he had been too engrossed in talking to Hockey Boy to feel as romantic as I suddenly did.

'Hey, Chloe,' he said as he got up and gave me a brief hug. Now wasn't the time for a long hug, I did realise that, so why was I so disappointed not to be clinched and snogged and generally made to feel like the love interest in the happy ending of a film? Maybe that's the difference between girls and boys, I found myself thinking. Maybe a girl would go for the long hug if she felt like it whatever the circumstances, and...

My Boy Watching analysis was interrupted by the sudden realisation that Hockey Boy was none other than Tom Hiddleston. At least, I assumed he wasn't *actually* Tom Hiddleston, because it was highly unlikely that a major film star was having a quiet coffee in the middle of a supermarket coffee shop. But as I examined him more calmly, I thought we'd been right, he did look very like him.

'This,' Mark was saying to him as he put his arm round me (which felt very nice), 'is Chloe Bennet. And Chloe, this is Oscar.'

'Oscar' gave a brief smile, stood up, looked down at the table and held out his hand. Slightly taken aback, I shook the hand (it was a nice hand, warm and with long tapery fingers, a bit like a pianist's. Not that I had any experience of pianists).

The pianist still wasn't looking me in the eye, so I looked at Mark for some social guidance. Normally if you're introduced to someone, you start to get the hang of them by the way they look at you, but this particular boy seemed to find his empty coffee cup a lot more interesting than me. I tried not to take offence.

'Oscar is my second cousin,' Mark said, 'he's Swedish, and he's over here on an exchange till half term. He's staying at Mum and Dad's. He plays hockey, and he's going to be training hard, but when he's got time off I thought you might introduce him to a few people. Show him how nice we are in this country.'

Thinking that Oscar had already met one person who wasn't very nice – he'd been sitting next to her at the pizzeria the previous evening – I could see that there was work to be done. So, first I needed to show him how very nice I was, so that he could feel relaxed and ready to meet new people.

'Hello,' I said in my best welcoming tone of voice, 'do you speak English?'

Oscar looked confused. So I thought I'd help him out a bit. 'I mean, I'm not saying you need to speak English to have a nice time here, but I don't think I know anyone who speaks Swedish, or plays ice hockey, come to that, so it might be an idea to—'

'Chloe,' interrupted Mark. 'Oscar can speak English, and he gets quite enough hockey talk with the team he's playing for. I was thinking more parties, hanging out with your friends, maybe a film or a play. You know.'

'OK,' I said brightly, looking hopefully at Oscar, who was still looking earnestly at his cup. Maybe I had started off on the wrong tack, but then Oscar hadn't yet shown any signs of speaking English, or indeed wanting to hang out with anybody.

'Do you know Pippi Longstocking?' I said. I thought this was a genius idea. My favourite English teacher, the one who actually taught us stuff we hadn't known before, had once told us about Pippi Longstocking, who is a very famous character in Swedish children's books, and I was sure that anybody Swedish would know about her. Surely this was the way to unlock the fluent English that Mark said was lurking beneath the silent surface of Oscar.

I was just starting to think that maybe we could talk about another Swedish person, Alfred Nobel – who could fail to be interested in the man who had invented both dynamite and the Nobel Peace

Prize? – when Oscar looked up.

I noticed he had piercing green eyes. And a frown.

'Actually, I'm only three quarter Swede,' he said, looking intently into my eyes.

For a moment I thought I was going to make a joke about vegetables, but thank goodness nothing came out.

'My other quarter is Croatia,' he said in a lilting accent that sounded like nothing I'd ever heard before, not even on television when the subtitles are on.

'Ah,' I said. My conversational skills were clearly on fire. 'Croatia? I don't think I've ever been there.' What was I SAYING? I knew perfectly well I'd never been to Croatia in just the same way I knew perfectly well I'd never been to Germany, or Denmark, or Australia, or any other foreign country except France. And that was only three days in Paris.

'I mean,' I went on, 'I haven't been to Sweden either.' This was getting better and better. I glanced at Mark, who was looking at me with a slightly dazed expression on his face.

'I think,' Mark said to Oscar, 'that what Chloe means is that there's lots for everyone to learn and she's looking forward to showing you around. Isn't that so, C?'

I looked at Mark, looking at me, and all I could think was how great it was to be called 'C'. And how any minute now I was going to say something – didn't matter what, probably something exactly as silly as all the things I'd said so far – and I'd call him 'M'. M and C. That's who we were.

And it was a clear 1.2 seconds before I thought that in roman numerals we'd be worth 1,100.

There wasn't time to be so romantic, though, because an officious CoCo-Coffee waiter called Clarence (if his badge could be believed) came up to clear our table.

I reckoned this was probably Fate's (and Clarence's) way of telling us to move on. And since coffee never held any real appeal for me – dark, bitter and slightly sick-making – I had no problem with that. In fact, I had a brilliant idea.

'I've just had a brilliant idea,' I said to Mark and Oscar. 'Amy's got a training session on the athletics track over at the park. Some amazing new trainer is checking out whether he's going to take her on. Charlie'll be there, and Sally. So why don't we all go there now?' I looked at Oscar, who at least seemed to be taking in what I was saying. 'Then you can meet some sporty people,' I finished brightly.

'That sounds good, Chloe,' said Mark (no 'C', I noted; perhaps I had to do something specially endearing to get a 'C'). 'Not that Oscar only wants to meet "sporty people" but I know what you mean. Amy and Charlie are great.'

'And Sally,' I said loyally as they gathered their things together to go. 'Sally's great too,' I said again, looking at Oscar, because I didn't want her left out when it came to great people I could introduce him to.

'OK,' said Oscar, looking down at his trainers. 'First I go to bathroom, OK?' And he slung his backpack over his shoulder and headed off to the toilets.

I found myself breathing out. I turned to Mark and said, 'Gosh, he's so SHY. Isn't he? I mean, is that why he's not talking to me, or is it that he doesn't understand? I'm sure he's very nice, but—'

'I think you're right,' said Mark looking thoughtfully towards the toilets. (I think you *can* look thoughtfully towards toilets, it doesn't mean you're necessarily *thinking* about toilets.) 'He's much more at ease when it's just me and we're talking about football or whatever.'

Football or whatever. That, to my mind and after a lot of Boy Watching studies, is one of the most major of differences between The Boy and The Girl. Mostly boys are fascinated and gripped by everything about football, and mostly girls aren't (and that's NOT because they're not perfectly capable of understanding the offside rule). This may just be me – me and football and everything that goes with football have never got along – but I do think it's responsible for a lot of rifts and upsets between the sexes.

However, now was not the time to dwell on all that. (And, besides, these were dangerous waters: Mark loved football.) I texted Sally to tell her to meet us at the athletics track, and then I messaged Charlie to tell him to look out for us all by the pavilion.

As Oscar emerged from the Gents, I gathered up the bags of empty calories and followed him and Mark out of the door.

And then – horrors. There was the dog pole. But no dog. Not a sign or a sound of Albert, not a snuffle, nothing.

'Oh my GOD,' I shouted as I stood frozen to the spot by the revolving door of the coffee shop. 'Oh my GOD,' I said again, because this was awful. This was double double awful, and if ever I needed God's help it would be roughly about now.

'What's wrong?' Mark was looking at me with the dazed and puzzled expression back on his face.

'Albert,' I gasped. 'There is no Albert here. And I left

him here. Here on the dog pole. He was fine. Alone. Happy.' I was starting to gabble.

'Okaaay,' said Mark. 'Well, he can't have gone far, can he? He can't have been dognapped or anything, because he's not exactly valuable.'

He IS valuable, I wanted to shout. He's special, he's his own self, and he's the nearest thing I have ever had to an actual pet, and he loves me... I wanted to say, but didn't.

'The police,' I said, vaguely aware that Oscar had gone back into the coffee shop. 'We've got to tell the police. Or, wait, they've got Mr Underwood. He'll murder me. I bet he's done that before. I bet that's why he's wanted by the police.'

I could tell that I wasn't making much sense. I wasn't even making much sense to me. But I did know a full-blown crisis when I was living through it.

Meanwhile, I could see through the window that Oscar was talking to Clarence, and then to the rather severe-looking manageress.

'Well it's probably not a bad idea to let the police know,' said Mark, seeming to be quite unflapped by the whole turn of events. 'Let's see if we can find a security guard at the supermarket, they might be able to help.'

The revolving door gave a squeak behind me and out came Oscar.

'Clarence think he see a man in long grey coat undo him and take him away just now,' he said.

A long grey coat? Could it be Mr Underwood himself? He definitely had a dirty old mac...one that made him look like the baddie in a black-and-white movie.

I pushed the bags of cholesterol into Mark's hands.

'Thank you, Oscar,' I just about remembered to say. 'I'm going to try and catch him up. See if it's him, and Albert's safe. I'll see you at the track.' And I dashed off in the direction Albert and the dirty old mac might have gone in if the mac really was Mr Underwood.

I ran up the hill faster than I ever remember running in my life, glad that it was a trainers day and not a showing-off-in-heels day. I felt at least two squelches under my feet as I headed up the path towards the road, which would normally have been very annoying as the trainers in question were quite new. But this time I just vaguely hoped they were Albert's squelches and that I'd see him round the corner any second.

Home was in sight when I finally saw what I thought might be my quarry. A slow-moving old raincoat was heading along the street in front of me and there was definitely a dog in tow. And lo, and brilliant, it was Albert and he WAS being led to our front door.

Panting with all the exertion (I don't normally do running if I can possibly help it; I leave that to Amy) I skidded to a halt beside the long grey mac just as Mr Underwood, for it *was* he, was putting his key into the lock.

'Mr Underwood,' I gasped. 'It's you. I'm very sorry. Is he all right?'

Mr U turned and looked at me with a thoroughly unpleasant stare. This shouldn't really have surprised me, because Mr U is in fact thoroughly unpleasant. But still, it wasn't very nice to be made to feel like a squelch on the bottom of his shoe.

'Yes, no thanks to you,' he said in his guttural, slightly scary drawl. (I imagine serial killers talk a bit like Mr Underwood – kind of slowly and threateningly while they hold flames to the soles of your feet or whatever they do before they actually kill you.) 'You were supposed to be looking after the dog, not leaving him tied up at the mercy of any old Tom, Dick or Harry while you go off and enjoy yourself with your boyfriends.'

There were so many elements to this that were unfair. Not least the implication that I had lots of boyfriends. When actually all I'd ever wanted was just the one. Still, now was not the time to tell him of my everlasting faithfulness.

'I'm very sorry,' I said again. 'I wasn't going to be very long, and lots of people tie dogs up to dog poles, that's what they're there for.' Too late I realised that this sounded rather aggressive.

'Oh, so you think it's all right to take charge of someone else's dog, and then just leave them randomly tied up somewhere, do you, young lady?' He looked even more unpleasant as he said this. 'Well, I'll tell you something for nothing. This dog's going to have to find a new home. I'm going away for some time, and I WAS going to see if you would help look after him. But now I'm having second thoughts. Irresponsible I'd say you are.'

'But I wouldn't—' Mr U didn't wait to hear what I wouldn't do, because he had opened the main front door, dragged Albert indoors after him and was turning round to shut the door.

'You wouldn't nothing, and there's an end of it,' he said and slammed the door in my face.

I could hear a slight buzzing sound coming from inside my head, just behind my eyes. And then a sort of ache as I tried not to burst into tears.

But it didn't work. Within seconds the tears were

pouring down my cheeks as I retraced my steps back down the hill towards the athletics track. I was being horribly punished for a moment's carelessness, and now I'd never see Albert again.

I felt an urgent need to be with Mark, and people who wouldn't drawl and snarl at me.

→ **3** ←

Life's Little Ironies

'You horrible little boy!' The big bald guy in the red tracksuit, standing by the edge of the athletics track as I approached, sounded exactly as frightening as he looked. If I'd come to Planet Athletics for some peace and tranquillity, I'd come to the wrong bit of it.

Then I saw Sally, heading my way but with her face pointing resolutely down at her phone. I felt a bit better at the sight of her.

'I didn't think they were allowed to say things like that,' I said to her when she'd got within earshot. She looked up, with the sort of dazed expression that people have when they're in the middle of something very difficult and important like updating their Facebook status. (Sally changed hers roughly ten times a day, depending on how or whether she'd seen Rob.)

'Who? What?' she said, still with the dazed look.

'"Horrible",' I said. 'And "little", come to that,' I added, looking over at the big bald guy. He was standing over a boy of about nine who was looking up at him with barely concealed fear and loathing. 'I mean boys that young don't mean to be horrible, they just come out of the packet like that. And it's not his fault if he's little. Being big is something for later on in life.' I looked thoughtfully at the boy, who now had an expression of anger mixed in with the fear and loathing. Perhaps he was going to survive after all.

'What on earth are you talking about, Chloe?' said my BFF, staring at me with genuine puzzlement. I could sense that this was going to be one of those days when I questioned my judgement in choosing my BFF. How could she not be interested in others' use of language and how it might affect people, especially very young people?

'The big guy over there,' I said, pointing at the big guy over there.

'Oh, that's Chester Dubrovonich,' said Sally knowingly. 'He's very famous. Apparently. Amy says he's coached most of the Under 16 regional winners this year. That's the guy she's got to impress if she's going to get into this year's trials.'

Lord. Poor Ames. She needed to please someone

like that, so that he'd take her on and shout at her full time? Besides, what sort of a name was Chester Dubrovonich? Half American football player, half Russian oligarch?

'Come on,' said the BFF (status pending), 'Charlie's over the other side of the pavilion, and I said we'd meet him there. Amy will be doing her run any minute.'

I followed her over to the decking at the back of the pavilion. There were loads of people standing around, mostly in tracksuits and looking very fit, with that sort of sheen that people who run about a lot often have.

There in the middle of a particularly healthy-looking group were Amy and Charlie. Amy in the pink again in her pink running kit, and Charlie looking cool in a navy blue tracksuit. They were talking to Mark and Oscar, but as soon as they saw us everyone greeted us in their own special way.

'Yay,' shouted Amy, waving enthusiastically.

'Hiya,' said Charlie, his big wide smile making his face go all lovely and crinkly. He came over to us and gave me a big hug. It was always nice being hugged by Charlie (second only to being hugged by Mr Darcy, of course). He was tall and strong and he always seemed to smell nice – sort of flowery, but also manly.

Oscar seemed to be carefully examining the boards

on the decking floor, but Mark came over and, once I'd had my flowery, manly hug from Charlie, put both his arms round me, kind of slowly in a looking-aftery sort of way.

'So what's the story with Albert?' he said. 'Was it Mr Underwood? Everything all right?'

'Sort of,' I said, feeling much better now my face was buried in his shirt. 'It was Mr Underwood, and Albert's safe, but I don't think Mr U is ever going to let me take him out again. Which would be terrible, because I love Albert.' I looked up at Mark, hoping he'd be looking down at me with a worried, caring expression on his face. But he was looking over at his Swedish second cousin with a bit of a frown.

'It's awful,' I said in a very sad way to get his attention back.

'I'm sure things will work themselves out,' said Mark, giving me a quick kiss on the top of my head.

I wasn't sure this was quite satisfactory. There were only three and a bit more days before he set off for Dijon-or-wherever, and one of those days didn't even count because I'd be back at school for more than eight hours of it. And then he'd be gone for weeks. Probably ten, as that's how long term is. And that's *seventy* days. Surely he should be hanging on my every word and generally making the most of me.

I watched him wander over to the others, and tried not to feel all twisted and miserable.

Mustn't worry about it; boys just aren't wired in the same way, I told myself sternly. They're not sentimental, they don't cry in movies, and they don't talk about their feelings unless it's when their team loses 5–4 on penalties. Maybe absence *will* make his heart grow fonder, I thought. And maybe Cecile *is* such a tomboy that she's only interested in football and not boys at all. But then (my inner pessimist was in charge now) if she likes football, doesn't that mean she'll get close to him and they'll bond over the World Cup or something? (I knew it was a World Cup year. Much though I tried to tune out Ralph's entire conversation, I was pretty sure that the words 'world' and 'cup' had featured a lot recently.)

I looked over at Mr Darcy, who was now standing next to his second cousin and listening to something Amy was saying very animatedly. Oscar actually had his head up and was looking at Amy as she talked. He even had an expression of interest on his face. I wondered what it was that Amy had that I didn't that made her so interesting. Then, smiling broadly, I heard her shout, 'Fartleg! Exactly!'

Oscar was now laughing and nodding and looking unexpectedly lively.

Fartleg? I knew The English Boy could rarely resist laughing at rude words, but felt vaguely disappointed that the strong, silent Swede and one of my best friends could really be finding this so funny.

'OK everyone, listen up.' Suddenly the big bald guy in the red tracksuit was in their midst. 'Intense interval training first. *Fartlek*, as the Swedes call it. We'll start at the 100-metre point and take it from there.'

You learn something new every day.

I was starting to feel distinctly chilly. Looking around me I could see everyone's breath coming out of their mouths in quick small clouds. Some people were jumping up and down and flapping their arms about as if they were on fire and only by giving themselves a good slap could they save their own lives.

As I watched Amy and all the other Under 16s fartlekking round the athletics track I almost began to see the point of exercise. At least they were all warmed up.

In the distance, by the other side of the pavilion,

I could see Amy's parents. Even from a long way away you could see how nice they were. Something about the way they stood, about the way Amy's lovely dad – The Dad Who You'd Most Like If You Didn't Like Your Own – was bending down to listen to something Amy's mum was saying to him. He looked just as wise and kind as he usually did.

And Amy's mum too – you could just tell, even if you didn't know, that her job was doing something very kind at the hospital, and that she was very good at cheering people up by smiling at them and making many trays of chocolate brownies. (I admit that I do have some insider knowledge when it comes to analysing Amy's parents, but still, I do think you could just tell the niceness from the way they stood.)

Mark and Charlie had disappeared off to check out the gym and/or whatever sporting event the big HD TVs were showing there. But I felt Amy needed my support as she tried to impress Chester. Somehow I had the feeling that if I turned my back it would bring her bad luck. Plus Sally and Oscar seemed to be quite happy out in the cold watching what was going on on the track.

When I was pretty sure he was concentrating on some distant people doing warm-up exercises,

I let myself have a bit of a furtive stare at Oscar. His profile was great, and so, come to that, was his front view. And he was just a little bit stubbly in the rugged outdoor way that film stars have, even if they're indoor film stars.

The breeze (did I mention the breeze? No wonder I was freezing) was ruffling his thick blond hair, and he looked the very picture of the healthy, handsome Scandawegian.

I was just starting to notice how expressive his eyebrows were when he suddenly turned away from watching the runners and caught me looking at him.

For a tiny split second we looked each other full in the eye. Embarrassed, I barely had time to pretend I was focusing on Amy, way in the distance. And was mightily relieved that the cold had already turned my face pink. For I could feel the familiar wave of heat rising up in me which, from bitter experience, I knew would end in a full-on, full-frontal blush.

Thank goodness for Sally, who was standing just behind me, clicking away on her phone in a way that would normally have irritated me very much indeed.

I turned to her, 'Hey, Sal,' I said. 'What's new in Phone World?'

'What's new,' said Sally in a preoccupied tone of

voice as she focused all her attention on the small screen in her hands, 'is that Gemma says are we around this afternoon, because she's had a massive row with Merv and she wants to tell us something.'

That was definitely enough to distract me from my embarrassments and sadnesses. 'Does she say what about?' I asked. A massive row with Merv did sound a bit serious. Generally Gemma kept her father pretty much under her thumb. But it sounded as if this time he had fought back.

'Nope,' said Sally. 'Just that she wants us to come over to hers. I'll say yes, shall I?'

'Deffo,' I said.

I looked back at the athletics track. Ideally, I would have spent the afternoon bonding with Mark. Perhaps we'd go for a walk in the country somewhere, and then – tired but happy – we'd be lying under a tree in a field, eating chocolates and looking up at the sky, talking great thoughts about life, the world and love. (Obviously, the climate would have taken a sudden turn for the better, and we'd be bathed in warm sunshine.) Then we'd talk about how brilliant my first novel was, and what we were going to do with all the money that my publisher had paid for it – perhaps we'd buy a boat and sail round Italy...

'Hey, Chloe,' the object of my beautifully imagined dreams was shouting from the entrance to the pavilion. 'I'm going to gather the guys to play some football in the park. Wanna come and watch?'

As invitations go, that one was right down there at the bottom of the pile. I must have looked as unimpressed as I felt because as Mark got nearer he gave what I think they call a rueful grin.

'Sorry, C,' he said – possibly knowing that the 'C' might improve my mood – 'but I've no idea if there's going to be any footie in France, so I want to make the most of it. And anyway, I thought Oscar might like to come and have an English warm-up before we go back home. His mother's going back to Sweden tonight, so we're having a bit of a farewell for her.'

So much information, and all of it seemed to exclude me. I suppose it shouldn't have surprised me that Oscar had a mother, many people do after all, but it all just seemed to emphasise how she and Oscar and Mark's family were all together – having New Year and everything – and all I had been doing was feeling sorry for myself at home with Mum and Ralph.

'I'll come and pick you up tomorrow,' said Mark. 'We'll do something fun on your last day of freedom. I've got to go to London to be ready for the flight out on Wednesday, so you won't be missing anything by being at school.'

Just as I thought I was going to collapse into the freezing mud in a sobbing heap, Mark put his arms around me.

It was amazing how magical the effect of that was. Such a simple act, and yet instantly I was transported into a realm of – well, if not heaven, then at least feeling much, much better.

And then he let me go. Suddenly and totally. He turned away to go back to the pavilion and gather the boys for football.

From not-quite-heaven I went back to feeling all sad and sorry for myself.

'Hey, Chloe.' I felt a tug on my sleeve. 'Look—' Sally was pointing to the other side of the track – 'isn't that Amy in front?'

Suddenly remembering the whole point of our being there, I guiltily looked where Sally was indicating, and sure enough the runner in the front of the pack was a small pink blur that could only be our friend.

'She's going to win!' shouted Sally, tempting fate as I knew there was another circuit to go. 'She is, she is! Look at her go.'

I noticed a few feet away that Oscar was still

standing outside the pavilion; he seemed to be concentrating on watching the race, but I also had a vague sense he was watching us watching the race. I decided to think about that some other time, because for now our friend needed us to send her some winning/impress-the-big-scary-trainer vibes through the chill winter air.

The runners were circling round for the last lap now, and we moved ourselves nearer to the side of the track to be closer to the action. Out of the corner of my eye I saw the Dad Who and Amy's mum move closer to the edge of the track too. They were with Charlie, and I had a moment of thinking how very lucky Amy was to have not just such a nice boyfriend but such a lovely family.

In between us was Chester the scary Russian oligarch trainer. He was staring intently at all the runners, and I wondered what was going on inside that big bullet head of his. Would he take on our friend? And if he did, was that a good thing or a bad thing?

There wasn't time to do much more thinking about the life of a professional athlete, and whether we wanted that for our friend, because the runners – about twenty of them – were coming thundering towards us.

Some of the healthy people in tracksuits the other side of me started shouting. And then Sally suddenly let out a series of huge whoops right next to my left ear. She had only just learned how to whoop, and I could tell that there'd be no stopping her if this race went on for much longer.

But it was all over in about ten more seconds. The runners came charging past, with our friend still in the lead. Everyone around us started waving and cheering and jumping up and down. I was amazed to discover that I was waving and cheering and jumping up and down too – who knew I could be so uninhibited, I thought, rather pleased at my own pleasure in someone else's success.

'Hey,' shouted Sally in my ear. 'Amy's won! How ABOUT that?'

It wasn't really a question, but I still answered – 'Yeah, it's great.' And then I gave another wave at Amy and shouted out, 'Well done, Ames, superstar!'

I was jumping up and down so uninhibitedly that after my last jump I landed on a solid object rather than the ground. Looking down I realised that the object was Chester-the-Russian-oligarch's foot. It looked so solid, and quite resistant to a (newly) fifteen-year-old girl landing on it, but I still found myself quite frightened at having invaded the big man's personal space.

I looked up at him (way up – he was incredibly tall

close to), prepared to do my best grovelling apology.

'Good work,' he shouted, seemingly completely unaware of having been trodden on. 'Over here, Amy.'

I watched Amy, now bright pink all over and gasping from her long fast run, walk towards Chester. The Dad Who, Charlie and her mum were heading our way too. It was clear that there was going to be Serious Talk about Amy's success and what was going to happen next.

I backed off to leave them to it. Mark and Oscar were now the other side of the pavilion and waving at me. They were See You Later waves; I could tell that the call of footie was getting louder and they had to go off and do what boys had to do.

That was fine, I told myself, because it was time to go and do what girls had to do.

'Come on,' I said to Sally. 'Let's go and see what's up with Gemma.'

The bus stop drops you off three doors away from Gemma's house. You would think that that would therefore be quite close to Gemma's front door, but in Gemma World, it's actually quite a walk away.

This is because Gemma is the only one of us who lives where the rich people live, and rich people's front doors tend to be a long way from other rich people's front doors.

It's always fascinating, almost in a horror movie kind of way, to go to Gemma's. She and her father, the slightly creepy Merv, live in a huge three-storey house, with a giant porch, a gravel drive and tall electric gates. It has an air about it of a place where dodgy deals are done, and criminals discuss their share of the take over glasses of whisky and overflowing ashtrays.

I know this is just my overactive (borderline feverish) imagination, but we did know that Merv had been in trouble with the Inland Revenue, and he always seemed like a man who was looking over his shoulder and was only seconds away from being Found Out.

But still, the quality of pizza, ice cream and dangerously sugary drinks was streets ahead of anything we had at home, so we didn't really question where the money to pay for it came from. (Merv had actually made his fortune from selling TV show formats, but the people who sometimes came round to the house for 'business meetings' bore such a close resemblance to Chinese mafia that we all thought there had to be something more to it than that.)

We stood at the enormous electric gates, as Sally pressed the keys on the keypad. We had been given the entry code some time ago, and it always amused Sally to operate the gates. Something about this huge mechanism responding to just a few touches from her forefinger seemed to fascinate her. In fact, I was fascinated by watching the gates slowly roll into action too.

Or they would have done if Sally hadn't forgotten the code.

By the time we'd phoned Gemma and been told how to reset the code, the novelty of Chateau Gemma's security system was starting to pall. It was a cold January afternoon, what sun there was had long disappeared, and I couldn't wait to huddle by the enormous fake log fire in the sitting room.

'Hi there,' said Gemma as we came into the room. Even though she was only wearing tracksuit bottoms and a plain white T-shirt, she managed to look glamorous as she lay on a sofa by the fire. She had her phone and her iPad on her lap in front of her, bottles of nail varnish and hair straighteners on the table beside her, and was running her fingers through her hair in an absent-minded fashion.

She put the electronic devices on the table, and

said, 'Let's go and get something interesting from the kitchen. What do you fancy?'

We followed her through into the state-of-the-art kitchen, where she headed straight for the enormous stainless steel fridge... Which was next to the enormous stainless steel cooker, deep freeze and microwave. Hanging all around the ceiling and walls were huge copper and steel pots and pans, more of which hung off hooks on the edges of a huge...island, I think they're called, in the middle of the room.

In between all these things were various remote controls – for the blinds, the ovens, and the fake fire (every room should have one).

It was like the set for a very smart cookery programme, except, to my certain knowledge, no one ever actually cooked here.

Armed with cans of some of the best and most dangerous sugary drinks we went back into the sitting room.

'OK,' said Gemma, sitting back on the sofa as Sally and I arranged ourselves on the fur rug in front of the fire. (By 'fur' I think I mean some kind of plastic acrylic made to look like the outside of a polar bear. Certainly whatever it was gave you the type of electric shock that no real polar bear would know how to give you.)

'Here's the thing,' said Gemma once she was quite sure she had our full attention. 'I was walking down the high street this morning with Merv.' She paused, so that we could absorb the full effect of this – she never went anywhere with Merv if she could possibly help it, so there had to be a good reason. 'Because we were going to the bank to open an account for me, so he had to be there.' Ah, all was explained.

'And we were just going past the entrance to the mall when this woman came up to us,' said Gemma. 'She was quite old, but she looked incredibly sleek, had on the kind of coat that looks very simple, but you know costs a fortune because it's got no buttons or belt or any means of doing it up because that would spoil the shape.' She looked a bit wistful at the thought of something so extravagantly minimalist.

She went on: 'Anyway, she said to Merv: "I'm so sorry to interrupt you, but are you this young lady's father?" So Merv looked a bit puzzled and admitted that he was. 'Well, I run a model agency called "Management2Model", and your daughter is just the kind of model we are looking for to front one of our clients' new campaigns." Well, I don't know which of us was more gobsmacked.'

Sally and I, gazing up at our friend from the

acrylic polar bear skin, must have looked a bit gobsmacked too.

'I thought this sort of stuff only happened in books,' I said.

'Well, quite,' said Gemma. 'But she looked absolutely the real deal, so Merv said, "What do you mean. I mean, what does that mean?" Or something similarly smart and on the ball. "If you're interested," said the model lady, looking at me, "perhaps we could have a meeting in London to discuss it further. Here's my card. I hope you can take this seriously, I'm quite sure I'm right and there is a future for your daughter." And she carried on looking at me, like she knew I was the one in charge.'

'So what happened? What did you say, what did Merv say?' Sally was still wide-eyed, and I guess I must have been too.

'She took a photo of me, and then went off, got into some sort of chauffeur-driven car, so I'm sure she was for real. And then Merv says, "I think we can say no to that straight away. You've got to focus on your exams, my girl. We'll have none of this flitting around modelling lark."'

Gemma took a swig of her sugar-rich drink, and went on: 'I said, "That's just where you're wrong. This

is MY chance, MY opportunity, and I want to go for it."
And then I flounced off. Got on a bus, came back here.
Really annoying that we hadn't set up my bank account,
though. Because I'm going to need that for modelling
fees and stuff.'

There was silence round the electronically crackling
log fire. This was huge. I felt sure the Model Lady was
right, and there was a future for Gemma. She always
moved like beautiful people did, and I could see that
she had the kind of features that would look great close
up on a billboard.

And then I had a sudden lurching sensation deep
inside. If Gemma went off and became a famous
model, and Amy went off and became a famous athlete,
then what about us? I knew it wasn't meant to be about
me, but, well, we are all we've got. And I suddenly and
passionately didn't want to lose my friends.

'So are you going to go to London then, Gem?'
I asked in a small voice, knowing the answer.

'Sure am,' said our supermodel friend. 'Mum says
she'll come with me. She's not too sure about it either,
must admit.' Gemma looked a bit downcast as she
said this. Her mother, Marianne, was actually pretty
glamorous herself. She had left Merv when Gemma
was eight and run off with a schoolfriend of hers called

Juliet, who was also glamorous, and was now a famous artist living in Cornwall. (Gemma does seem to supply all the glamour in our lives.) Marianne was not only beautiful and wise, she was also just a tiny bit scary, and though Gemma was very happy to be reunited with her, I knew she was quite frightened at the thought of displeasing her mother.

'But it's so exciting,' said Sally from the tail end of the polar bear. 'You're going to be the world's best supermodel. And they'll be wanting to interview us in all the magazines because we knew you before you were famous. And you'll go to Hollywood parties, and you can introduce us to all the film stars, and you'll be on all the chat shows. It's going to be amaaaazing.'

'Yeah,' said Gemma. 'Except first, they've got to decide they actually want me, and second, Merv's got to stop interfering.'

As if he'd been listening outside the room – and I wouldn't put it past him – in came Merv, right on cue.

He was wearing his trademark black denim: top and bottom and all the bits in between. As usual, the denim was one size too small, so you could see the seams glowing white from the pressure they were under from Merv's expanding flesh.

His long grey hair was tied back in a ponytail, and

he was wearing the kind of glasses that turn black in the sun. Only for now they were orange, which gave his whole head the rather sinister look of a bug just emerging from his underground hole.

Merv walked into the room rubbing his hands with the air of a man who was determined to be brave and confront his demons. In this case, Gemma.

'Hello, girls,' he said in the hearty way he had when he was surrounded by us lot. 'You warm enough in here? Got everything you want?'

He looked at us as if he genuinely cared whether we were warmed by his electronic fire or needed something out of his huge metal fridge. For a moment, I had an attack of guilt. Were we possibly and perhaps a little mean about Merv, just on Gemma's say-so?

'We've got everything we need,' said his daughter in chilly tones. 'Except having this room to ourselves.'

Merv looked put out. But, rubbing his hands again as if to give himself courage, he said, 'I'll leave you girls for now, but, Gemma, we must talk. You can't just go off in a flounce if you don't like something. I'm your father, I've got a right to try to look after you, you know.'

It was quite a speech for Merv. Especially in front of an audience. I think even Gemma found it a bit impressive, because she muttered, 'OK, OK, but later. We've got stuff to do now.'

Merv seemed to take this as some sort of victory, because he smiled, almost a proper smile, raised his hand in a mock salute and turned and went out of the room.

'God,' said Gemma in the special drawl that she used whenever Merv was around or being talked about. 'He always plays that I-care-about-you card when I do something he doesn't like. Especially if there's a chance I'll go to Marianne about it.'

I wasn't sure she was quite as dismissive as she sounded, but nothing was ever entirely as it seemed in this family.

Perhaps that's true of every family.

I decided to stop trying to have deep thoughts as we settled down to watch the first *Hunger Games* movie for the fourth time. It's always nice to know there are some things you can rely on, even if it's the terrors of District 12.

⇢⇢ 4 ⇠⇠

The Threat of Pleasure

It's a sign of a good movie if you spend more of your time looking at the big screen than you do looking at the small screen of your phone. We'd all managed to achieve this, even Sally. This was because we'd decided – or, anyway, I'd decided and the others agreed – that we'd all put our phones underneath the polar bear so we weren't tempted to fiddle with them during the film.

But by the time the end credits rolled I was starting to feel guilty and I decreed that we could all look at our phones as a reward. (I know, I know, but it's just that sometimes it's nice to live in the real world. Even if that *is* just the one you're following on the small screen.) I think we all opened our messages at exactly the same time, because we all gave a yelp of surprise at pretty much the same moment.

'**Truth** or **Dare** Affair', the message was headed. And then lots of little messages written on pink hearts: 'If you **dare**...come to a Valentine's Party... Tuesday 14 Feb...**dare** or be square... Don't be left out...7pm... Bring your **true** love...and see what happens... Maggie, Party Girl'

There was a silence in the room which had until recently been so loud with the noise of people trying to kill each other.

Sally, now sitting cross-legged on the polar bear's head, was looking in consternation at her phone. Me too. And even Gemma looked a bit put out.

Who knew that an invitation to a party could be so full of veiled threats and the fear of public humiliation? Even if the words could have a benign interpretation you only had to look at the name of the person who wrote them to know that something seriously threatening lay behind them. 'Party Girl' indeed. The only reason the QB Maggie would have asked us all to a party would be to make quite sure there was the widest possible audience for whatever it was she had planned for us in her evil little head.

'Gosh,' said Sally. 'Maggie's having a party.' Sally always had a way of getting straight to the point. 'And she's invited us.' Yup, finger on the pulse all right.

'Quite,' I said. 'Normally you'd think that an invitation to a party would be a Good Thing. So why is it that I feel ever so slightly sick?'

Gemma had opened one of the bottles of nail varnish and was starting to apply a particularly bright green to her nails. 'Because we know,' she said, 'that "Party Girl" Maggie has got some sort of scheme up her sleeve. Either something horrible is going to happen to us, or we're going to have to watch her triumph in some way, or both.'

'It doesn't say where it is,' I said scrolling through the page of horrible pink hearts.

'Yes, it does,' said Sally frowning over her phone. 'Or at least there's a small heart at the bottom that says, "You Know Where!"'

'That's great,' I said. 'So it's like an invitation, but not an invitation. If you're not in with the in-crowd you don't even know where the party is.'

'Not to mention who we're going to go with,' said Sally. 'I mean, who ARE we going to go with? Rob has hardly texted me all holiday. I've only seen him once and that was just when we were making a toboggan for his sister. I don't see us suddenly getting all loved up for a Valentine's party.' Her voice was going all down at the edges, which is what happens when you're feeling really miserable.

And it was true that Rob had made a very disappointing showing on the Boy Watching charts over Christmas – scoring practically zero. We had thought that he and Sally were going to see lots of each other and if not actually Go Out together, then at least go out (lower case) together a few times, but instead he'd been off air, on holiday with his family, and hardly called Sally at all.

'I know,' I said, because it was hard to offer any comfort. Especially when you had your own problems to worry about. 'And Mark's going to be in France, in Dijon-or-wherever. Probably well on the way to being in love with this girl he's doing his French exchange with.'

'But we've GOT to go,' said Sally, wailing a bit now. 'Can you IMAGINE if we weren't there? We'd be the only people in the year, in the school – probably in the world – who wouldn't be there. And we'd look like total, utter losers. Like the losers of losers. We'd be—'

'Yes,' said Gemma from the sofa, 'I think we get the picture. It's kind of weird she's asked us, but of course we've got to go. If only to see what her slimy little game is. You surely don't care whether Maggie thinks you've got a boyfriend or not, do you?'

It was all right for Gemma, I thought, but didn't say, because that would have made me look like I cared whether Maggie thought I had a boyfriend. But it *was* all right for Gemma, who only had to beckon with her bright green fingernail and the devoted gangly Jezza and or the Cornish surfer-boy Jack would come running – to name but two.

This is why, I thought to myself, people hate Valentine's Day so much. It's like the day when you have to say, 'Here he is! He's The One! Look at us – we're so together and so happy! Look at the lovely presents we've bought each other! Aren't we loving and generous!'

Whoever invented Valentine's Day had a very cruel sense of humour, I reckoned. And the person who has a Valentine's Day party is even more cruel.

'Nightmare,' said Sally, picking the nose of the polar bear. 'Absolute nightmare. I don't think Rob's ever going to ask me out again. I mean, if he doesn't when we're on holiday what hope is there in term time? It's all hopeless. *Total* nightmare.'

I was thinking that Sally was quite right, especially because it was very possible that there would be karaoke at the QB Maggie's party (she loved karaoke; people could look so stupid doing karaoke, and Maggie loved nothing more than for people to look stupid), when I suddenly had an idea.

'I've had a thought,' I said, not trying to disguise my excitement at my absolute brilliance. 'Listen, Sally. Do we or do we not know an incredibly handsome single boy? Not just incredibly handsome, but one who I'd SWEAR I saw looking at you very interestedly in the last twenty-four hours? I can't BELIEVE I haven't thought of this before, but I'm SURE that any minute now Oscar is going to be very brave and ask you out. I'm SURE of it!'

I was almost breathless by now – I don't normally speak in capital letters, but I was absolutely sure that I'd solved Sally's party problem for her. And not just her party problem but her whole life! She liked watching sport (well, if her favourite boy was playing: that's why she liked football so much, because Rob played it), she liked a bit of mystery (she had thought there were hidden mysterious depths to Rob because he was generally quite silent) and she liked boys who were tall. It's true that Oscar was a lot taller, but then Sally, as discussed, was really quite short, so it was only to be expected that there'd be a bit of a height difference somewhere along the line with any boy.

'But how do you know that?' said Sally, a little

ungratefully, I thought. 'How do you know Oscar likes me, and anyway, why should he, and won't he be going back to Sweden one day?'

'I saw the way he looked at you,' I said, increasingly confidently, 'and anyway he doesn't HAVE to go back to Sweden, he could just as well stay here. I'm sure there are plenty of people who play ice hockey here too. I mean, that's why he's here, isn't it?'

'But...but...what about Rob?' Sally said. 'He's single and handsome too, and...'

'An awful lot more single than handsome!' I said without thinking.

Sally's face fell. The corner of her mouth drooped.

And I felt instantly terrible. I was right, of course. On a scale of one to a hundred, where one is a deformed amoeba and one hundred is Zac Efron, Rob scored something in the middle. But now was obviously not the time to dwell on that.

'I'm sorry,' I said quickly. 'I didn't mean that like it sounded.' I crossed my fingers behind my back, in the way people tell you to if you don't want to be punished for lying. 'I just thought...well, it's just that Oscar does seem to like you, and he is so very beautiful, and a touch exotic what with his funny accent.'

Sally still looked crestfallen and unconvinced.

'Now you've sorted out Sally,' said the voice from the sofa, 'what are you going to do about *you*, Chloe? Come to think of it, what shall I do about me?'

Gemma had put down the nail varnish and was waving her green fingernails about in the air to dry them.

'Can't you ask Jack to come up from Cornwall? He can't be surfing in the middle of February, can he?' I said.

'Jack can be surfing in January in the Arctic Ocean if the waves are right,' said Gemma. 'He says he'd do anything for me, but apparently that's only true when he doesn't hear the call of turbulent salt water. And before you say can't I summon up Jezza, no, I can't. Partly because I've told him I've had enough of him. I've definitely and finally had enough of his selfish, rubbish ways. And partly because he'll be back at home in Scotland and at school that week.'

'Well, that's it then,' said Sally. Having finished with the polar bear's nose, she was now picking its claws. 'It's a disaster. We'll be social outfits.'

'Outcasts,' I said miserably. 'Although you might have meant "misfits".'

'Whatever we're going to call it, Little Miss Dictionary,' said Gemma, 'Sally's right. It's got all the potential of a complete disaster. I've got a bad feeling about all this. Anyway. Let's worry about it tomorrow. Merv's laid in some pizza. I fancy having something with heaps of cheese on it. May be the last pizza I ever have. It'll be supermodel celery from now on.'

We headed back to the shiny expanse of kitchen and opened up some of the shiny cupboards in search of empty calories and killer carbs.

That evening, as I put the key in the lock of our front door, I heard a little bark from Albert's flat. I was sure it was a 'Hello, why aren't you coming to see me?' bark, and I felt sad all over again at the thought of being separated from the one reliable male in my life.

How difficult life is, I thought. All these worries about being publicly humiliated, or abandoned by the boy in my life, or separated from the terrier in my life were bad enough. But as I opened the door and heard Mum give a small apologetic cough from the kitchen, I knew that there was something worse. I realised that I half dreaded getting home in case Mum was having one of her bad days when the treatment made her feel terrible. I hated it when she couldn't disguise how weak she was feeling, not least because it meant that I couldn't pretend to myself either that everything was all right. And I realised that this inner nagging fear for Mum lowered my resistance to life too.

If only everyone I cared about were well and happy, if only everyone were nice to each other, then I could get up every morning with a spring in my step. It wasn't much to ask for. Was it?

'That you, love?' Mum called out from the kitchen as I shut the front door behind me. It was a question she must have asked me hundreds of times when the only possible answer was yes, but now wasn't the time to point that out.

'Yup, I'm back,' I said – because stating the obvious is a family trait. 'How are you feeling?' I said as I came into the kitchen and saw Mum, looking rather pale, sitting at the table.

She had a Sudoku puzzle in front of her and her special Sudoku pencil in her hand, but I couldn't help noticing she hadn't made much progress with it.

'Not too bad, love. Had some of your birthday cake, and that perked me up a bit,' she said. 'You don't mind, do you? There's plenty left.'

Oh, if only birthday cake was all it took to make you feel better. Is what I thought, but didn't say.

'Course not. We've been pigging out at Gemma's, so I reckon you need it more than I do,' I said, trying hard not to sound like I might cry.

'I've got another session tomorrow, love,' said Mum. 'And they say they're going to keep me in overnight to make sure I don't have another turn. So I'm afraid you're all going to have to fend for yourselves tomorrow.'

A 'turn' was a typical Mum understatement. It was what happened when the chemo made her faint, and made her white blood cells do whatever they weren't supposed to do. She'd had one of these 'turns' when we were all at home, and it was so frightening that I was glad to hear the doctors were going to look after her.

'Don't worry about us, Mum. I'll make dinner. It'll be brilliant.' And I smiled confidently at Mum. 'Better than Gran's meatballs anyway,' I added for good measure.

Gran's meatballs were the only thing she actually made herself. Everything else came out of a tin, a packet or a box. They were large brown lumps of unspecified meat, fat and gristle, that she mixed with onions and moulded into large balls with her hands before dunking them (the meatballs) into a bowl full of tinned tomato sauce. The red and brown result looked like the by-product of a particularly brutal shoot-out on a pig farm. And tasted so squelchy and fatty that even brother Steve – whose ability to eat anything so long as he didn't have to prepare it or wash up after it was legendary – found them hard to get down.

'And just *what* is that supposed to mean, young lady?' came a voice from behind me. I turned round. Framed by the kitchen doorway, giant pink spectacles trembling in indignation, was Gran. She was wearing her bright pink nightdress and her green dressing gown that looked like an inside-out duvet cover. Horrified though I was to be caught out like this, I still managed to notice that her ancient slippers were on the wrong way round. You'd think by the time you got to Gran's great age, you would be able to tell left from right.

'Sorry, Gran, I mean I'm going to try to make something *even* nicer than your meatballs.' I felt quite pleased with that. I looked hopefully at her expression to see if she was in any way taken in.

'You're an ungrateful little girl, that's what you are,' said Gran. So I guessed that would be a no. Not taken in.

'Now, dear,' said Gran, turning to Mum with an altogether nicer expression on her face. 'Time for your cocoa, and then it's bed for you. You've got a big day tomorrow.' As Gran turned to put the kettle on, Mum caught my eye and gave me the tiniest suggestion of a wink.

I decided it was time for me to go to bed too. I had a big day tomorrow as well, what with saying goodbye to Mark, worrying about Mum, and cooking something nicer than meatballs. Plus, it was my last day of freedom before being dragged back into the unrelenting clutches of full-time education.

'Night, Mum, night, Gran,' I said, and headed off to my room to look up 'How to Survive Valentine's Day' on the internet.

Tuesday 3rd January.

Day 3 of being Fifteen Years Old.

Last Day of Holidays.

Last Day with Mark Anderson/Darcy.

Last Day to do all the holiday homework that hasn't so far been done, which is to be frank pretty well all of it.

In short. The very worst day to wake up feeling like someone has stuffed cotton wool in your head, blocked up your nose, and put two large lumps in your throat so that swallowing involves huge and painful effort.

I lay there in bed, staring at the damp marks on the ceiling that I'd never noticed before. If I moved my head to the left I felt marginally less uncomfortable than if I moved my head to the right. But whichever side I turned I still couldn't breathe through my nose.

There was a knock on the door and Gran's voice: 'Up you get, missy, it's getting late.'

'Missy.' And there was I thinking nothing could annoy me more than her calling me 'young lady'.

'Just getting up now, Gran,' I said in a voice that sounded like I was breathless, underwater and hoarse all in one go. Oh lord. Suppose I lost my voice? On this day of all days. When I needed to say so many meaningful and lovely and loving things to Mark. I wanted him to go off to France with memories of all the brilliant and adorable things I'd said ringing in his ears, not a series of croaky splutterings.

I decided to try again and say something else – see if I could get my voice to work properly. I cleared my throat, drew a deep breath and out came an enormous sneeze.

Great. It was as if a seal had been broken...out came sneeze after sneeze after sneeze, so loud that I almost didn't hear the *ping* of an incoming message. 'Pick u up @ 12. OK? M xxxxcxxv'

It was lovely to see so many *X*s in Mark's message (although this time difficult to translate into Arabic numerals – maybe 115 if you counted it as 90 and 25), but less lovely to think I only had two hours to make myself well and beautiful.

'Great!' I texted back in the middle of another three sneezes.

I threw back the duvet, got up and padded my way to the bathroom. There was nobody around, so I had plenty of time to look at myself in the mirror.

I'm sure the older generation thinks our generation spends *way* too much time looking at ourselves in the mirror. But I'd argue that it's not about vanity, but more about a dreadful presentiment that all is not as it should be.

On this occasion I was quite right. A fetching red border round my eyes and a bright white complexion were rounded off with the lankest hair I'd ever seen. And once I'd blown my nose I could see that there'd be a nice redness there that could only get worse as the day wore on.

Gloomily I got out all my top-of-the-range concealers and darkest eye make-up and set to work. If I couldn't look all glowing and healthy for my Last Day With Mark then I'd have to settle for looking like an over-made-up party girl.

Finally, the job was done. An orange face and panda eyes were a small price to pay for not looking like I was at death's door. I still felt rotten, and knew I sounded croaky, but I wasn't going to waste our last day together, whatever happened.

Once I'd put on my favourite black crop top and my new white jeans I had convinced myself that I was starting to feel better. With my hair up in the latest vlogger-approved ponytail, I even thought I looked pretty OK.

I went into the kitchen to find Mum, Ralph and Gran sitting at the table surrounded by the remains of a major fry-up. The air was thick with the smell of recently burnt bacon and toast. Clearly Ralph had been in charge. He always had a heavy hand with the grill.

He was looking down at the sports pages, which was where Ralphs normally looked of a morning, and Mum had the same Sudoku puzzle open in front of her – which left Gran to be the first to comment on my appearance.

'Chloe!' Gran cried out. 'Whatever have you done to yourself? And at this time of day!'

You could always rely on Gran to make you feel better.

'I've got Mark...' *...coming to pick me up in less than an hour* is what I was going to go on and say. Except nothing came out.

'Oh, poor love,' said Mum. 'You've got a cold on you, haven't you?'

Gran was less sympathetic. 'Stay well away from your mother,' she said. 'The last thing she needs is to pick up germs from the likes of you.'

I understood Gran's worry, but did wonder who 'the likes of me' could be if they weren't actually me.

'Got a bit of a cold, yes, Mum.' I found that by making a big effort I could overcome the hoarseness. 'But I'll be fine and I won't come near you.'

I turned away to fill up the kettle. There was never a bad time to fill up the kettle and make a cup of tea in the Bennet household, and it was the only thing I could think of to do that wouldn't annoy everyone else, or depress me.

As I wrestled for the millionth time with the curly lead of the kettle (I hated that lead with a passion people normally reserve for serial killers or overcrowded trains), I wondered what surprise Mark had up his sleeve for our last day together. I hoped it wouldn't involve anything too active, or too much talking, or too many bright lights.

Ideally, it would be just us in a quiet corner somewhere with him doing all the talking, and all of it about how much we mean to each other. I was just getting to the bit where he had his arms round me and was whispering into my ear – we were in a restaurant by this stage, or perhaps a darkened cinema – when the doorbell rang.

Thinking it might be Mark, early because he couldn't wait to see me, I said I'd go, and dashed to the door.

I must have rearranged all my internal organs to prepare for the joy of seeing the most handsome boy in the world on the doorstep. So it was a bit hard to disguise my disappointment when I opened the door to find Sally and her newly rediscovered father standing there.

Sally was carrying a small suitcase, and looking vaguely embarrassed. James, the mysterious newly returned spy who also had loud arguments with his newly rediscovered wife, was looking tall and macho and stern. His red hair, the exact same shade as Sally's, was still wet from the shower which gave him even more of an outdoors look.

He looked at me and smiled – one of those sudden

smiles that people produce when they suddenly remember the occasion requires them to smile.

'Hi there, Chloe,' he said in the faint Scottish burr that I rather liked. 'Bit of a situation here, I'm afraid.'

I saw Sally look up at her father with an aggrieved expression on her face. I guess she didn't like being called a 'situation'.

'Fact is,' and now James was sounding properly embarrassed. 'Liv's a bit under the weather, and the twins have got to be taken to hospital. Harris and Jock have come out in some bad rashes and the doctor wants them to be taken in for tests. It's a specialist hospital a hundred miles away, and the tests might mean they're kept in overnight. So I'm afraid...' He looked down at his daughter with a frown.

'He's *afraid*,' said Sally rather crossly, 'that he's got to dump me on somebody. And that somebody is you. Sorry, Chloe. And it's your last day with Mark, too.'

Somebody up there had clearly decided that a last romantic day with the most handsome boy in the world just wasn't going to happen. Harris and Jock weren't my favourite terrible twins at the best of times. But though I didn't wish them ill, I did wish them ill a couple of days later.

My mental image of Mark and me lying on a grassy

bank somewhere murmuring sweet nothings in the sunshine was beginning to appear impossible at every level, but Sally was looking so miserable that I thought I mustn't take it out on her. Not her fault, I told myself.

'That's OK,' I said heroically. 'Sally can have the blow-up bed in my room, and we can go to school together in the morning.'

James's face suddenly relaxed, and he gave a much more real smile. 'Thanks, Chloe,' he said. 'I know you didn't plan on having my daughter around today. We'll bring you something nice to make up for it,' he said, putting his arm round his daughter who by this stage was looking really cross.

I wondered vaguely what a newly returned spy's idea of 'something nice' might be – night vision goggles, or sunglasses with a camera in them perhaps? – and made myself give him a real smile back. After all, it was clear that this whole parenting thing was completely new to him, so we couldn't really blame him for not having quite got the hang of it.

James gave Sally a quick hug and went back down the stairs.

'You sound awful, Chloe,' said Sally. 'Also, you look a bit weird. Like you're going to some cool all-night party, except it's only 11.30.'

Great. With BFFs like her, who needs Queen Beeyatches?

'I'm not feeling great, Sally,' I said, leading the way to my room for Sally to dump her bag. 'So what would be fantastic would be if you didn't tell me I look awful, and then I might not *feel* awful. I mean, this IS my last—'

'I know who you remind me of!' Sally interrupted. 'The Penguin! In the Batman movies! Same raspy voice, same big eyes!' And she started to giggle – uncontrollably, I think is the word.

It was at that point there was another ring on the front doorbell.

Brilliant. The love of my life has arrived, and I've just been told that I look and sound like an evil, elderly cross between man and beast.

I just had time to give my ponytail a tug and check the mirror in the hall (not a good idea: all I could see were my panda/penguin eyes) before I opened the door.

And there he was, looking taller and more beautiful than ever in a denim jacket and skinny jeans and carrying a big box of chocolates. He was smiling a lovely smile, which was just starting to show the lovely dimple on his right cheek. I had just a moment to see it before it disappeared completely and was replaced with an expression of concern.

'Hey, Chloe,' said Mark, frowning a little. 'You OK?'

'Yes, I'm fine!' I said, just about stopping my voice cracking and croaking. 'Just a bit of a cold, and anyway, much better now you're here.' I gave Mark one of my best dazzling smiles.

It didn't seem to reassure him, and he just looked even more concerned. He leant forward and gave me a kiss on the cheek. I couldn't help feeling that it was the sort of kiss that didn't want to get too close.

'I've brought your mum some chocolates,' said the perfect boyfriend. 'She might not feel like them now, but perhaps later on when she's back from hospital.'

We followed the still-giggling Sally into the kitchen, where Ghastly Ralph and Gran had cleared up the remains of fried beast and were standing over Mum as she got to her feet.

'There you are, Mark,' said Mum with a warm smile on her pale face. I think even if I didn't already love Mark for being Mark, I'd love him for the effect he had on Mum. Her smile was so nice that I hardly noticed that she greeted him with one of her trademark Mum-isms.

'Hello, Mrs Bennet,' said Mark. 'Brought you something to cheer you up for when you feel like chocolate.'

'Bless you,' said Mum as she struggled into her favourite brown coat, the one she had darned and stitched so many times she was almost like a walking needlework lesson. 'I'll look forward to those when I get back.'

'Right then, you lot,' said Ghastly Ralph, putting a proprietorial hand on Mum's arm. 'Time to let us get off. Chloe, I'll see you this evening. Don't be late back and don't forget you're in charge of dinner.'

I went over to Mum, gave her a hug and buried my nose in some stitches by her right shoulder. I hated the way Ralph ordered me about, but I didn't want Mum to see how much.

After they'd set off for the hospital, and Gran had retreated to her/Steve's room for a quiet lie-down, Mark turned to Sally and me and said, 'Now, Chloe, I know it's our last day together, but I think I've got to look after Oscar. He's off to training camp tomorrow, and he's a bit down, what with his mum having just gone back home. You don't mind, do you, if we go skating this afternoon?'

'Oh, yay!' said Sally. 'Brilliant. I love skating!'

I looked at Mark, looking at me, and I knew he knew that my heart had sunk, because I couldn't really disguise the downward turn of the corners of my mouth.

I had only ever once been skating, and had been utterly mystified as to why anyone would do that sort of stuff for pleasure. Perhaps I didn't have a proper centre of gravity, because whenever I let go of whoever I was holding on to, my legs started trembling uncontrollably and I fell over on to the ice, into the side of the rink or on top of whichever friend was lucky enough to be in falling distance.

'We'll go and get pizza, first, though,' said Mark, 'then we'll head over to the rink. Then maybe we'll see a movie. Eh? Chloe? How about that?'

It was all a million miles away from the sunlit orchard, the whispering of sweet nothings, the lying on the grass looking up at the sky...

Ice-skating with Sally and Oscar, and then probably no time for a movie because I was 'in charge of dinner'.

Plus, I had a sore throat and looked like a penguin. Miserable didn't begin to describe it.

⇥ 5 ⇤

Cold Comfort

An hour later and we were in a pizza parlour that was so noisy I couldn't even hear myself sniff. I'd already used three napkins to blow my nose, and I now began to wonder if my croaky penguin voice could make itself heard even to Sally or Mark who were sitting right next to me. Never mind Amy and Charlie and Oscar who were sitting opposite.

Because, yes, my romantic last day *a deux* with Mark had somehow turned into a raucous sports day and a day-long last-day-of-the-holidays party. After we all went skating, we were all meant to be going to a movie which Oscar's mother had apparently said was the most brilliant movie ever made. It was in Swedish, she said, but we mustn't let that deter us because it was so exciting.

All this and being home in time to be a dutiful daughter.

I looked over at Oscar. He was staring silently at his knife and fork, and had a rather soulful frown on his face. He looked handsomer than ever, but still seemed sad and awkward. When we'd all said hello, I'd noticed that his black sweater seemed to emphasise the bright green of his eyes. He really was looking his best, and it made me think how well all that green would look next to Sally's auburn (we always call it auburn these days) hair.

It all seemed to make so much sense: Oscar the Silent Awkward Type and Sally the Chatterer. I thought they would make each other very happy. And if Sally was happy, then obvs I, as her BFF, would be happy, but also to the point: if Oscar were happy, then his cousin Mr Darcy would be happy – and pleased with his girlfriend who had made it all happen. I was absolutely determined to make Project Oscar my life's mission.

I was just marvelling at the fact that I had actually allowed myself to use the word 'girlfriend', even if only in my head, when I felt a nudge in the ribs on my left side. The Mark side.

'Don't you think, Chloe?' he was saying, looking at me as if there were something rather worryingly wrong with me.

As it happened, he was right. When I opened my mouth to ask him what I thought about what, I was instantly doubled up by a crippling bout of coughing. As I choked and spluttered and felt myself getting redder and redder in the face, I thought: what a horrible way to die – turning purple, incoherent with splutters, and suffocated by your own spittle.

Mark poured me a glass of water. I managed to swallow a mouthful but my cough wasn't put off. On and on it went, until suddenly someone walloped me on the back so hard that my coughing instantly stopped. Blearily and still sniffing I looked up at my saviour and saw Oscar looking down at me with a concerned expression on his face.

'Sorry, I am too hard hitting,' he said. 'But this is what must be done with the hysterical cough.'

I wasn't at all sure about the 'hysterical' bit, but didn't have time to dwell on it. 'You've saved Chloe's life!' said Sally, gazing up at Oscar. 'I'm sure she'd have choked to death if it hadn't been for you.'

'Slight exaggeration, Sally,' said Mark, a little coldly, I thought. 'But anyway, main thing is she's all right.' He put his arm round me. 'You are all right, aren't you?'

'Yes, thanks,' I croaked. 'All right now.'

The waiters chose that moment to deliver armfuls of

platefuls of food. I was mightily glad that everyone's attention was so easily diverted towards tomatoes, mozzarella and carbohydrates, all thoughtfully served on what looked like pieces of roof tile. ('I wonder who thought of that,' said Charlie. 'Do you suppose they looked up at the roof of the church or whatever and said, "I bet all those tiles would look really great underneath a rocket salad."')

Whether it was my illness or my sadness I didn't know, but I felt incredibly unhungry, and could only toy with the tiny tomatoes sitting on top of my salad.

I looked over at Amy and Charlie as they goofily grinned at each other between virtually every mouthful. They believed in sharing, I knew that, but it seemed that each had to taste every forkful of whatever the other was eating. Fond though I am of both of them, the sight of this was making me feel even sicker.

We couldn't be too long on the tiny tomatoes and the loving looks because Amy's father, the Dad Who, was soon coming to pick us all up to take us to the skating rink. He taught photography, and always seemed to have a huge amount of kit. This was good because it meant he had to have a huge van, which could always give a lift to his beloved only daughter and all her beloved friends.

'How's your dad, Amy?' Mark asked her as everyone was coming to the end of their pizzas, and the restaurant was starting to get a bit less noisy. 'Is he still trying to teach people to photograph sunrises from the middle of a wood? None of us could ever actually do that, but he seemed to be able to.'

People said Mark was good at photography (obviously I thought he was *brilliant* at photography), and I loved that he had been taught by my friend's lovely dad.

Amy was in mid goofy giggle with Charlie as Mark spoke, but she suddenly seemed to stiffen and go all serious. She looked Mark in the eye for a moment, and then seemed to come to some sort of decision.

'He's fine,' she said quietly. 'He's been taking loads of pictures lately. Yep, he's fine. But anyway, aren't you going to ask me about Chester Dubrovonich?' She looked at Mark in a more cheerful way.

'OK,' said Mark, smiling. 'So, Amy. How's that lovely chap Chester Dubrovonich? Do you know yet if you're going to be lucky enough to be on his team?'

'Well, it's funny you should ask,' said Amy smiling back, 'but he sent a message this morning saying there was a really good chance he'd take me on. He said he was really impressed by my trials, and he thought I showed real promise. So hey! How about that?' She looked much more cheerful now. Amazing that the thought of spending time with a bullet-headed bully had that effect on her.

Charlie meanwhile, smiled fondly at his GF, and then said to us all, 'OK, everyone, listen up. Pizzas are on me. They gave me a massive tip at the hotel, so this is your last-day-of-the-holidays present. Plus, it's au revoir to Mark, and congrats to Amy for being so brilliant.'

Charlie got a cheer from us all for that. He'd earned money during the holidays being a doorman at the big hotel on the high street, where he had had to wear a yellow uniform with a red waistcoat. I reckoned that anyone who had to spend the day dressed up like Winnie the Pooh deserved every penny of his tips.

As Charlie parted with untold wealth (those roof tiles didn't come cheap apparently), we gathered ourselves up to go outside to find the Dad Who and his giant van.

'There he is!' Sally yelled as soon as we came out of the restaurant. It was pouring with rain, so we ducked down and ran across the road, following Sally as she scuttled towards a big van with the words 'The Purple Photo Shop: Capturing Your Magic Moments for Ever' printed on it in large droopy purple letters.

The Dad Who was holding the back door open, like a farmer herding lambs into the back of his truck. Although I hoped that's where the analogy ended, as there was only one place lambs in a truck were going...

'Well done, everyone!' said the Dad Who, rain dripping down his dark hair and on to his purple jacket (all wetly droopy like his van).

As the last of us, Sally as it happened, climbed into the back of the van, the Dad Who climbed in with us.

'Dad,' said Amy as she snuggled up to the world's most handsome Winnie the Pooh impersonator, 'if you're back here with us, who's driving us to the rink?'

'Ethan,' he answered. 'You know Ethan, don't you, Chloe? Steve's friend from the army? He got in touch with me wanting to earn some money to help pay for his acting course. I think he thought photography would be suitably arty to go with the acting. But I'm afraid all he's been doing so far is driving vehicles and lifting heavy machinery. He must feel like he's back in the army.'

I remembered Ethan all right. A nice guy, who had seemed too spindly for the army. Steve had once brought him back when they were on leave. Ethan had seemed the most unlikely soldier you could wish to meet, and had shown a completely unexpected familiarity with the novels of E. M. Forster. Well, one novel by E. M. Forster, but that was definitely one more than Steve had ever heard of, let alone read.

I later heard that Ethan had decided that the army wasn't for him, and that he had left to become an actor. But I guess acting is never going to be a full-time job, and driving purple vans would be a great way of filling in the time when you're 'resting' between jobs.

But we clearly must all have looked a bit puzzled. Because the Dad Who looked a bit awkward.

'You may as well know,' he said, sounding as awkward as he looked, and directing his words mostly to Mark, 'but the college has decided that a teacher who teaches photography is a teacher too many. Apparently photography isn't something that really needs teaching anyway' – he sounded the nearest thing to bitter I had ever heard him sound – 'and now that it's off the curriculum, so am I.'

He looked around at us all as we bounced around on the rough bench at the back of the van, and went on, 'So now I do a nice line in wedding photography. When you and your beloveds take the plunge I'd ask you to remember me and the Purple Photo Shop. I'll "make your wedding memories special".' He still sounded a bit cynical, but he was smiling at us as he spoke.

I could see Amy looking a little bit relieved at all this. I guess she hadn't wanted to tell us about the family worry, but at least now it was out in the open.

Charlie put his arm round Amy at this point, and looked deep into Amy's eyes. 'Best photographer in the world, your dad, I reckon,' he said and he gave her a hug. What did I say about Charlie being so wonderful? In one (slightly corny, but there you go) sentence, he had shown sympathy and solidarity with the Dad Who, and he'd sort of implied that, yup, they would be needing his photographic services one day.

Awwww, I thought. But there wasn't much more time to dwell on the romances and worries of Amy's family (and there would be worries – I knew they had been very short of money even when the Dad Who had had a teaching job) because we'd arrived at the skating rink.

I followed the others out of the van. Added to my rotten cold, I was feeling slightly queasy at the thought of going ice-skating when I couldn't really ice-skate. And then I felt even more queasy when I looked at the flashing lights of the sign over the ice rink. 'Slide 'n' Glide' it said in quivering pink letters. I guess whoever had come up with that one must have been mighty pleased with it, judging by the giant size of the sign.

I looked back at the van to see if Ethan was going to get out and come with us. But he didn't even look out of the window, and in moments he had put the van in gear and driven off. Perhaps to park it, perhaps to go and lift some heavy machinery.

'Come on, Chloe,' Sally was shouting from halfway up the steps. 'Time to show us your moves!'

Mark put his arm casually but carefully over my shoulders. 'Don't worry,' he said. 'I know you can't really skate. Just hang on to me.'

Needless to say this was absolutely the best thing I could hope to hear.

I went into the sweaty, smelly changing room feeling marginally less miserable about everything than I thought I would.

An hour later and I wanted to be anywhere in the world but in the Slide 'n' Glide ice-skating rink.

It had all started well enough. I actually had got my skates on, got out on to the rink and, with Mark's arm round me (of course Mark was a brilliant skater, did I mention that?), I was able to totter on to the ice, and actually start to go round the rink.

We were going slowly and carefully behind Oscar, who of course skated like the skates were a part of him. He was so confident, and fast, and able to do twirly things that I thought he must be soooo bored being with us.

Then I saw him go over to Sally, and grab her arm just seconds before she was about to skid into the sides. He's rescued her! I thought to myself. It just goes to show how much he looks out for her, even when he doesn't show it.

After a few minutes, the business of staying upright was all starting to come back to me. I was beginning to feel a bit better – the sheer effort of not falling over seemed to stop me sneezing and coughing. Soon I told Mark that I was going to go it alone. He should go off and do twirly things with Oscar, and generally show off and look cool.

I set off round the rink, following everyone else. As I sped along, really quite pleased with myself by this stage, I thought what a good system it was that everyone goes round the rink in the same direction. Imagine, I thought to myself as I slowed down for a young four-year-old in front of me and an old fifty-year-old behind me, if someone bucked the system and deliberately went round the rink the wrong way.

Imagine that, I thought, as I saw two boys in hoodies, aged about eighteen, dressed all in black, coming from the opposite direction, going the wrong way and dodging in and out of the crowds. They were shouting and grim-faced and seemed to love it when people had to dodge out of their way.

Maybe it was the cold, maybe it was *my* cold, but something made me determined to play them at their own game. They were heading straight towards me, and I was heading straight towards them.

They were going faster than I was, but I was sure I could see their expressions of malice and enjoyment. Two middle-aged women only just avoided a collision ahead of me, and both of them fell over. The boys just flew past without stopping.

I headed straight for them. They were in the wrong. I was in the right. I put my arms up in front of them and accelerated towards them. I had nothing to lose. Mark was going away, I hadn't done my homework, Mum was in the hospital, there was nothing to look forward to but public humiliation at the hands of the QB Maggie... Someone was going to pay for all this... I thought.

They say at moments like this – before a major accident or before you fall over – everything moves in slow motion.

Well, so it was. I could see the expressions on both the boys' faces change from grim determination to outright disbelief. Then from outright disbelief to proper alarm.

I gave another push with my right leg, put my head down, and aimed straight for the boy who was tallest and looked the meanest.

I collided with him, hard, with my left arm. He was knocked off course and skidded over to the edge of the rink, swiftly followed by his mate who looked back at me with an expression of fury and loathing.

Sliding (and gliding) further on I felt a huge sense of exhilaration. I was right, and they were wrong, and they were shocked and catching their breath by the side of the rink.

Moments later, I was surrounded by Mark and Charlie, closely followed by Amy and Sally.

'Chloe, you're a dingbat,' said Charlie. 'Did you do that deliberately? Do you actually want to get us all thrown out and very possibly beaten up?'

'They were going the wrong way,' I said, starting to feel a little less brave now the adrenaline and sense of righteousness had died down a bit. 'Weren't they? I mean, they were the ones who were a danger to everyone?'

'I'm afraid Charlie's right, Chloe,' said Mark. 'You are a total dingbat. They were ice stewards. That's why they're in a black uniform. They were heading over there to sort those guys out.' Mark pointed to where there were some boys shouting and waving cans of beer.

'We'd better all quietly get off the rink and move on out,' said Mark. 'Come on, everyone, game's over.'

Head down, with my snuffly cold now back with a vengeance, and not feeling a trace of my former bravery, I followed him off the rink. There was no sign of Oscar – perhaps he had gone off to be brilliant somewhere else – but all the others crowded round me as we went back to get our skates off and our shoes on.

'Hey, you,' came a shout from behind us. It was the taller hoodie, the one I'd barged into. Now I could see that he had a big 'Slide 'n' Glide' badge on his tracksuit. I could feel a huge wave of redness wash over me, and I knew it wasn't a fever from my cold.

'I'm very sorry,' I said, my evil penguin voice sounding more raspy than ever. 'I didn't mean to.'

Which was of course not very clever as I'd obviously very much 'meant to'.

'Get off the ice right now,' said the tall one. 'You lot are all banned. Don't ever, any of you, try to come here again.' And he turned on his heel and shot off into the distance – going, I couldn't help noticing, the wrong way round the rink.

'You're a dork, Chloe,' said Sally helpfully as we undid our laces. 'Honestly, I can't believe you didn't see their badges. They're so cross. They might call the police. And then we'll get arrested. And then we'll have to spend the night in jail. And it'll be All Your Fault.' She looked up at me triumphantly.

I opened my mouth to say something in my defence, but before I could say a word, out came an enormous sneeze coupled with a cough. It was a strange and unpleasant sensation which only added to all the other strange and unpleasant sensations I'd had in the last day or so.

'OK, Chloe,' said Mark as we emerged from the changing rooms. 'Let's get you home. You need to have an early night if you're going to get better.' He manoeuvred me out through the crowds and into the freezing air outside.

We seemed to have lost Oscar completely, but I

didn't have the energy to think about that. All I could think about was that these were the last few precious moments with Mark, and we were spending them in the freezing cold, with loads of other people, and very probably fleeing for our lives thanks to my moment of madness on the skating rink.

The Dad Who was standing by his purple van, concentrating hard on his phone and – I couldn't believe my eyes – smoking a cigarette. The perfect dad was not so perfect.

'Daaaaaad,' said Amy as we approached. 'What are you *doing*? You're supposed to have given up!'

The Dad Who looked up, shamefaced. He dropped the cigarette and ground it out with his heel.

'Sorry, love,' he said. 'Been a bit stressed. That's the last one, though.' He looked her in the eye. 'Honest,' he added.

It was pitch dark by now, and gently sleeting. There was no sign of spindly Ethan. The Dad Who got into the driving seat and told us to settle ourselves in the back and he'd take us home, with me and Sally as first stop.

As Charlie shut the doors I sat on the bench next to Mark, trying to get as close to him as I could. With his arm round me, and feeling his warm breath in my hair,

I started to feel a bit better. And then overwhelmingly sad, knowing that I wouldn't see him for weeks and weeks – not until the Easter holidays, which seemed like another world away.

'Hey,' he said into my hair. 'You won't miss me that much – you'll be busy looking after your mum, and Oscar. Don't forget to look after Oscar. Show him a nice time, make him into a happy Oscar with fluent English and lots of friends. And I bet there's the perfect girlfriend for him out there, too.'

'Sure,' I said, looking down at the camera boxes and tripods bouncing around on the floor of the van. 'Sure,' I said again, trying to sound like I could achieve all these things, and also determined to make a success of Project Oscar.

'And we can Skype lots,' Mark went on. 'We can make plans for the Easter holidays. You never know – perhaps Ralph could pay for you to come to France and see me at half term?'

The chances of that happening were about one in fifty-seven million. Which only made me feel even more miserable. Especially when I remembered that the only thing planned for half term was QB Maggie's horrible party.

I felt the corners of my mouth turn down in the way

that they will keep doing when I'm trying hard not to cry.

'Don't be like that, C,' he said, bending down so he could look me in the eye. 'It's not for ever. We'll talk to each other all the time. It'll be OK.'

He was so grown-up, but even as he was comforting me I could just tell that actually he was excited about going away. Excited – I couldn't stop myself feeling – at the thought of being in another country, meeting new people, getting to know his (probably glamorous) exchange…

Just in time I stopped myself thinking like that, and let myself be kissed. It was a lovely kiss, it was just a pity that the Dad Who put the brakes on hard right in the middle of it, and we were all thrown against the back door.

'Hey, everyone,' he said from the front. 'First stop, Chloe. You can open the doors with that green catch on the inside.'

Mark leaned over, opened the door and let in more freezing air. He jumped out and then held his hand out to Sally, who jumped enthusiastically out of the van and straight into a puddle, soaking her coat and Mark's trousers.

But at least she had the tact to walk away and go

and sit on the garden wall.

As the sleet and rain poured down on us, Mark and I had a long hug. He felt all wet and warm and I absolutely didn't want to let him go.

'OK, then,' I said, pulling myself together and trying to sound all bright, and not too coldy and crying-y. 'Have a great time in France.' And then I took a deep breath. 'Love you,' I said in a tone of voice that could be taken as just an affectionate goodbye, or might, just might, be read for what it was: a full-blown declaration of actual love.

Mark drew back and looked down at me. 'Me too,' he said slowly and warmly. Then he gave me a quick kiss, and disappeared into the purple van.

The gears creaked and screeched as the Dad Who took off for his next delivery.

I stood in the sleet for a few moments longer, looking after the tail-lights as they disappeared into the distance.

Then, trying not to sniff, I found my key and headed towards my front door, my tactful friend and an evening of home cooking.

'What,' came a voice from the direction of the living room, 'is that *revolting* smell?'

I looked at Sally, and Sally looked at me.

Gran could be pretty loud when she wanted to be, and even though she had her favourite TV programme (*Great Baking Disasters*) on at full blast, she still managed to drown it out with her shouty voice.

I put down the spatula, which now had a black crusty edge round it from where I had tried to scrape some burnt sauce off the cooker, and headed out of the kitchen. The last thing I wanted was for Gran to come and inspect the damage. There was a lot to do before a grown-up could be allowed anywhere near the kitchen.

There *was* a pretty revolting smell hanging around, though.

I shut the kitchen door behind me and went into the sitting room. Gran was sitting in the middle of the sofa looking very cross. Ghastly Ralph was dozing in the armchair to her left, holding his mug of tea at the sort of angle that meant it probably wouldn't be long before it woke him up.

'Sorry, Gran, just over-heated something, that's all,' I said in my best apologetic granddaughter tone. 'Won't be too long now. Hope you're hungry!' I added cheerfully, as if everything were under control.

'Hungry is as hungry does,' said Gran, using one of her favourite utterly incomprehensible expressions. (I once looked it up, and I think you're meant to say 'handsome is as handsome does', which at least has the advantage of making some sort of sense.) 'I just hope you know what you're doing in there, my girl.'

Which of course I didn't, but I smiled sweetly at grumpy Gran and comatose Ralph and scuttled back to the kitchen.

'It's all right, Chloe,' said Sally looking up from the cooker with a confident smile on her face. 'Look, I've re-boiled the sauce so the burnt bits don't show, and I've broken up the spaghetti into little bits and now it's all cooking together nicely.'

I looked down at the red and black and yellow mess bubbling away in Mum's best pan, and could see that quite a lot of it was sticking to the sides and turning dark brown. I bent down for a closer inspection and could see that the little bits of spaghetti were still dead straight. As I reckoned they needed to be bent and curly, I turned the heat up a bit, which just had the effect of making more stuff turn dark brown round the edges.

'We should put this on Instagram,' said Sally,

peering down at the pan. 'Doesn't it look delicious?'

I looked sideways at Sally, just to make sure she was joking, but she looked her usual cheerful self as she got out her phone and took a picture of the pan.

I turned on the extractor fan, gave the brown mixture a last stir and went to tell Gran and Ralph dinner was ready.

'Well, that wasn't too terrible,' said Ghastly Ralph twenty minutes later, giving a small burp of satisfaction. 'That could have come out of a tin, that could.'

This was probably the highest praise possible from a Ralph, and Sally and I exchanged a glance of amazement or satisfaction depending on which one of us you were looking at.

'I don't know about that,' said Gran, because whatever Ralph said you could rely on Gran to take the opposite point of view. 'You wouldn't find crunchy spaghetti in a tin, I don't think.' She looked over at the cooker and said to me, 'And I hope you're going to give your mother's pan a good scrubbing, because if I'm not very much mistaken there's all sorts of burnt bits on it.'

Mention of Mum made me feel all sad and worried again. I knew the day had been OK, and she was fine and being looked after in hospital, but I suddenly wanted her back. I know she would have gently stopped us making such a mess of cooking dinner, and then given us all the credit for getting it right.

But apparently there wasn't time to dwell on that. 'Right, you two,' said Ralph getting to his feet in a business-like fashion. 'I'll come and help you get the spare bed ready. Tomorrow's your first day back at school, so you need a proper night's sleep.'

In case that sounded too much like a proper caring parent, we should remember that that night was the night of the European Cup Final something or other, so Ghastly Ralph was anxious to get us properly out of the way before kick-off.

But he did at least operate the rather elderly pump to blow up the 'spare bed' – an all-in-one mattress that featured characters from Steve's favourite cartoon.

By now I was starting to feel desperate to go to sleep, and began to get ready for bed in the hope that Sally would do the same.

Eventually, I turned off the light in an encouraging way, and heard Sally snuggle down in between the Teenage Mutant Ninja Turtles (perhaps it was a love of their mighty weaponry that had started Steve on his mission to join the army). Having established that breathing through my nose if I lay on my right side was impossible, I turned over on to the other side and waited for sleep to make me feel better and make me forget all my troubles.

It was not to be.

'So, Chloe,' said Sally, 'are you very sad about Mark? What do you think I should do about Rob, and how am I going to get out of swimming this term?'

I turned over on to the side facing Sally, the one where I couldn't breathe. 'I think—' I started to say, but Sally hadn't finished.

'Also. WHAT are we going to do about Maggie's party, and do you think everyone will be talking about it tomorrow? Also. Have you finished all your holiday homework?'

I could see that going to sleep would have to wait a little longer. 'I am very sad about Mark,' I said, 'but I don't think you should worry about Rob. After all, you know what they say about other fish in the sea.'

'No,' said Sally in a rather puzzled tone of voice. 'What do they say about other fish in the sea?'

'That there are some,' I said slowly and patiently and sleepily. 'I mean, remember when we worked it all out with our Boy Watching charts? We never really had enough points for Rob to be absolutely certain that he's the one for you, did we? I think you can never really tell, because you just never know.' I think I was getting my clichés muddled up, but I wanted Sally to stop thinking that Rob was The One.

'Well, I think I AM sure,' said Sally rather crossly. 'It's just it's not going very well at the moment. And anyway, HAVE you done all of your holiday homework? You'll get in awful trouble if you haven't, won't you? And if you're going to be a famous author hadn't you better win the English Prize this year?'

All of which was exactly calculated to make me feel all stressed and worried all over again.

Sally went on. 'I've done my Ecosystems essay, *and* my Dairy Food project *and* my African Wall Hangings project,' she said in a horribly self-satisfied tone.

Honestly, you could go off people.

'But you haven't told me how I'm going to get out of swimming,' Sally said. 'I hate swimming,' she added unnecessarily.

'I think you're going to have to get a massive fungal infection,' I said. 'The kind of thing that looks really, really horrid, and makes everyone want to keep well away from you because you smell so much and look disgusting.'

This wasn't really very helpful of me, but it made me feel better.

'I think you're being horrible,' said Sally. And on that sour note, we turned over on our respective coloured sheets and went to sleep.

⇴ 6 ⇷

Education Matters

The wintry sun was streaming through my bedroom window the following morning. It made everything in my room, including Sally and the mutant turtles, look all bright and cheerful, as if nothing in the world were wrong, and nobody had to go to school.

I had managed to breathe all night, and even go to sleep and not dream of Mark, Mum or undone homework. I wasn't feeling brilliant, but not quite as bad as I had the morning before.

School seemed so long ago that it was like another world, and I couldn't remember what the day held. No doubt Fate and the school timetable had some horrors up their sleeves – like Maths (with the vile and vicious Miss Grunbar) or Chemistry, or swimming, or Geography.

Sally was struggling with the zip just by

Michelangelo's nose (at least I think he was called Michelangelo, although why you would name an armed turtle after a Renaissance painter I can't imagine). 'Help,' she said crossly. 'Get me out of here, Chloe.'

I got out of bed, sneezed and released her. Muttering to herself, Sally set off in the general direction of the bathroom.

'Oh my god!' Sally screamed moments later. 'Help!'

I dashed out of the room, thinking that she'd been attacked by a dead body, or at the very least had trodden on an enormous spider.

Sally was standing by the airing cupboard next to the bathroom. She'd clearly opened the wrong door. Of course in a normal household you would expect to find things being aired in an airing cupboard – sheets, pillowcases, that sort of thing. But not chez Bennet when Gran's in residence.

Facing out of the inside of the cupboard was Gran's collection of china dolls. Rows and rows of bright white faces, some with deep black eyes or straggly hair, some with torn old-fashioned costumes, all gazing implacably at whichever hapless soul opened the door.

In this case the hapless soul was Sally, who was standing in front of the cupboard, motionless with shock.

'Chloe,' she said in a small voice. 'It's like a horror movie. Are they all dead?'

'Absolutely,' I said, realising that Sally was in quite a state and trying to be vaguely reassuring. 'They really, really aren't going to come and get you.'

Sally continued to gaze wordlessly at the bright white faces.

I tried to sound relaxed and cheerful, although the rows of staring black eyes were starting to unnerve me too. 'They are rather gruesome, though, aren't they?' I said. 'But they're Gran's pride and joy. Love Gran, love her china doll collection, she says. Apparently they're really valuable. Collectors' items.'

'Yuck,' said Sally, backing away from the cupboard. 'I can't imagine why anyone would want to collect such revolting things.'

I heard a rustling sound from Steve-now-Gran's bedroom. Thinking it would be better for Gran not to hear all this, I said to Sally, 'Best go to the bathroom and try to forget about it.' I pushed her gently away and shut the door on the staring faces.

By the time we had had breakfast, let the air out of the mutant ninja turtles and packed our school bags, we were running late. Not a good start to a new year and a new term.

Catching the bus by the skin of our teeth we settled ourselves on the top deck and opened up our phones. Sally was jubilant because she had posted her picture of dinner on Instagram and had got two 'likes'.

My phone was telling me altogether more serious things.

Starting with a message from Mark – 'On train to London. Thinking of you. Will call. Take care. Love + hugs xxxxxxxcxx'

I suppose it was exactly the sort of message you'd hope for from the love of your life who was heading off into the depths of a foreign country. But knowing he was now definitely and certainly on his way made me feel suddenly so miserable that I gave an enormous sneeze. No amount of Xs could cheer me up, I thought, and then couldn't believe that my inner mathematician was at it again and had already calculated the Xs as adding up to ninety.

But next door to Mark's message was one guaranteed to take my mind off my sadness. 'Timetable change' it said: 'Lesson 1 Wednesday 4 Jan now Maths not English'. Great, the evil Miss Grunbar would be welcoming us into the new year after all.

The bus rolled up to the familiar bus stop by the school gates. The good news was that Amy and

Gemma were standing just inside the gates, and the bad news that the QB Maggie was standing just outside them.

The QB looked as she usually did: short, short-skirted, heavily made-up and extra high-heeled (*way* more heels and make-up than we were supposed to wear; sometimes I think the staff are even less anxious to take on Maggie than the rest of us) and was holding forth to five or six girls who were surrounding her in a circle.

Each one of them had exactly the same expression of anxious malevolence on their faces. As if to say, 'Exactly how bitchy would you like us to be? Because we can be that bitchy, or even more so if you'd like, just so long as you don't turn on us.'

As Sally and I got off the bus I could see Maggie point at us and say something to her cohorts. As one, they turned round, looked at us and started sniggering. The sort of snigger that is utterly mirthless and terribly relieved to be on the side of the sniggerers. With their long hair, their high heels and their frightening eyeliner, they managed to look exactly the same as each other.

'Did you know,' said Sally to me, with only a tiny quaver in her voice, 'that research shows that popular girls are the most likely to be mean?'

Sally was a great one for surveys, most of which seemed to come from the University of the Bleeding Obvious. This was an interesting one, though, because while being extremely mean, Maggie wasn't exactly popular.

'I don't think we're really talking *popular* with Maggie, do you?' I said, glancing at the short one in centre of the group as she tucked her hair behind her ears and smirked in a self-satisfied fashion.

I tried to ignore the sniggering and tittering as we got nearer to the QB's cohorts. 'I mean,' I went on, trying to pretend they weren't there and that anyway Sally and I were so deep in conversation we hadn't noticed them, 'nobody actually likes Maggie, do they? They're just very frightened of her.' I looked determinedly ahead of me, hoping to catch Gemma's eye as she talked to Amy.

But as we got nearer it was impossible not to hear what the QB's cohorts were saying: '...they'll find out when no one's talking to her!' 'Yeah, and just imagine what'll happen when she tells them at the party!' '... Little Miss Lonely, here I come...!' '...put it on Facebook and then let's see what "Mark's girlfriend" makes of that...'

Every part of those sentences carried a hidden

menace, a mystery and a threat, as well as reminding us of the dreaded Valentine's party. If they'd been carefully constructing dialogue for a masterclass in psychological bullying, they couldn't have done it better. But come to think of it, of course that's exactly what Queen Beeyatches are so good at doing.

But at that moment Amy looked round, saw us and waved with a cheerful, friendly grin. There was someone uncomplicated and happy, I thought, and I felt a bit better when we got past the gates and into the school yard.

'Hey, Chloe, guess what?' said Amy, as she bent over and touched her toes – I suppose if athletics is your thing, there's never a bad time to stretch your muscles.

'Can't guess,' I said. 'What?' Amy had now started on another set of muscles and was drawing her right knee up to somewhere near her ear.

'Gem's going to London on Saturday to meet the model agency people,' said Amy. 'Merv's taking her in the big car and says we can all come too.' She had put her right knee down and had started on the left.

'That's great!' said Sally, 'Perhaps when they see us they'll want us to be supermodels too!'

Amy put her left knee down and looked at Sally with

the sort of expression you might have on your face if you saw a dog trying to stand on its hind legs. You know it's hopeless but you have to admire the optimism.

'Let's just see what happens with Gemma first,' I said. 'They probably only want one supermodel at a time.'

'Anyway,' said Gemma, trying to look bored with the whole subject but not quite succeeding. 'We'll go from mine first thing Saturday, and meet Marianne in London.'

This was definitely something interesting to look forward to – not just being in at the beginning of whatever was going to happen with Gemma, but also to see Marianne. Altogether definitely something to take our minds off Maggie and her plots, and our general boyfriendlessness.

'And now, girls, we're going to have some fun.' This was the extraordinary statement that came straight out of the mouth of the evil and vile Miss Grunbar, she of the rasping voice, the huge nose and the cruel way that she had of making us feel tiny and stupid with her mighty sarcasm. We had been in her Maths class for only ten minutes, but already it felt like we had been back at school for weeks, if not years. I was not hopeful that Miss G's idea of fun was mine.

'Look at this equation,' she was saying, writing on the whiteboard.

'5 + 5 + 5 + 5 = 555,' she wrote. 'Now,' she said, 'draw just one line on this equation to make it correct.' And she stood back from the board with a self-satisfied smile on her face. And she waited. And waited.

Silence reigned.

Eventually, and with a deep sigh, Miss G moved to the board, and drew a line which made the middle plus sign into a 4. '5 + 545 + 5 = 555' 'Five plus four hundred and forty-five plus five is five hundred and fifty-five,' she said with an even deeper sigh.

I had a moment of feeling vaguely sorry for someone who obviously did actually love these things called numbers, but spent her days entirely surrounded by people who didn't.

Just as all good things come to an end, so do all bad things. Eventually we were released from the morning's classes, leaving us just enough time to bunk off to the local shops before Geography.

We were on a tight schedule. Sally was convinced that if we timed it right we would get to the shops at exactly the moment that Rob and his friends from St Thomas's Year 12 would be buying their illicit cigarettes. I thought the chances of us bumping into him accidentally on purpose were remote to the power of remote, and besides if Sally was going to bump into anyone I wanted it to be Oscar. But it was always interesting to be somewhere where the St Thomas's boys might be, so I was still happy to do it.

But first we had to head off to the changing rooms to put on enough make-up for the outside world. It would be unthinkable to step out of the gates in the middle of the day without at least eyeliner, lip gloss and maybe foundation if our complexions were being at all awkward.

Soon we were ready. All we had to do was creep out of the gates without being spotted by some tiresome member of staff. But happily it started to pour with rain, freezing cold rain, which was almost always guaranteed to keep old people, like teachers, indoors.

We made it to the shop just after it had started to rain so hard that even young people like us would rather not be outside.

Dripping all over the floor, we huddled together near the 'Personalised Retro Sweets' (it wasn't clear how you personalised a retro sweet, but judging by the price of them it was obviously an extremely expensive business), the Belgian chocolates and the DIY magazines. From there we could get a good view of people coming in and out, especially ones in the distinctive St Thomas's uniforms trying to look as if they were eighteen and old enough to buy cigarettes.

Gemma, being Gemma and therefore much cooler than us, was standing near the counter practising her supermodel flick of the hair. The rather tired-looking old guy behind the counter didn't look that impressed when her supermodel hair flicked water all over his lottery ticket machine.

'Hey, Chloe,' Gemma called over to me, completely unaware of the glance of hatred the shopkeeper was giving her. 'Come and see this.' She was looking at a noticeboard that was stuck all over with cards and ads. 'Someone you know, I think.'

I thought it highly unlikely that anyone I knew was stuck to a noticeboard, but made my way over to the other end of the shop. Looking at the ad Gemma was pointing to, I saw a picture of an adorable border terrier gazing into the camera with an expression of innocent curiosity.

For a moment I thought, What an incredibly sweet-looking dog. And then in the next moment I thought, But that's Albert!

And then I saw the words 'for sale' in spidery writing just under his right paw. 'Due to unforseen cirkumstances, and family illness, this dog nedes a home. House trained and cheep.'

'I don't believe it!' I cried out. 'He's selling Albert! This is awful. We've *got* to rescue him.'

Sally came up and looked over my shoulder at the noticeboard. 'That's not how you spell cheap, is it?' she said.

I couldn't believe that Sally didn't see the utter horror and tragedy of the situation. Nor that she was actually asking a question about spelling. Ignoring her, I turned to Amy, who I thought was the person most likely to understand.

'What can I do, Ames?' I said. 'How do you go about rescuing a dog? And what does it cost?'

Amy looked sympathetic. 'I don't know, Chloe. There's a phone number: let's ring them now. Put him on speakerphone so we can hear what he says.'

I pulled out my phone and started to press the numbers written on the bottom of the card. I knew I'd be getting through to Mr Underwood, and I knew he wasn't about to make a deal with a fifteen-year-old girl who he'd stopped speaking to after she'd abandoned his dog. But I was desperate, and I had to stop him selling Albert to someone else.

'Underwood,' said a man's rough voice at the other end of the phone. Unmistakeably our horrible downstairs neighbour.

I put on my best grown-up voice and adopted a plummy accent to try to sound like I was rich enough to own a dog. I reckoned I sounded a bit like a cross between a character in *Downton Abbey* and a villain in a Bond movie. Or at any rate, someone with a big house, possibly capable of destroying the world if they chose to.

'I am ringing about the dog in the advertisement,' I said slowly and carefully. 'The one for sale. I am interested in acquiring it.'

'Oo's this?' said Mr Underwood. 'This some kinda joke? Oo do you think you are, taking the mick? You can get off the line, that's what you can do.' And he hung up.

'Twit,' said Gemma unsympathetically. 'Now you've got his back up even worse than if you'd been yourself.'

'Great,' I said. 'Disaster. Now what can we do?' I looked helplessly at the others.

'Well, you've got to get someone to buy him first, and then we can work out what to do with him later,' said Gemma, being amazingly practical, I thought.

'I can ask Charlie,' said Amy. 'He can sound even posher than you, Chloe...'

'Ha,' I said. 'Not funny. But anyway, that would be brilliant. We can get him to ring this evening, can't we?'

'We can,' said Amy, smiling. 'But I don't know what we do for money. Are dogs expensive, do you think – even when they're cheap?'

'I'm sure Ralph can get me a weekend job at the JobCentre, or I can ask Mum. Or...something...' Thinking of it all made me feel a bit overwhelmed. With Mum ill, Gran already hating Albert and everything to do with him, and Ralph hating everything that interfered with a quiet life in front of the telly, we were hardly an Albert-friendly household. Even if I could earn the money to pay for Albert and whatever Alberts ate.

'We'll have to work that out later,' said Gemma, looking out of the shop window, 'Right now the sun's coming out and so are some of our favourite Year Twelve St Thomas's boys. Look.'

She was right. Walking down the street as if they owned it were five St Thomas's boys in full football kit, swigging from cans of energy drinks and laughing like drains at something the tall one in the middle had said.

Gemma, being Gemma, knew them all. The rest of

us, being us, didn't know any of them.

'Who's that good-looking boy on the right?' said Sally peering over the piles of newspapers to look out of the window. 'Doesn't he look a bit like Rob?'

I was thinking that the sooner she got over Rob and found her true love with Oscar the better, when one of them called out to us, 'Hey, Gem! Come over here and see what we've got!' They all stopped where they were and were squinting against the sudden sunshine. All of them were now focused on the group of us still standing in the protection of the shop's doorway.

'OK, Chloe,' said Gemma, half sarcastically, half amused. 'What does your Boy Watching manual say we should do in cases like this? Did we ever get to the chapter dealing with "Inspection of Unknown Objects"?'

'I'm not sure this is a good idea,' said Amy. 'And anyway we need to get back soon or we'll be late for Geography.'

'Oh no, let's go and have a closer look,' said Sally. 'I'm sure the one who looks like Rob must be nice, because look, he's got big ears.' I couldn't remember when we'd decided that 'big ears = nice' any more than I could remember what we should do about inspecting unknown objects.

'Come on then,' said Gemma as she squeezed her

still wet hair over the shop floor. 'Let's go and see what they mean.' And she led the way down the street towards the boys.

As we approached, all of them looked at her, and didn't seem at all interested in us.

'So what's the story, Robin?' said Gemma to the tall one. 'What's going on?'

The tall one, Robin, looked down at her and said, 'Nothing, Gem. We just wanted a closer look at you. Someone said you're going to be a supermodel, and we just wanted to see what a supermodel looks like close up.'

The one with big ears, who on closer inspection didn't look at all like Rob, started laughing. And then all the others started laughing.

Gemma looked them up and down and gave her absolutely best eye-rolling look of utter scorn. And then turned on her heel, saying to us, 'Come on, you lot, we're going to be late.'

It was a masterclass in cool. Even I was a bit frightened by Gemma's expression of total contempt.

'That was interesting,' said Sally cheerfully, as she trotted along beside us. 'Don't you think, Chloe? I mean for your Boy Watching skills. Who knew that you could get a group of boys behaving a bit like Maggie and those cows she's always surrounded by?'

'I suppose so,' I said. 'Yes, it was like they were all showing off to each other. Because, the fact is, they all really, really fancy Gemma, but because she's not interested in any of them they have to pretend they're not either.'

I could see Gemma give a small smile at this, but there wasn't time to dwell on The Boy as Beeyatch because we had exactly minus thirty seconds to get back into the school grounds and ready for Geography.

We were, in fact, properly late. By the time we'd found out there'd been a classroom change, picked up Sally from the bottom of the stairs (she had tripped over the laces on her trainers. I guess something like that could happen to anyone. But it did always seem to happen to Sally), and had waited for Amy to finish texting Charlie, we were more than five minutes behind schedule.

The corridors were eerily silent as we made our way to the right room. As we walked past all the firmly shut doors, our footsteps echoed through the building. It felt like the whole world could hear that we were in trouble.

I opened the door of Room 211A. There was more silence as everyone looked up. Standing by the whiteboard, Miss Bartlett – six foot two, orange hair, and a permanent expression of scorn on her horse-like face – watched us fumble our way to the four empty desks in the front row.

'Glaciation,' she said icily. 'Some of us are learning about glaciation here. But perhaps you already know all there is to know about glaciation? In which case, I think we would like to hear your definition of a glacier, and how it affects the landscape. Chloe?'

'Striations,' I said with a mixture of confidence and fright. 'They cause striations. And also freezing and thawing. Which makes things like the Peak District.' I had absolutely no idea where I'd got this from, but it's extraordinary what the subconscious can come up with in moments of desperation.

'Well, that's rather amusing: somebody's been doing some lucky Googling,' said Miss Bartlett, sounding not in the least bit amused. 'But I don't think that means we're entitled to miss the beginning of our lessons, do you?'

'No,' I said quietly and, I hoped, humbly. Although there was something about her use of the first person plural that annoyed me intensely. I thought, I am not a 'we'. And then I started thinking maybe I should call my next Creative Writing essay that. 'I am not a "we"', the story of a single girl abandoned by the love of her life who goes off to a foreign country and leaves her on her own, and so she is no longer the 'we' she had hoped to be. Brilliant, I thought to myself. Then I can write about what it means to miss someone and be lonely, to miss out on the togetherness of being part of a couple, missing that sense of knowing someone is there for you—

'Isn't it, Chloe?' Horse-face was looking intently at me, with an expression of pure malevolence. My lucky Googling luck had run out, and I was in old-fashioned trouble. I had no idea what she'd been talking about.

There was a sniggering and a tittering sound coming from the back of the class. I could hear the tones of the QB leading the sniggers, and I felt a kind of tingling in the back of my neck, as if the looks of spite coming from the back row were actually physical.

'I... I...am not sure,' I said glancing desperately at Sally sitting beside me. But she was no help. She was just looking at me open-mouthed, as if fascinated by the sight of a small vulnerable creature (me) being slowly eaten by a massive boa constrictor (Miss B).

'You are not only late, you are inattentive, and you are deliberately avoiding engaging in my lesson,' the boa constrictor said. 'Somehow you girls need to learn a lesson, and I will make an example of you, Chloe. You will take seven detention points.'

Just great. Amy, Gemma and Sally looked at me sympathetically. After all, there but for the grace of me went them. And I bet they couldn't even spot a striation if it bit them in the bottom. Although, come to think of it, neither could I.

Eventually the gruesome Geography lesson was over, but as everyone got their books and bags together I stayed sitting, still slightly poleaxed by the great unfairness of Miss Bartlett and calculating that seven detention points would mean that I now had so many points (all for the kind of lateness that makes mums buy their daughters alarm clocks) that I would have to go into school on Saturday morning for the dreaded Saturday detention. A hideous punishment, as much for the members of staff who had to supervise it as for any of us, and particularly horrible for anyone wanting to go to London for the day.

'Nightmare,' said Sally as we packed up after our last lesson of the day. It had been History. The bitterness of the working classes towards the Poor Law. (An appropriately miserable way of ending the day, I thought.)

'What is a nightmare?' I said, thinking that if anyone had one of those it would be me. I'd been right about detention: our form teacher Mr Carson – the man who made nervous blinking into an art form and who should never, in my opinion, have taken up teaching – had confirmed my fears. I now had fifteen detention points which meant I automatically had to spend ten till eleven on Saturday morning at school and in detention. There was a very real danger of missing going to London.

'Well, it's all right for you,' said Sally, rather inaccurately, I felt. 'But I've got to go home to Harris and Jock, Mum being ill, and James being all weird. Apparently they still don't know what the rashes are, but the twins need to stay in bed and have stuff put all over them. So it's *all* about Harris and Jock and nobody else gets a look-in.'

I thought I knew who she meant by 'nobody else'.

'And I'm going home to try to cheer up Mum, avoid Gran and Ralph, and hope for a message from Mark, who I know I'm not going to see for *ten* weeks. AND I've no idea if we're going to be able to save Albert's life,' I said, not wanting her to have the monopoly on misery.

'That's a slight exaggeration,' said Amy, coming up behind us, already in her quilted coat and ready for the freezing outdoors. 'But we need to go now because Charlie's waiting and he says we should make a plan so we can ring Mr Underwood together.'

Moments later the three of us were heading towards the bus stop to meet Charlie. Gemma had melted away in the way that she sometimes has when she's got things to do and people to see.

'Hi, girls,' said Charlie, looking as warm as his GF, all wrapped up in a big black coat with a big black scarf round his neck. 'Ready for me and my super posh accent?'

'I'm always ready for you whatever your accent,' said Amy in her special goofy tone of voice that Charlie loved and we all found incredibly irritating.

''K then, let's do this,' said Charlie. 'By the way, do we know why he's really selling Albert? What ARE these "unforeseen circumstances"?'

'I dunno,' I said. 'Mum said he had to have an interview with the police that day I lost him. But I don't know what for.'

'I think he's going to jail,' said Sally cheerfully. 'I've

always said he looked like a mass murderer, haven't I, Chloe? I reckon you can always tell a mass murderer by the way their eyes go together in the middle.'

'I kind of wish,' said Charlie slowly, 'that I hadn't asked the question. Maybe I'll just concentrate on doing the deal. How much am I supposed to be paying for your cheap border terrier, Chloe?'

'Oh dear, I have absolutely no idea. Except as little as possible because I haven't actually got any money,' I said, not very helpfully but a little desperately.

'I bet you we could get Gemma to ask Merv to pay,' said Sally. 'After all, he's always trying to please her and he IS awfully rich.'

'Right,' I said. 'And she *was* the one who said we should just buy him and worry about everything else afterwards.'

Charlie had his phone in his hand and was starting to dial the number I'd taken down from the newsagent's. I heard a ringing tone.

'Oh, hello there,' he said after it had rung a couple of times. He sounded like he owned at least a thousand acres and a couple of stately homes. 'I'm ringing about the terrier you have advertised. He looks just right as a companion for my mother who lives in the countryside. He will be good with elderly ladies, I take it?'

I was so impressed. In my mind's eye I could already see a small elderly lady sitting by the fire in a grand library, looking fondly at the little terrier sitting in her lap.

We heard a low guttural voice saying something the other end. I longed to know what as Charlie raised his eyebrows in disbelief and amusement.

'Oh, that's remarkable! What a splendid coincidence,' said Charlie. 'I should think that would work out nicely. Let's say I will come round to your house on Sunday... Yes. Thank you so much. Goodbye.' And he shut off his phone just in time before bursting out laughing.

'Apparently,' he said, 'Albert used to be owned by a ninety-year-old duchess who lived in Scotland on an estate. So his aristocratic roots make him perfect for us. Apparently.'

'He probably thinks you'll pay an aristocratic price for him, then,' said Amy.

'Don't worry about that,' said Charlie. 'I'll plead aristocratic poverty, what with the leaking roof, the crumbling stables and the terrible gambling debts Great Uncle Fergus left us with...'

Charlie's own personal episode of *Downton Abbey* was interrupted by the arrival of my bus. Hurriedly waving goodbye to the others I climbed on and made my way towards the only empty seat, which was at the back of the bus – just next to the boy with big ears who didn't look like Rob.

He was bending over his phone, but looked up as I approached. There was a tiny moment of recognition, and then he looked quickly back to his phone and didn't move a muscle when I sat down next to him.

I thought back to our Boy Watching conclusions about The Boy (On Its Own), and the contrast between him and The Boy (In Its Pack). The one with its pack being so much more fearless than the one on its own. Big Ears wouldn't have dared to laugh at anyone if he wasn't with his mates.

I glanced sideways at his phone. I could just make out the words 'girl next to me' in one of the Snapchat bubbles.

Looking hurriedly away, I got out my own phone and started writing a message to Sally. It was important to tell her that 'big ears' does not mean 'nice'.

➤➤ 7 ⬅⬅

Model Pupil

By the time we got to Saturday, it felt like the winter term had already gone on forever, and I was way overdue a holiday. As it was, I had to make do with a weekend – even though it was one that started with a dose of detention.

'We'll pick you up at eleven on the dot,' Gemma had said. 'And don't be late. I know how you can't tear yourself away from school, but my appointment's at two, and I DO NOT want to be late.'

Mum had come back from the hospital looking paler than ever but swearing she was feeling much better. I had so wanted a hug, but as I was still sniffling and snotty (Sally's sweet description) I wasn't allowed anywhere near her.

I had had two messages from Mark, and the promise of a proper Skype conversation with him on Sunday.

Apparently Dijon-or-wherever was actually in remote countryside, Cecile played cricket and football, his French wasn't as good as he thought it was, everyone drank red wine, and it was sunnier than it was in England. Which made me instantly imagine him lying on a grassy bank, bathed in sunshine, drinking claret with a beautiful blonde girl called Cecile who had just scored two goals and a hundred runs.

Also, he wanted to know if I was missing him like mad (yes) and if I had been looking after Oscar (not really). I felt guilty that I hadn't made as much progress with Project Oscar as I had intended to. So I made a plan for us all to take Oscar and Albert for a run in the park on Sunday. Sweet Albert, who I very much hoped would be properly rescued by then.

I arrived at school at quarter to ten that Saturday morning. Perhaps if I were early, they'd release me early, I thought. Making my way to the side entrance, and slightly spooked by the complete emptiness of the playground, I wondered what grim tasks they would have lined up for me.

Maybe I would have to write loads of lines in chalk on a blackboard like Bart Simpson, or maybe I'd have to empty all the rubbish bins, or run round the playground wearing a special badge of shame...

But before my imagination went into overdrive, I got to my classroom, where I saw that my form master, the blinking Mr Carson, had drawn the short Saturday morning straw. He was sitting by the window reading a battered copy of *Thinking Outside the Box: How to Be A Brilliant Teacher*. He was about halfway through and frowning so hard you couldn't see his eyes. For a moment I did think of telling him that if nature had intended him to be a teacher, it wouldn't have made him so blinking terrified of us.

But when he looked up I saw the moment had passed. He was obviously very unhappy at having to spend his Saturday morning in room 311. So I suppose we had that in common at least.

'Chloe,' he said in a voice that managed to sound both weary and hate-filled. 'Your task will be to read a passage in French, answer some comprehension questions, and learn three pages of vocabulary. Here it is.' And he handed me an alarmingly large pile of paper.

With a deep sigh, I sat down at one of the desks as far away from Mr C as possible and looked at the papers. '*Combien je suis heureux d'être en France*', the passage was called – it was all about how a boy was having a wonderful holiday in France.

I suppose they weren't to know what an entirely

appropriate punishment they'd dreamt up.

It was hard, slow work, but eventually I heard an alarm bell from Mr Carson's phone at exactly the moment there was a *ping* from mine. Mr C stood up, came over my desk to take the papers back and said, 'That's it, Chloe. This'll be marked by your French teacher. You may go now.'

I reckoned that it was very unlikely that Madame de B, our distinctly unenthusiastic French teacher, would ever see my French comprehension. She was as unkeen on extra-curricular work as I was. Which was just as well, as I hadn't made much progress beyond a sentence which read 'I stepped out of my homework and had a drink in the wood'. Or perhaps it said 'There was no time to pay the duty on the box of weather'.

I couldn't help thinking that what I really needed was help from some kind, handsome boy whose knowledge of French was so much better than mine.

But at least it was now time to focus on other distractions, starting with a short, sharp message from Gemma. 'Outside,' the message said. Never one to waste words, Gemma.

Gathering up my stuff, I rushed out of the classroom, almost knocking over the blinking Mr C as I went, and headed for the playground, where I could see Merv's enormous black car throbbing away just by the main entrance.

Gemma was sitting in the front with Merv, and Sally was waving away at me from the back. I climbed up into the car beside her. I could see that Gemma was looking even more amazing and supermodelly than usual. In fact, I had no idea she owned that much make-up, never mind knew what to do with it.

'All right, Chloe?' said Merv from the front, his grey pigtail gleaming in the sudden winter sunshine. 'Didn't beat you or anything, did they?'

'Merv,' said Gemma, turning to him with disdain, 'they gave up beating schoolgirls before even you were born. Chloe's probably just had to have a dose of mild French translation. Probably featuring some boy who's on a French holiday.'

I was amazed. How did she know? 'How on earth…?' I said.

Gemma turned round to me. 'It's too much like hard work for them to come up with new detentions, and I pretty much know that passage off by heart.'

'Are you trying to say you've had lots of detentions then, Gemma?' said her father. Fortunately, he didn't pursue that line of inquiry because just at that moment he was brought to a screaming halt by a motorbike overtaking him on a left-hand bend and then slowing down to turn right just in front of him.

Merv wound down the window and shouted out a series of unprintable insults at the top of his voice.

The bike came to a halt and slowly and deliberately turned round and came towards Merv and our car. Hastily, Merv wound the window back up, put his foot on the accelerator and shot off ahead and past the bike.

'Jeez, Merv,' said Gemma. 'Maybe next time keep the window shut if you're going to scream abuse at the nearest boy racer.'

The rest of the drive to London was a quiet affair; we all had a range of different things to worry about, and Sally had her Instagram account to update. (She had posted a picture of the twins' rashes, and was constantly checking for likes. Although why anyone should be delighted at finding a picture of mysteriously orange skin on the internet I couldn't imagine.)

Finally, at 1.30 on the dot, with less than half an hour to spare, we turned into the central London street where Management2Model had their offices. It was one of those streets that had grand old-fashioned houses in it that were now all offices. It was full of huge trees and builders making basements, and there was absolutely nowhere to park.

'You drop us off and go and get rid of the car,' said Gemma to Merv. 'I seriously don't want to be late, and Mum's already there waiting for me.'

Merv, used as he was to doing Gemma's bidding, came to a halt outside the imposing front door of the offices, and the three of us got out.

Perhaps it was because it was lunchtime, perhaps it was because London's always like that, but the pavement seemed to be jammed with people all in a hurry, all pushing each other out of the way, and practically all of them on the phone. It was a relief to push open the huge wooden door and enter the air-conditioned peace of the reception area.

There were a dozen or so people dotted around on various state-of-the-art leather chairs. Some of them were thin, beautiful, young and heavily made-up and the rest of them were rather anxious-looking and middle-aged. This could only be the reception area of a model agency, where the young and beautiful disguised their nerves with industrial quantities of make-up, and their parents looked on with naked expressions of pride and anxiety.

On a white leather sofa to the left of the reception desk sat an elegant blonde woman. Dressed entirely in black, she sat with her legs crossed in the self-confident way that only rather beautiful people or professional models did. She was reading a book, and seemed to be so engrossed in it that she hadn't noticed the front door open.

'Mum,' said Gemma quietly as we shut the door behind us. She walked quickly towards the woman, who looked up with a preoccupied expression that was quickly replaced with a smile of such unguarded happiness that it almost brought a lump to my throat.

'Gemma,' she said as she got up and put her arms out to her daughter. She hugged her tight and long. And then stood back from her, and looked her daughter up and down. 'You're looking lovely, darling. Everything all right? Still sure you want to do this?'

'Yes, Mum, quite sure,' said Gemma, although her smile wasn't quite as self-confident as she sounded.

At that moment a girl came out from one of the doors at the side of the room. Silence descended on the reception area as everyone looked curiously at the blonde girl with the skintight white trousers and black jacket. She looked at least thirty until you looked again and saw that underneath it all she was more like our age. She went over towards a woman who really did look about thirty, and who asked anxiously,

'Well, love? What did they say?'

'Two for and one against,' said the girl tensely. 'Which means no. Apparently. Definitely no, they have to be unanimous.'

She looked upset, but was trying hard to disguise it. I felt momentarily thankful that being medium tall, medium size, with medium brown hair, no one was ever going to suggest I go through this tormenting selection process.

'So not even hand modelling? Or feet?' said her mother anxiously.

'Nope,' said the girl. 'Wrong proportions. Wrong measurements.'

I could see some of the other mothers looking slightly gleeful as they looked at what they thought were their perfectly proportioned daughters. The buzz of conversation got louder; half the mothers seemed to be talking in a foreign language.

We followed Marianne back to the sofa where we all squeezed up next to each other.

Sally seemed blissfully unaware that the two of us must have looked distinctly out of place in all this high-tech glamour and make-up. But I was rather fascinated by the difference between us and them. Looking at a particularly skinny girl sitting opposite me I wondered if you had to practise her air of vacant seduction, or whether looking into the middle distance with mouth half open was just her natural expression.

Just as I was noticing that her lip gloss was arranged in four separate layers, she caught my eye. 'Vat are *you* lookin' at?' she said in a deep, aggressive voice that seemed to come from somewhere east of Bulgaria. Her look of vacant seduction became naked aggression. Blushing, I looked away and felt thankful again that Nature had determined I didn't have to compete in this world.

Eventually they called Gemma's name, and she disappeared into the door at the back of the reception area just as Merv came in the front door, looking sweaty and hassled. Clearly parking in central London had been more of a challenge than he'd thought.

'Hello, Mervyn,' said Marianne politely but coldly. 'There's a stool over there if you want to sit down.'

Merv, looking even more out of place among the highly groomed women than we did, sat down where he was told. There was an awkward silence.

'Tricky chappie, Johnny Parking, round here,' he said eventually. Nobody seemed to have a view about Johnny Parking, so we lapsed back into silence.

Merv bowed his head and focused on the floor,

frowning and looking worried. He glanced up with an expression of relief and concern when eventually Gemma emerged from the fateful door. She had a completely unreadable expression on her face. Everyone went quiet and looked at her as she stalked in her special extra-supermodel way towards us.

'OK, everyone,' she said. 'We can go and have tea now.'

'Hey, Miss Super Cool,' said Sally, twisting her auburn hair round her forefinger in an anxious way. 'What happened? Are they going to take you on, are you going to be super rich, and will you be on the cover of *Vogue*?'

There was now total silence in the high-tech reception area of Management2Model. The vacant expressions were all pointed towards Gemma, and the older versions on the faces of the mothers looked the other way and tried to pretend they weren't interested.

'Sure,' said Gemma, smiling at our orange/auburn friend. 'Catwalk work in Milan next week, Paris the week after.' And she reached for her mother's hand and started to walk towards the main door. We all got up and followed her, some of us giving the sea of faces behind us something that might have been mistaken for a triumphant smile.

Later, sitting in the comfort of a hotel tea room, Gemma confided that actually, although the agency had said yes to her, her first job wouldn't be on a catwalk in Milan. In fact, she'd be going to a basement studio to be photographed in twenty-seven different shades of cotton dress for a catalogue.

But it was the first step on the ladder to superstardom, and we drank a toast of tea to our friend's future.

Two hours later, we got into Merv's giant car, now festooned with parking tickets ('Tricky chappie, Johnny Parking Ticket?' said Gemma sarcastically when she saw them), all sad after saying goodbye to Marianne. She had set off for beautiful Cornwall giving us strict instructions to go and see her in the Easter holidays, and we were feeling tired but happy after all the excitements of our day in London watching the beginning of Gemma's Brilliant Career.

It was a long drive home, made even longer by Merv running out of petrol on the motorway ('Johnny Petrol' obviously being as tricky as the rest of the Johnnies). So by the time I got back, everyone at home was asleep – in front of the TV or actually in bed, depending on their age and identity. So what with the sniffling and the sneezing I was glad to go straight to my room.

I had a feeling Sunday was going to be a difficult day from the start, and I was right.

Firstly, I only had two hours to make progress on my Creative Writing for the English Prize before we were going to meet up for the Acquisition of Albert and Project Oscar. I had a deadline for my essay of two weeks' time, and there is nothing more killing to the creative instinct than the deadline, I thought as I sneezed quietly over my keyboard.

'Write about what you know,' they say. Well, that's all very well, but 'Difficulties with Eyebrows', 'Great Swimming Disasters' or 'Growing up with Ralph' didn't really have the right literary ring to them.

So I started to write an epic poem (surely a poem would be just as able to win a creative writing prize) on the theme of love and loss. But it just made me dwell on the loss bit, and quite unable to write about the love bit. And by the time I'd tried to inspire myself by reading The World's Greatest Love Poems online I was feeling thoroughly sad and hadn't written a word.

There was half an hour to go before we were meant to be meeting Charlie, the laird of many acres and the odd abbey, so I thought I'd cheer myself up with a quick look at Mark's Facebook page. Perhaps there would be pictures of some beautiful French countryside, or an epic musing on the subject of love and loss...

There were nearly twenty new pictures on the Facebook page of Mr Darcy. All of them outdoors, bathed in sunshine and one of them featuring a blonde girl waving a tennis racquet and a glass of some dark liquid which was obviously making her feel very cheerful if her beaming smile was anything to go by.

I gazed at the pictures, vaguely aware that with my mouth half-open I might have looked as if I wanted a job on a catwalk or in a catalogue. Admittedly there were other people in the photograph, and maybe it was just the way the sun shone on her hair that made her look like the star of the show, but there was no mistaking the fact that whoever she was, she wasn't a tomboy by any stretch of the imagination.

I swore. Quite loudly and using words that I didn't know I knew.

Rather unluckily Ghastly Ralph walked past my open bedroom door at precisely that moment. He jerked to a halt.

'*What* did you say, young lady?' he said in a tone that managed to be both disapproving and self-righteous at the same time. I also hated the fact that he'd adopted Gran's ghastly (of course) habit of calling me 'young lady'.

'Nothing,' I said in the time-honoured fashion that people of our generation have of denying the truth even if it's staring them in the face. Although actually I don't think it's a habit peculiar to our generation.

'Nothing?' said Ghastly Ralph, obviously enjoying every moment of being in the right. 'Nothing?' For a mad moment, I thought he was going to launch into the speech from *King Lear* that we'd just learned at school – 'Nothing shall come of nothing'.

'We'll see about that, my girl,' said Ralph. So obviously I was wrong about the speech from *King Lear*.

'Anyone who uses language like that shouldn't be allowed out,' he said. 'You are grounded for the rest of this weekend.'

Aaaaaah. But what about Albert? And Oscar? And all our plans for making Oscar perfect, and sociable, and happy, and properly in love with Sally? There were people out there who needed me, and I needed to be released.

'Please,' I said, sounding like a frightened schoolgirl.

Which I suppose wasn't that surprising, seeing as...

'Please, I have to go and rescue a dog from a terrible fate, plus there's a friend who desperately needs my help. And we've only got today...'

'I shall talk to your mother,' said Ralph, still in his ghastly self-righteous tone. 'We shall see what she has to say about this.'

I breathed out. Surely Mum wouldn't punish me for something she hadn't even heard me say. Surely...

The pattern on my screen had changed. The arrangement of pictures on Mark's Facebook page had moved to accommodate two new pictures. This time they were of Mark in the centre of a group of people, none of whom I knew and all of whom would not look out of place in the Reception area of Management2Models.

Mark was smiling at the camera and now he, too, had a glass of some dark liquid in his hand. 'Cecile's anniversaire' it said in bold capitals underneath. 'Toute la ville celebre!'

I zoomed in on the photo and examined the faces one by one. Nope. Not a single one looked anything other than older than me, more beautiful than me, and – I could swear – cleverer than me. They looked like they could find a rhyme for anything, had never missed a deadline in their life, and could translate anything English into French and anything French into English.

Despair didn't begin to describe it.

My feeling of utter hopelessness must have shown in my face, because the next thing I knew was a soft voice saying, 'You all right, love?'

There was Mum in her favourite electric blue nightie that made her look a hundred but we would never say so, standing over me with a concerned expression on her face.

'Is it something on that Facebook thing that's upset you?' she said.

'Just me being silly, that's all, Mum,' I said, trying to summon up a cheerful smile. 'I think when you're separated from someone you just assume the worst, don't you?'

'If this is about Mark,' said Mum, knowing perfectly well that it was, 'then you mustn't jump to conclusions. You've done that before, haven't you? And you know where that got you.'

She was right. As always. I smiled again, this time a bit more convincingly.

'You're right, Mum. You're always right,' I said. 'I'm sure it's not what I think. Not that I think anything, of course...'

'All right, love,' said Mum. 'Now, Ralph says you've been using terrible language. Well, I think I know what that's about, but you really must try not to swear. It's not funny, and it's not—'

'Clever,' I said. 'I know, Mum. Sorry.'

And we smiled at each other just as Ralph came into the room.

'Well?' he said gleefully. 'Grounded, I said. This sort of thing can't be allowed to go on.'

'No, it's all right, Ralph,' said Mum quietly but firmly. 'Chloe knows she mustn't do it again. I don't think we need punish her on this occasion.'

God bless Mum, I thought as I closed down the dreaded Facebook page, and went back to worrying about the English prize

Then I realised that it was getting late and it was now time to move on and start worrying about Albert.

What with one thing and another, I hadn't even begun to formulate a plan for how we were going to fund the Acquisition of Albert. It was hardly good timing to ask Mum and Ralph, Gran was completely out of the question, and my fallback scheme of somehow getting Gemma to ask Merv during the long car journeys of yesterday had been rather scuppered by Merv being in a terrible temper pretty well all the day.

The plan was to meet Charlie at the bus stop (it always seemed like a good plan to meet Charlie at the bus stop), so I needed to leave the agonies of Facebook behind, put on my thickest waterproof (it always seemed to be freezing and raining whenever I had a plan to execute) and head off into the outside world.

Padding quietly past the kitchen where Mum and Ralph seemed to be having a not very friendly conversation, I unlocked the front door and walked downstairs as quietly as I could. There was no cheerful bark from Albert's front door as I walked past, and I had a horrible moment wondering if he had already been sold.

The rain was pouring down Charlie's face when we caught up with him and Amy at the bus stop. It had the effect of making him look more like a boy doing his A-levels at St Thomas's and less like the heir to a large country estate, but it was too late to worry about that now.

'Right,' said our hero. 'Obviously you two can't be anywhere near when I knock on his door 'cos he knows you, so let's meet back at the coffee shop in the park in an hour's time. If I've got him, then we'll have to worry about what happens next. I think Gemma's dad's our best hope. But first things first. I've got the details of my parents' account if he wants a guarantee of a money transfer, and anyway I can always say we want to take Albert for a test run. Possession nine tenths of the law and all that.'

I wasn't sure that that would stand up in an actual court of actual law. It was all starting to feel more and more like we were stealing Albert, but I decided to worry about that later as I watched Lord Charlie head confidently off to Mr Underwood's.

'Come on, Ames,' I said to Amy more cheerfully than I felt. 'Let's get to the park. I'll tell everyone to meet us there.'

Such is the speed of electronic communication these days, also the fact that no one had anything better to do on a wet January Sunday, the others were already there when we arrived at the coffee shop.

It was in the middle of the park, in a place designed to enjoy the views, with outside decking and wooden tables that in sunnier times would be covered in people and their coffee cups. But on a day like today it was dripping with rivulets of water that were being cheerily blown about the tables and floor by a howling gale. It was horrible weather for being outdoors – so horrible that even Amy hadn't wanted to go running in it – so we scuttled inside as quickly as we could.

Gemma and Sally were sitting in a corner, still in their coats and huddled over their phones. In a not very fetching bobble hat, Gemma was looking a lot less like a supermodel, and Sally was looking like, well, Sally.

Both of them glanced up as we approached.

'Where's Albert?' said Sally, looking as if she were only half-interested in the answer. Her relationship with Albert was an ambivalent one. (I think I mean 'ambivalent'. It's one of my new favourite words and I have started to use it a lot. At some point I must find out exactly what it means.)

'We hope that Charlie will be bringing him here very soon,' said Amy. 'But it's touch and go, and it all depends on Charlie being very cool and clever.' She looked as if there were every chance he'd be precisely that.

Seeing her proud expression, and her happy grin, suddenly reminded me of how much I missed being with someone who was cool and clever. The sunny French photos flashed before my mind's eye, and I gave a sigh.

''S'matter, Chloe?' said Sally, who, amazingly, was staring at me and not at her phone. 'You look like someone who hasn't got a Boy to Watch.' She paused, seeming to think about that and all sorts of sad things, judging by the droopy nature of her mouth. 'Let alone bring to Maggie's Valentine's Day party.'

We hadn't talked about the dreaded party for two whole days. Nobody had said anything about it at school, although the QB and her cohorts had done more whispering and sniggering together than ever before. And they had seemed to deliberately say the words 'party' and 'it'll be hilarious' and 'get *such* a surprise' very loudly so that everyone could hear. But it seemed like everyone else was deliberately not talking about it, either through fear, or through being on the 'in' side and wanting it to look like they knew something we didn't.

'Not going to think about that now, Sal,' I said, *really* not wanting to think about it now. 'Going to worry about that later. Today is Albert Day.'

I looked around the café, and saw in the opposite corner a sight that reminded me that I had something just as important to do as saving Albert. Sitting on his own, underneath a sign that read 'Breastfeeding mothers welcome here', was Oscar.

He was dressed in a white tracksuit that had, as Mum would say, 'seen better days'. Probably just after she'd said that white was a difficult colour 'because it shows the dirt'. (In this case, she'd be right, I thought, looking at the grass stains on his shoulder.)

Oscar was gazing out of the window at the pouring rain with an expression of puzzlement. I wondered if perhaps they didn't have pouring rain in Sweden, and then I wondered why he didn't have the weapon of choice of every person on their own – that is, some kind of electronic device to make him look like he didn't need the company of humans.

This is Mark's second cousin, I thought. Not a close relation, but still family. He's handsome and alone and awkward and sad. And I must not forget that Project Oscar means that it is my job to make him happy. And then I looked at my auburn friend as she tapped away on her Instagram page (she'd had her first 'like' for the picture of the twins' rash, and one more for our spaghetti dinner. Sally was clearly on a roll). And I thought, It must surely just be a matter of time before they discover each other and dance happily off into the sunset/the Valentine's Day party. Plus, with Sally's auburn colouring and Oscar's dark blondness and green eyes, they would have beautiful children.

At that moment Oscar looked up. Of course I had to blush – an enormous blush, as if he somehow could know that I'd been speculating about the precise colouring of his children. I looked back at our table to check that no one had noticed, and was for once relieved to see that everyone was looking down at their phones.

Once I'd let the colour in my face die down a little bit, I looked up again and turned round to Oscar's table. He was still sitting there, still with nothing in front of him, not even a camouflaging cup of coffee, and he was looking straight at me. I smiled at him as if I'd only just noticed him, and got up to go over to his table.

'Hi there,' I said in my best breezy voice. 'Going to come and join us? We're going to get a dog soon, and then we can all go for a walk in the park.' I made it all sound so simple, rather like a children's story with a happy ending.

Oscar was staring blankly up at me. Perhaps he was trying to think of how to say, 'Thank you, I'd love to' in English, or perhaps I had a large spot on the end of my nose. Surreptitiously, I gave my nose a quick rub. There didn't seem to be any sign of anything pustular. So I carried on with our one-sided conversation.

'It's the dog you saw being stolen by his owner the other day,' I said, probably only confusing him more. 'You know, the one by the pole when we were with Mark.'

Oscar continued to stare at me.

I started to feel like I was in the middle of a particularly tricky piece of French translation. Soon I would be inviting him to 'step out of his homework and have a drink in the wood'.

I could hear the others talking to each other in the other corner of the shop, and made myself even more confused as I tried to make out what they were saying. I felt I was starting to look a little desperate, doing all the talking to a very handsome but completely non-responsive boy.

Suddenly Oscar stood up. This is it, I thought. He is now going to turn and walk silently away from me, and I am going to look like a stalky pest who wouldn't take no for an answer and who has single-handedly driven away the only handsome boy in the café.

'I will buy you some drinks, yes?' said Oscar, looking at me and then over to the others.

'That would be lovely, thank you very much,' I said. My relief at being spoken to was obviously bringing out all my best middle-aged tea party conversational skills. 'You're very kind. Shall we go over and see what the others want?'

I thought we were going to have a bit of a setback when Oscar just stared silently back at me. But then he said, 'Yes, of course. We must.'

Giving him one of my brightest and most brilliant smiles, I led the way over to the table where the others were pretending to talk to each other in between glancing over at Oscar and me.

'Hi, everybody,' I said. 'Look who I've found.' As if it was pure coincidence that he was there at all.

'Cappuccinos is good, yes?' Oscar said, looking down at the floor, as if he were frightened of actually catching anyone's eye.

'Yes, please,' said Amy and Gemma and I.

'Could I have a half decaff venti with an extra shot and some sprinkles if they've got them?' said Sally.

I gave her a glare. I knew she actually hated coffee, which is why she kept trying to find ever more complicated variations in the hope that the more complicated it was the less it tasted like a cup of coffee.

Only, poor Oscar wasn't to know that. He gazed uncomprehendingly at Sally, mortified and probably thinking he was being set up.

'I'll come with you,' I said quickly. 'Help you carry the cups.'

By the time we were back at the table, a silent Oscar having paid for all our coffees, the air of awkwardness was getting worse.

Oscar looked sooo beautiful, but as his default

position was carefully examining the floor, it was hard to get a proper sense of all the fun he and Sally were going to have with their beautifully coloured beautiful children.

Sally wasn't looking at him either, she was too busy picking out the sprinkles on her complicated coffee.

I gave a small sigh, and realised there was a lot of work to be done before we had a happy Oscar fully integrated into the social scene.

➤➤ 8 ←◅

Barking up a New Tree

The awkward silence didn't last long. It was broken by the sound of some very loud yapping coming from the general direction of the decking outside. It had stopped raining, and I could just about make out the sight of Charlie, talking to somebody sitting at one of the tables.

'He's back!' I announced to everyone. Abandoning my cappuccino, I got up and dashed towards the door.

Charlie had tied Albert up to a table leg, and was talking animatedly to Ethan, Steve's friend who'd run away from the army and was now working for the Dad Who. Ethan was looking wet and thin, but was gazing up at Charlie like a small boy who's suddenly met his hero.

'...scored yet another goal from the other side, straight through three defenders...' Charlie was saying.

I couldn't *believe* anyone could talk about football in the middle of the world's tensest Animal Rescue operation, but Ethan was looking transfixed.

Charlie saw me come out of the café. 'Hey, Chloe,' he said, smiling at me. 'This is Ethan, who's working for Amy's dad. He says he knows you 'cos he's a friend of Steve's.'

By this stage, Albert was bouncing up and down, yapping his heart out and pulling so hard on his lead I thought his head would come off.

I still couldn't believe Charlie had been so easily distracted from the job in hand. 'Hi, Ethan,' I said. 'Nice to see you again.' Even in the midst of dog crises, it seemed I couldn't stop myself sounding like I was at a tea party.

I bent down to give Albert a proper Hello Cuddle. He somehow managed to carry on barking and lick my face at the same time. His little brown ears were bouncing up and down in his excitement, and his paws scratching my arm as he jumped up at me.

'So what happened?' I said, looking up at Charlie, anxious to stop him launching into another episode of football World Cup commentary. 'What did he say? Have you had to pay money? Did you keep up your posh accent?' The others had come out too now, and were standing behind me, looking expectantly at Charlie.

'Well,' said Charlie, turning away from Ethan, 'it was all a bit tricky, I must say.' Charlie seemed to be relishing the prospect of another commentary. 'For a start Mr Underwood wouldn't say anything about why he was leaving, but he wanted to know all about my house in the country, my elderly mother who was once lady-in-waiting to the queen, and my experience of breeding border terriers.'

'Oh, *Charlie*,' said his beloved in disbelieving tones.

'Yes,' went on Charlie, 'and I think he was quite impressed that one of my ancestors has a town in Australia named after him, and my uncle played cricket for England.'

'You're mad,' said Amy in even more disbelieving tones. 'Supposing he knew something about cricket and the England cricket team?'

'No chance,' said Charlie. 'Boxing's his sport.'

I gave Albert another cuddle. He was quiet now – probably waiting for Charlie to get to the part of the story where he came in. I felt rather the same.

'And then what?' I said.

'And then he told me Albert was a red grizzle border terrier, which of course I told him I knew already, and that because of who I was and because I could offer him such a nice home, he'd sell him to me for only six hundred pounds. I explained as carefully as I could that I was posh but not stupid, and that because Albert was quite old and didn't have any paperwork, the going rate would be more like one hundred pounds. We settled on one hundred and fifty pounds. Payable tomorrow.'

'You're brilliant, Charlie!' I said giving Albert a congratulatory cuddle. 'That's so great. So he's ours now!'

'Yup,' said Charlie. 'Just got to find him somewhere to live, and the money to pay for him and yup, he's yours now.' He smiled as he said this, but I suddenly felt so deflated. At least Albert was freed from horrible Mr Underwood, but he wasn't out of the woods yet.

I looked around at my friends. Amy, Sally and Gemma were all watching Albert as he snuffled around and settled himself at my feet. Oscar was standing in the doorway looking inscrutable (I think I mean inscrutable), Charlie was looking smug, and Ethan was picking bird droppings off the table.

I had twenty-four hours to find a lot of money, and a place with at least a medium-sized garden (I'd looked up border terriers on the internet, and they like their exercise) and a houseful of tolerant dog lovers.

'Tell you what, Chloe,' said Gemma. 'I can smuggle him back to mine, and keep him in the garage till we can decide what to do with him. I don't suppose Merv will notice dog poo in among his four-by-fours and his Harley-Davidsons.'

'Albert's house-trained!' said Sally indignantly. I felt suddenly proud of my BFF for standing up for Albert, and grateful to Gemma for trying to help with the Find Albert a Home problem.

'That's a great idea, Gem,' I said. 'But I'm not sure we can feed him and take him for a walk and stuff at the same time as secretly tying him up to a motorbike.'

We stood around looking downcast. I was just about to wonder if we'd have to throw ourselves on the mercies of Ralph after all, when there was a Swedish-sounding cough from the doorway of the cafe. It was Oscar, who had raised his head and was looking around him, blinking in the watery sunshine.

'I'm thinking,' he said. Certainly this was an encouraging start.

'What are you thinking, Oscar?' I said, momentarily glad that he felt able to join in the conversation.

'At Andersons', there is many dogs,' he said. 'Perhaps Albert have room there.'

Genius. Mark's home, where Oscar was staying while he was in England for his ice hockey training, already had two puppies in it, so it was certainly dog-friendly. Perhaps Albert could stay there while we tried to figure out what to do next. And I would just somehow have to make time to take him for a walk early in the morning and on the way home from school, because he mustn't be a burden to Patricia, Mark's lovely mother.

But Oscar hadn't finished. 'And I could take him for the walks,' he said, looking down at the ground again.

If Oscar had been looking at me, he would have seen me give him another of my best dazzling smiles.

As it was, Charlie got there first. 'Oscar, you're a superstar,' he said. 'As an experienced breeder of border terriers, I can tell you that they like puppy company, gardens and long walks with Swedish ice hockey stars. Well done.'

'Clever old Oscar,' said Sally. Which wasn't quite how I wanted her to think of her future husband. There would be time enough for her to appreciate how 'old' and 'clever' he was when they were sitting on their rocking chairs watching their grandchildren play nicely together. But I supposed one step at a time; she obviously appreciated his solving some of the What

Shall We Do With Albert problem.

'And now you've rescued Albert from a mass murderer, all you've got to do,' said Sally to me, 'is find all that money to pay for him.'

'I'll talk to Mum and see if I can borrow it from her,' I said. 'Perhaps if I promise not to eat or drink anything or use up any heating or electricity, I can pay them back by the time I leave school.'

'Come on, everyone,' said Charlie in a commanding tone. Clearly he'd inherited the masterful genes of the ancestor who had Australian towns named after him. 'No time like the present. Let's all go to Mark's house and see if we can make this happen.'

He dialled a number – as an old friend of Mark's he was practically family – and had a conversation which, annoyingly, I couldn't hear. But Charlie was nodding and smiling, so it must have gone roughly according to plan. When he'd finished, he turned and untied Albert from the table leg, and tied the lead firmly round his wrist. I felt a little bit jealous, but guessed there would be time enough for me to bond with Albert. And anyway, at that moment Charlie was definitely our hero and he could do what he liked.

Besides I had something else to think about. I felt slightly trepidatious at the prospect of going off to

Mark's house so suddenly and unexpectedly. I rather thought I needed more notice to prepare myself for properly seeing his parents or his sister Georgie or the house where he lived.

As we started to get ready to set off on the walk, my phone gave its extra special Mark Buzz of an incoming message. 'Wifi terrible here! But will try Skype tonight. M xxxxxxxxxcx'

Which left me feeling half excited at the thought of seeing and hearing him, if only electronically, and half suspicious. If the wifi in France was so terrible, how come he managed to put loads and LOADS of pictures up on Facebook?

I saw Ethan get up to follow us all, and, feeling guilty that I'd pretty much ignored him, I turned to him with what I hoped was a bright and friendly smile.

'How's it all going, Ethan?' I said. 'Not regretting leaving the army or anything? Are you at acting school now?'

He was looking at Charlie as he flung his arm casually round Amy's shoulders. 'What?' he said as if he'd just been woken from a dream. 'Oh. Yes. In my first term at acting school. It's quite hard actually.'

He seemed to suddenly remember his manners, and turned to me with a proper smile. He looked as spindly as ever, and I found myself wondering again how he could possibly have thought it was a good idea to go into the army. Perhaps he had had the same careers adviser as Mr Carson. Someone who thought it a great celestial joke to put young men into The Least Appropriate Job Possible.

'Do you have to pretend you're a tree? Or a baby?' I asked him as we headed out of the park and in the direction of Mark's house. 'Or do you have to learn great chunks of Pinter and Shakespeare?'

'Actually,' said Ethan, 'you have to go to rhythm and singing classes and things. It's not like you play Hamlet on Day One. It's really exhausting.'

Oh dear. So, way too spindly for the army, and probably a bit too spindly for acting too.

'How's Steve?' said Ethan, obviously keen to change the subject. 'He's still training, isn't he? I haven't heard from him for a few weeks.'

I felt suddenly bad that I couldn't answer Ethan's question. I had been so preoccupied with Mr Darcy, my plans for Oscar, my brushes with the education process, and of course Mum, that I'd hardly given a thought to my brother.

Oily and oiky he might be, but he was still my only sibling, and it had been a while since he had last come home on leave, or since I'd had any contact with him.

'I think he's OK,' I said truthfully – because I guessed someone would have told me if he'd suddenly been posted to Iraq or Afghanistan or Crimea or whichever holiday hotspot was on the army's list. 'How was he when you last heard from him? How do you think he's getting on?'

We were coming out to the edge of the park now, with Charlie and Amy leading the way (obviously highly honed athletes always want to be at the front even on a walk in the park) and the rest of us keeping up as best we and our shoes could. (I'd noticed that Gemma's heels were almost impossibly high. I supposed a trainee supermodel must keep in practice when it comes to heels. But looking at the way they sank into the mud made me glad yet again that my all-round mediumness meant I could wear a pair of comfortable trainers.)

'I think he's still finding the five-mile runs a bit rough, but not as rough as Maths and Navigation. Not a great one for studying, your brother,' Ethan said with the sort of smile that implied he meant this in a caring rather than a critical way.

Ethan himself was a bit of a studier, I seemed to remember from our hasty conversations when he came back for that day with Steve. I'd been surprised (but pleased, obvs) that a trainee soldier should have had such a detailed and sensitive insight into the novels of E. M. Forster.

Still, it all made me resolve to write to Steve and see how he was getting on. Who knew, perhaps he had a supply of handsome new army friends who were free on the fourteenth of February...

'Come on, you lot,' Charlie was shouting from the front of our cortege. He and Amy were waiting at a pedestrian crossing just outside the park. Just behind them was Gemma, her supermodel catwalk elegance slightly undermined by her mud-encrusted high heels. Either side of her were Sally and Oscar.

I wished I'd separated Gemma from the two (trainee) lovebirds so they could get to know and appreciate each other, but it was too late now as we were getting very near the Andersons' house.

Knowing I would soon be On the Street Where He Lived almost made me want to burst into song.

And then nervousness took over good and proper. I started to worry about meeting his mother, Patricia, again. She was a truly elegant lady – like her friend Marianne – and very wise, and also something very important in the television world.

And then there was Mark's father, a barrister, who

I'd never met. But I imagined he must have a big brain (because of the barrister thing), was probably handsome (because of the having a handsome son thing) and who was probably scary (because that that's what I'd come to expect from the family).

And then perhaps Mark's sister Georgie might be there – who was older than me, and who I really liked and who I really wanted to like me. (So far, so good on that front – she was always nice to me whenever she saw me, and I hoped that wasn't just because she was being kind to her brother's friend. I mean girlfriend. Or friend anyway. No. Girlfriend. Definitely girlfriend.)

Georgie was going to be in a TV comedy series, and had already started rehearsing. Which meant she wasn't in school very much and was the object of much speculation and admiration. Amazing how television has that effect on people.

We turned a last corner, and it was time to stop my feverish internal speculation. I realised it had been a while since I'd said a word to Ethan, who was plodding quietly along beside me, probably unaware of the all the inner turmoil going on inside his silent companion.

As we got nearer the house – which was old and slightly run-down but so covered in ivy and other things I couldn't identify that stay green in winter that it looked a bit like a film set – Albert started barking and pulling at his lead. I could see Charlie heave him back to heel, but clearly there was something that was making Albert extremely over-excited.

I caught up with Charlie. 'As a breeder of border terriers,' I said over the loud and increasingly hysterical barking, 'isn't there anything you can do to stop him making this noise? They'll never want to give a foster home to a little barker like him.'

It was too late. The front door opened, and Patricia stood in the doorway, hanging on to the lead of two small puppies who were making almost as much noise as Albert. (Obviously dog must bark unto dog when they smell one behind a door.) Behind her was a tall, handsome man with distinguished greying temples (I've always wondered whether I would recognise 'distinguished greying temples' when I saw them, but these were unmistakeable) who had a phone in one hand and a pipe in the other.

I just had a second to think how perfect it was for a barrister to have a new-fangled phone and an old-fashioned pipe all in one go, when Patricia said, 'Welcome, everyone. Come on in and let's have a look at this dog of yours.'

With grey hair, an old blue polo-neck jersey and

jeans, she looked like the presenter of a casually upmarket gardening series. In fact, the two of them looked so Casual Distinguished that I think we were all overawed. But then again that might just have been my overactive imagination.

'Hello, Mrs Anderson,' said Sally bouncily. Yes, quite wrong about overawed. 'What brilliant puppies. Do you think they'll be nice to Albert and let him share their toys?'

'Hey, Sally,' said Charlie, pulling on Albert's lead. 'You might be jumping the gun a bit there. Not sure if Patricia and Gabriel are actually up for taking on Albert yet.'

I looked crossly at my gun-jumping friend, at the same time as thinking, 'Gabriel' – how cool is that? Hardly anyone is called Gabriel. In fact, just the one angel, and the handsome shepherd in *Far From the Madding Crowd.*

'Hello, Chloe,' said the angel/shepherd, putting his phone in his pocket and holding out his hand, 'Gabriel Anderson. I've heard a lot about you. I'm sorry we haven't met before, but I'm very glad to do so now.' And as he shook my hand, he gave a smile that crinkled up his whole face, right up to the DG temples.

'Hello, Mr Anderson,' I said, looking up at him with

what I strongly suspected was a goofy schoolgirl sort of expression. 'It's nice to meet you too.' There. I knew my facility with middle-aged tea-party conversation would come in handy one day.

'Come into the kitchen and have some tea,' said Patricia, as if on cue. 'Georgie's in the sitting room talking to the producer of this show she's in, so we're not allowed in there for the moment.'

Amazing, I thought, how this family had every aspect of cool down to a fine art. I'd never met a TV producer before, and now there was one just calmly sitting in the next room.

'Oscar,' Patricia was saying, 'you know where everything is. Why don't you get out the plates and cups and put them on the table. I'll boil the kettle and let's see if we can't calm down that dog of yours, Chloe.'

Albert was still bouncing and barking in his excitement at seeing a new place and some new dog company. Charlie let him get a little closer to the two puppies, and Albert started sniffing and snuffling at them in that eager way that dogs have when they first meet each other – usually focusing intently on the front and back ends.

Soon all three dogs were sitting down together, still

in an exploratory but now in a friendly way, and we humans were left to get on with our tea party.

I noticed with satisfaction that Oscar and Sally sat down next to each other. Also that Oscar seemed to be looking up a bit more – not actually catching anyone's eye, but definitely less focused on different patterns of flooring and the ground generally.

'So are you all going to go to Oscar's hockey match next weekend?' asked Gabriel as we sat down to cups of tea and some things on plates that were either scones or crumpets (I can never remember which is which).

There was a bit of a silence, and we all – naturally – looked at Oscar, who was slowly and very obviously just starting an absolutely massive blush. I knew the signs. And though I was half fascinated by the way the brick red colour was building up beneath his handsome stubble, I thought somebody needed to say something to deflect attention from this biology lesson going on in front of our very eyes.

'Definitely,' I said cheerfully, though I had no idea when the match was, or where it was, or indeed *that* it was. The only thing I knew for sure was that this would be an essential part of Project Oscar – to support and observe and help at all times. 'We'll get a whole gang together and all sit together and make a lot of cheering noises, and—'

'I've never seen an ice hockey match,' interrupted Sally, looking at Oscar and not seeming to notice his beetroot colour. 'I expect it's all quite violent, is it? Do people fall over and get terribly injured? And do you have fights and barge into everyone like Chloe does when she goes skating?'

Oscar turned his brick-red face to Sally, looking her full in the eye, I was pleased to notice. 'It's hurting sometimes,' he said. 'But we fight for puck, not each other.'

I had a vision of the small impish character from *A Midsummer Night's Dream* sitting in the middle of the ice, watching huge figures waving sticks at each other as they fought over him.

'A puck is disc of rubber,' Oscar was saying in his slightly singsong accent, almost as if he'd heard what I'd been thinking. 'And if people fight there are bad penalty. If fight, they take man off pitch. You only have six man, so man off pitch very bad.'

It was the longest speech I'd heard him make. Clearly ice hockey was his favourite subject, and I decided that anyone who showed an interest in it was well on the way to stealing his heart.

I looked expectantly at Sally, hoping she would follow up on her slightly bloodthirsty question. But her attention was now firmly focused on her crumpet-or-scone, on which she seemed to be trying to build a raspberry jam tree.

'I think, Sally,' said Gemma, looking up from her phone which had kept her preoccupied ever since we'd arrived, 'that if you tried really hard you could get at least another spoonful of jam on to that scone.'

Sally looked up guiltily. There was now a huge pile of jam on her plate, completely hiding what I now knew to be a scone.

'We must definitely go and watch Oscar,' she announced, obviously keen to get away from the subject of jam trees. 'Are you going to win, Oscar? What will happen if you win?'

This was excellent. She was asking him a direct question about the thing he did best. Oscar's blush had now almost subsided, and he looked Sally in the eye again as he answered.

'Big important match. If we win we will yump in the air for happiness,' Oscar said.

There was a pause. I imagined everyone was trying to pretend not to notice Oscar's different way with consonants. But I found myself secretly determined to get Oscar to say another word that began with J. Perhaps, I thought, I could get someone to start a conversation about those old British aeroplanes I'd read about somewhere called Harrier Jump Jets.

But that would have to wait. Charlie, Amy and Patricia, who had been focusing on the dogs in the corner of the kitchen, came back to the table. 'So far so good,' said Patricia. 'I don't think anyone's going to kill each other. Let's see how Georgie's getting on, then we can talk about what happens to Albert, Chloe.'

I stood up and went over to give Albert a cuddle. He sniffed my hands, gave them a lick, and then went back to exploring the two puppies.

As everyone got up from the table the kitchen door opened and in came Georgie, dressed in jeans and a man's oversize white shirt, her long dark ponytail swinging behind her as she walked towards the plate of scones.

'Hi, everyone,' she said, looking round at us all and smiling the sort of confident smile that people have when they look great and are about to star in a TV comedy drama. 'Hi, Chloe, how's it going?' she added, giving me an extra smile, which had the unfortunate effect of making me start to blush. If only I weren't so anxious to please, perhaps I'd be altogether cooler. And less red.

'Chloe's brought us a new friend, darling,' said Patricia. 'Look. Isn't he adorable?'

Everyone turned to look at Albert, who was indeed looking at his absolute butter-wouldn't-melt sweet best. I thought 'adorable' coming from Patricia sounded distinctly promising for those of us who worried about Albert's future well-being.

'He's gorge,' said Georgie. 'Is he yours, Chloe?' And then, before I had had time to reply, 'Donald's just making a call, but he says it's all go with the series, they're very pleased with the pilot.'

'That's brilliant!' said Sally excitedly before anyone else could say anything. 'What's it about? Is anyone famous in it?'

'Well, nobody's famous yet, but who knows what might happen if they schedule it properly,' said Georgie, still with her confident smile. 'It's kind of half improvised, about a young family – a boy and a girl (that's me) – living an ordinary life, but funnily.' Looking around at everyone's smiling faces, I decided I was definitely not going to be the one to say that this all sounded a little bit familiar. And anyway, just at that moment in came the Very Important Producer person, Donald.

I'd always imagined TV producers to be skinny, stubbly, about forty, surgically attached to their phone, and wearing tight denim and an air of self-importance. Donald didn't disappoint.

'Hi, everyone,' he said to the room, as if addressing a board meeting. 'All good. It's going to be great. Your daughter,' he said with a condescending smile to Patricia and Gabriel, 'is a star. She's really nailed this role. She's so cool with the improv. Networks are going to love her.'

We all looked at Georgie, who was smiling modestly.

'If the scheduling's good and the networks love her,' said Patricia just a little bit coolly, 'that'd be fine. But for the moment Georgie's got to schedule a bit more school and a bit less improv. So see what you can do with your rehearsal times, Donald, and let's discuss tomorrow.'

'Right,' said Donald-the-producer, just a little less cockily. 'Sure. Talk tomorrow then, Patricia. See you soon, Georgie.' And with that he went off to wherever cool TV producers go on a Sunday afternoon.

As everybody started making getting-ready-to-go noises, Patricia took me to one side. I thought this was going to be the big Albert moment, but I was wrong.

'Nice to hear that Mark seems to be getting on all

right over there in Dijon, isn't it, Chloe?' Patricia looked intently at me as she spoke.

'Yes,' I said not really knowing what else to say. 'Going to be talking to him tonight, I think.'

'That's nice,' said Patricia. 'He'll be pleased we're all taking good care of Oscar too.'

'Yes,' I said. And then, because I wanted to change the subject, and anyway there was something more urgent on the agenda, 'And Albert? Can we take good care of him too?'

'I think so,' said Patricia, smiling tolerantly, 'Yes, let's say we'll certainly look after him for a couple of months, but then we might have to find him more of a permanent home. But we can worry about that later.' Her tolerant smile took the edge of this prospect of future worry. The main thing I told myself was that Operation Albert had had the best possible start.

Sally and I walked back through the park slowly, full of thought (me) and scones (her). Ethan had gone off with Charlie and Amy to get his Monday work schedule from the Dad Who, Gemma had gone back to Chateau Merv, and Oscar had stayed at the

Andersons' where he did, after all, live.

We'd all made a plan to go to Oscar's match *en masse*, which was a good step forward for Project Oscar & Sally, but there was still a lot to do before I'd got anywhere near joining them together in holy – well, if not exactly matrimony, then at least romantic attachment.

And then, of course, there was the vexed question of the Price of Albert. Twenty four hours to find £150. Given that it was very unlikely that I could find a job that paid £6.25 an hour, lasted all day and all night, and which started immediately, I knew I would almost certainly do what I always do when life was just too difficult. Ask Mum.

I sighed. And then I remembered all the homework I hadn't done, and I sighed again.

And all this before I even began to worry about what I was going to say to Mark. Did I admit to looking at his Facebook page, and feeling suspicious? I was pretty sure that the internet would tell you that you should trust your BF and not spy on him. And I bet there wasn't a novel or an opera plot where spying on your loved one ended well.

This time my sigh was of epic – possibly even operatic – proportions.

'Chloe,' said Sally, as she trotted by my side, narrowly avoiding a huge pile of dog mess. 'You haven't said a word since we left the Andersons'. Obviously you're worrying about something and I bet it's to do with Mark.'

Sometimes the wisdom and sagacity of my BFF surprises me. I told her about my latest worry – that Cecile the tomboy appeared to have grown into a fully formed French sex goddess. Which perhaps was a slight exaggeration, but Sally, being Sally, immediately got the picture.

'I read somewhere,' she said, 'that in cases like this you mustn't automatically assume the worst and you must trust your boyfriend and you mustn't be manipulative and in fact you should try to get to know her and maybe even be friends with her yourself and be honest with him and also it's very important you don't make any ultimations.' Sally paused for breath.

It was such an impressive piece of research, and such a great feat of memory – and breath – that I almost resisted my urge to correct.

'That's brilliant, Sal,' I said. 'And quite right, I'm sure. Definitely won't be making any…ultimatums.'

Sally was all for discussing my problems over a bucket of ice cream and a film at hers, but I felt the responsibilities of life and the urgencies of my worries hanging so heavily on me that I knew I would get no pleasure from those things.

'No,' I said, 'much though I would love to get ice-cream indigestion in front of a movie, I have things to do. And I must go home.'

I waved goodbye to my BFF feeling the weight of the world on my shoulders. Where was a boy's hug and £150 when you needed them, I wondered to myself.

⇉→ 9 ←⇇

Matchless

'What do you think you're gawping at, young lady?' Gran sounded even more cross with me than usual. But there was every possible excuse for gawping. Lying in front of her, completely covering the kitchen table, was her entire collection of china dolls. It was like suddenly coming upon the aftermath of a mass poisoning in a Victorian workhouse – lots of little people, dressed in old-fashioned clothes, lying stiff with lifelessness.

Gran was cradling a particularly scary example. The doll, with its wide-open black eyes and a red crack in its bright white cheek, was the stuff of a low-budget horror movie. Gran had a large yellow duster, which she started to wipe fondly over the revolting creature's face.

'Nothing,' I said in time-honoured fashion, but

pleased not to have said an involuntary 'ugh' or 'yeuch'. 'Just wondering where Mum is, that's all.'

'She and your stepfather,' said Gran, now rubbing so energetically at the forehead of the creature that I feared she might rub it alive, 'have gone out to celebrate.'

This was good news. Or at least it must have been, because generally it's only good news that one tends to celebrate.

'That's good,' I said. 'Celebrate what?'

'Your stepfather,' said Gran lingering over the word in a disapproving fashion, 'has started a new business, which he *assures* us will result in all our money worries being over.'

Gran pursed her lips in a way that indicated she very much doubted this.

'What sort of business?' I asked. Ghastly Ralph had previous when it came to disastrous (and faintly illegal) business ventures.

'Apparently…' – more lingering in a disapproving fashion – 'it involves selling something called virtual wheat in Mongolia. *Apparently*, the father of a friend of yours is funding this business.'

She looked at me as if the whole thing was very bad and it was all my fault.

But I could only think that the friend had to be Gemma, and the funder her father. And then I could only think, how frightening to depend for our financial security on someone like Merv. And *then* I thought that if Merv was able to afford an enormous house, electric gates and gold-plated pizza, he must be doing something right.

'Okaaaay,' I said warily. And then I had a thought. 'Does this mean that he's got actual money to start his business? I mean, does a virtual business mean it's virtual money? Or is it real money?'

I suddenly had a vision of Ralph rolling in twenty-pound notes, several of which he would peel off so that I could settle my Albert score.

'I have no idea,' said Gran, putting down the original revolting creature and picking up another one. 'But he seems to have made your mother feel a little more cheerful about life, so I suppose we must be grateful for that.'

She picked up her yellow duster, spat on it lustily, and set to work on the grey face of a doll that had large brown teeth and very little nose.

'They'll be back soon,' she went on. 'So I suppose you can ask him yourself.'

I thought this was a good moment to retreat to my

room. It wasn't as if Gran needed any help in her ghoulish task, so this might be the time to try to tick off at least one homework box. At least focusing on my education would take my mind off Mark.

But it was as if Someone Up There wasn't going to let me off that lightly. Whether it was French homework ('write to your penfriend in France') or English ('explore the theme of jealousy in Shakespeare') or even Maths ('find a constant in a variable'), everything seemed designed to remind me of Someone Down Here.

I was just about to return to my non-progress on my award-winning creative writing when I heard the sound of voices. I couldn't make out what they were saying, but I could tell that Mum sounded a bit tired and Ghastly Ralph a bit slurred. But on the whole the timbre (I think I mean 'timbre') sounded cheerful enough. Perhaps it was a good time to go and find out if there was actual money in virtual wheat.

'Hi, Mum; hi, Ralph,' I said in my best dutiful-daughter-just-taking-a-quick-break-from-hard-work-and-generally-being-good voice as I came out of my room. 'Have you had a nice time?'

'Oh hello, love,' said Mum, looking up from taking off her favourite furry ankle boots. I often borrowed these boots because they were warm and surprisingly 'cool' and, I couldn't stop myself thinking, looked better on me than they did on her.

'Gran says you've been celebrating,' I said in my nice voice to make up for the nasty thought. 'What's going on?'

'It's business, my girl,' said Ralph, failing to stop a loud burp. 'But good business, I don't mind telling you. There's money in them thar wheat.' He started to chuckle at his own non-joke.

'It's true, love,' said Mum. 'Ralph's started this business venture. And Merv's already put up the money for it.'

'So,' I said, taking a deep breath, 'would this be a good time to tell you that we've rescued Albert? He was going to be sold, to someone horrible, because Mr Underwood's going away. So we rescued him and he was very glad to be rescued. And he's now safe at the Andersons' for the moment. But the thing is, well, the thing is that somehow we've got to find £150 by tomorrow afternoon.'

At almost the exact same time that Mum sighed, 'Oh, *love*...' Ralph said, 'Who's this "we"? Eh? Who's been encouraging you to do such a daft thing? Cos whoever it is came up with the idea can come up with the money. Eh? Can't they?'

'No,' I said, looking helplessly at Mum. 'Not really. It was just us, and it was really my idea. So, I'm sorry it was all my fault.'

'Oh dear,' said Mum. 'Just when we were thinking we wouldn't have to worry about money.' Which of course made me feel absolutely terrible. Especially as she really was looking very tired now. 'But I don't know. What do you think, Ralph? Albert means a lot to Chloe, and I'm sure he's going to be much better off at the Andersons' than he would be anywhere else.'

'Better off is as better off does,' said Ralph crossly, unwittingly adapting one of Gran's more idiotic expressions. 'I may have an investor, but I'm not made of money.'

Feeling desperate, I said, 'It's only a loan. Honestly, honestly. I will take all sorts of jobs and I will pay you back. I will, I will.'

Ralph was looking down at the floor. He seemed to be lost in serious thought. And then he suddenly gave the most enormous burp, and I realised that all his energies were in fact being concentrated on the proper expulsion of a massive amount of wind.

'Oh, *Ralph*,' said Mum, whose patience I could see was being sorely tried that Sunday afternoon.

'Well, I don't know,' said Ralph, looking very slightly

shamefaced. 'I really don't. Maybe I've got the money. But it's a loan, my girl.' He wagged his finger at me, like a villain in a cartoon. 'We'll draw up a proper IOU. You'll have to learn the value of money.'

I smiled at him, a strangely genuine smile that I didn't know I could give Ralphs.

'Thank you,' I said. 'Thank you, thank you. That's wonderful. I'll bring Albert round tomorrow so that he can thank you himself.'

'Absolutely no need for that,' said Ralph. 'Now. Leave me in peace, I've spent all day avoiding people who know the result of this afternoon's match, and the recording's just finished so I'm off air for ninety minutes. Not to be disturbed.'

At that moment Gran emerged from the kitchen, carrying a large pile of china dolls, all of whom seemed to gleam in an extra scary way from the attention of her spittle and the yellow duster.

'All done now,' she said to no one in particular. And then, seeing Ralph going into the sitting room, said, 'Shame about your team losing like that, isn't it, Ralph?'

Ghastly Ralph looked at her with an expression of such intense hatred that I wanted to run away and hide. And then he turned to go into the sitting room using words that I hadn't known I knew but wasn't surprised he did.

Gran, pretending to be quite unaware of what she had done, started to put her monsters back in the airing cupboard.

'Come on, Mum,' I said. 'Let me make you a nice cup of tea.'

It was absolutely the least I could do.

Once I'd settled Mum with a large pot of tea and her favourite Sudoku puzzle book, there was only an hour to go before Mark was meant to call me. I retreated to my room to prepare myself. I knew he was only going to be seeing my face and shoulders, but I needed to make sure that they were looking their best. And at that moment with greasy hair, another spot coming along on my chin, and all my make-up worn off by excitement and rain, I was looking anything but my best.

As I started to get a choice of tops out of my wardrobe (the white one probably made me look too pale, the dark blue one had a tear on the right shoulder, the black one was just too, well, black...), my laptop sprang into life. Listening to the familiar cheery tune of the Skype call, I suddenly realised that, what with France being an hour ahead, I was exactly an hour behind on my preparations.

Great.

I clicked on 'answer' and there he was. Like magic. His handsome smiling face filled the whole screen, and for a moment I couldn't say anything, or even think anything, so lovely did he look.

'Hi, there,' he said, the words coming out a good two seconds after I saw him say them. I tried not to look at the video picture of me in the corner of the screen. With any luck the light in my room was bad enough for him not to see the zit, the hair, the blank pale face...

'How you doing, Chloe? Looking good!' Was he being sarcastic? Or did I really look better with greasy hair and no make-up? But there wasn't time to answer these existential questions. Mark was looking expectantly at me.

'Looking good yourself!' I said, instantly regretting this awkward compliment. 'How's France?' I said at the very moment he started to say something.

'What? Oh, France is brilliant. And my French is coming on too. Everyone's being very nice to me, too, which helps.'

'That's great,' I said. And then because I needed him to know how seriously I was taking Project Oscar, plus I really didn't want to hear too much about how nice everyone was being to him, I said, 'I'm looking after Oscar. But who knew someone so handsome could be so shy? He's getting less shy, though. I really like him.'

'Right...' said Mark slowly and thoughtfully. 'You "really like him", he's "really handsome". You trying to tell me something, Chloe?'

'No!' I said. 'I mean I do really like him, but not like *like* him.' I was now straining to see him properly as the signal came and went. 'I only want him to be happy to make *you* happy—'

The laptop gave a burping noise, and up popped a sign saying the connection was lost. Mark's face flashed back on the screen, and then everything went black.

I tried redial and call-back and nothing worked. Perhaps it was true about terrible wifi in France – or his bit of France anyway.

I sat there gazing at the blank screen, surrounded by a pile of crop-tops in various shades of various colours, and felt a sense of mild despair. If only Mark were here with me in real life, I thought, I could reassure him, tell him how I was never going to 'like *like*' anyone else. Ever. Electronic communication can be so great, and then again, so not great.

As if on cue, my other means of electronic communication leapt into life. It was a message on my phone from Sally – 'help. swimming 2moro nEd gd excuse'.

I went back to the laptop and looked up 'symptoms of fungal feet' glad to have a sense of purpose and a distraction.

I decided to keep a low profile the following morning. I didn't really want to witness any further fallout between Gran and Ralph. (I made a pact with myself that I would try not to call him 'ghastly' if he lent me my Albert money).

But as luck would have it, Gran was feeling 'poorly' so was keeping to her room. This meant that I could try to seal the deal with Ralph over breakfast. I waited until he was good and full of sausage and bacon. (I was fairly sure that there was a connection between this part of his daily diet and his world champion belching, but I was also sure I wasn't going to be the one to point this out.)

'So, Ralph,' I said, checking that Mum was listening, so I had a witness. 'I've written this IOU for the Albert money. Is that all right? Can we have it this evening? So I can pay Mr Underwood?'

'All right, missy,' said Ralph, slurping a huge mouthful of tea-with-four-sugars, 'when I'm back from work.'

I set off for the bus stop with a spring in my step. If we had saved Albert, then that was a huge thing ticked off my list of Things To Do. I could now concentrate on some of the next ones: make Oscar happy/in love with Sally; make Sally happy/in love with Oscar; find someone to go to the dreaded Maggie party with; make sure Mark was still my BF and knew I was still his GF; win the English prize; make Mum better.

But as soon as I got to school, I realised that I'd already failed in my mission to make Sally happy.

'That was hopeless, Chloe,' she said crossly as soon as she saw me come through the school gates. 'That thing you sent me. It said I've got to have peeling, cracking, scaly skin, and blisters, and brown toenails. How am I going to get all that in one morning?'

'Well, I don't know,' I admitted. 'Perhaps you should

make it more of a long-term project? I'm sure you could pick up an infection if you really tried. Perhaps you can find some old school towel...'

'Hey!' a voice behind me shouted. There was no mistaking the tones of the QB. 'Chloe! Sally! How rude are you?'

We both turned round, Sally looking as sick as I felt.

'I don't know,' I said lamely. 'How rude are we?'

'Don't you know it's manners to reply to an invitation?' said Maggie, walking towards us, closely followed by at least six of her favourite sycophants. 'Don't tell me you get sooooooo many invitations, that it just slipped your mind to reply to mine?'

Since Sally was just gazing at Maggie with her mouth a perfect O, I knew I wasn't going to get any help from that direction.

'Sorry, Maggie,' I said. And I really was. She had an expression on her face of such confident malevolence that it was frightening. 'It would be great to come. Thank you.'

'Ah,' said Maggie, smiling a small triumphant smile. 'So it would be great, would it? Well, that's *great*.' She emphasised the word in what I took to be an imitation of my voice. 'Next week I'll tell you where it's going to be. And I'll let you and your *boyfriends* know what the dress theme is. It'll be fun.' And she turned to the six sycophants. 'I can't *wait*, can you?'

'No, Maggie.' They all giggled as they looked pointedly at me and Sally. 'Can't wait.' And they all turned on their heels, still giggling and with some of them looking back at us as if to make quite sure that we knew they were laughing at us.

'Cripes,' said Sally. And even in the middle of feeling so miserable, I found time to wonder where Sally got her old-fashioned vocabulary from. 'That was horrid, wasn't it, Chloe? Do you think she's got some sort of special horribleness lined up for us, and anyway WHAT are we going to do about boyfriends?' A determined look came over her face. 'I'm going to text Rob. I'm going to throw myself on his mercy and just ASK him.'

'No you are not,' I said very hastily. 'You can't invite him to a party when he hasn't been in touch with you for ages. That would be dreadful. And anyway, he'd probably say no – or not answer, which is what boys normally do if anything's remotely awkward – and then how would you feel?'

Sally's look of determination turned into one of misery. ''Spose you're right. This is awful. What ARE we going to do, Chloe?'

It wasn't the time to explain that help was at hand in

the form of a handsome, but shy, Swedish boy. And anyway the bell was ringing for registration, a sign that we needed to start thinking about a different set of horrors, starting with Maths and finishing with swimming via Biology, Geography and French.

It was a long old Monday, as Mondays so often tend to be. With so many things to worry about it was almost a welcome distraction to have to worry about glaciation, variable constants and the past participle of the verb 'to hate'.

But still, the Angry God of School Timetabling had saved the worst till last. We dragged ourselves slowly in the direction of the swimming pool like the snail in Shakespeare's 'seven ages of man'. (I think it was a snail. At least I'm sure a snail comes into it somewhere.)

I found myself walking next to Gemma, who was doing her best supermodel stalk – no doubt, I thought slightly bitterly, anticipating the moment where she was going to look great in a swimming costume.

'By the way, Chloe,' she said, semi casually. 'I can't come to Oscar's hockey match, as they say they want to photograph me for the ads on Saturday.'

'That's exciting,' I said, meaning it. But also annoyed that she wasn't going to be part of my army of Oscar Fans. 'Shame, though. All those ice hockey players you won't meet. You never know, some of them might be even more handsome and charming than Jezza. Or even more available for parties than Jack.'

'I'll meet them some other time, Chloe,' said Gemma. 'Don't tell me you're really panicking about who to bring to Maggie's party, are you?'

I told her about the QB having sneered at Sally and me, and how it had made us feel a bit sick. But she seemed serenely unconcerned and simply said that that reminded her to text Maggie...some time.

As we got ready for the dreaded swimming, I thought about how Gemma continued to just be so much cooler than us. Or certainly a lot better at hiding it if she wasn't.

I was dwelling on all this, when my thoughts were rudely interrupted by a disgruntled voice. 'It's all your fault, Chloe,' said Sally, struggling with her electric pink swimming costume, the one that clashed with her hair, not that I'd ever tell her that.

'What's all my fault?' I said trying to keep the sigh out of my voice.

'You said you'd find out about infectious diseases. You said you'd tell me how to get the best ones,' she said, totally illogically, but then she really did hate swimming and sometimes I think that clouded her judgement. 'You've let me down,' she said crossly.

I followed her out to the pool, thinking how extraordinarily unreasonable she was being.

Miss Dinster, the sports teacher who had the uphill task of teaching us swimming, was at the other end of the pool, busy shouting at someone as about six of us emerged from the changing rooms.

Amy, as usual, was first and went to stand by the edge of the pool, obviously – but inexplicably – excited at the thought of jumping into all that water. I suppose if you're athletically inclined, then any opportunity to move about competitively, even if it's slowly and in lots of water, is a source of excitement.

'Come on, Sal,' she said with her incredible cheerfulness. 'Let's you and me do a pencil jump. Here, I'll show you how.'

Sally walked reluctantly over to Amy, who was standing straight as an arrow, arms above her head. 'Like this,' she said. 'Arms up and then to the side, and then straight into the water. Look, watch me.'

And she walked to the edge of the pool, took a breath and jumped out, rigid and straight, into the water. She was so neat she hardly left a ripple.

'Well, that looks easy,' said Sally. 'And the sooner I get in, the sooner I can get out.' And she went to the edge of the pool, put her hands in the air and, standing still and straight, stepped forward into the water.

She went down all right, pencil straight, just like you're supposed to, but a second later shot back up to the surface spluttering and yelling.

'Ow, ow, OW!' she cried, pink in the face. 'Oh, ow. That hurts sooooo much!'

We stood stock still in horror. Miss Dinster was at our end of the pool in about 1.5 seconds.

'I've broken something!' Sally was shouting. 'Ow, ow!'

Without breaking step Miss D dived into the pool and grabbed Sally. She gently pulled her out of the pool as Sally continued to shout and scream.

Sitting her on the side of the diving board, Miss D inspected the foot and announced that she thought there was a good chance Sally had broken her big toe.

'Ow,' said Sally, but a little more calmly now. 'Ow. It hurts.'

I went and sat down beside Sally and put my arm round her. 'Poor Sal,' I said. 'But hey. Bright side! This'll get you out of sport for *weeks.*'

Miss Dinster looked down at me and pursed her lips disapprovingly. 'That is not at all helpful, Chloe,' she said. 'Now we'll have to take Sally to have an X-ray to see what damage has been done. You can get changed and come with us to the hospital.'

Amy was looking mortified while all this was going on. Dripping with water and sympathy, she said, 'Oh, Miss Dinster, it's all my fault. I thought we could all do pencil jumps and, well…' Her voice trailed off.

'These things happen sometimes,' said Miss D gruffly, but not unkindly. 'We'll get Sally to the doctor, and she'll be fine.'

We took Sally into the changing rooms, where she got dried and dressed very slowly and carefully, making a great deal of noise as she did so.

I thought the sooner we handed her over to A & E, the better for all of us.

I suppose it shouldn't be altogether surprising, but that day I realised that the Great British Public must surely not like spending its weekend in the A & E department of a hospital. Instead, it saves up all its ailments and injuries and brings them in on a Monday.

We were *hours* in A & E – well, two or three anyway – and by the time a nurse came to inspect Sally, we were also a little bit fed up. But such is the magical effect of the medical profession, as soon as the nurse and then a doctor came into the cubicle where Sally was waiting, everything gradually felt better – even Sally's toe, which she had indeed broken.

She was given painkillers, which seemed to take effect quite quickly, and was then told that her toe needed rest, elevation and an ice pack. So we decided to go straight from A & E to her bedroom, to bandage her foot, and put it on top of a pile of cushions and underneath a packet of frozen peas.

'Darlings!' cried Liv when she opened the door to us. 'You're frightfully late, where on earth have you *been*?' She was wearing white jeans and a jersey that either had a very unusual pattern on it or was on inside out.

'We left loads of messages, Mum,' said Sally sulkily. (And I could sympathise with the sulk on this occasion. After all, surely one of the things mothers are for is to come and rescue you when you find yourself unexpectedly wounded.) 'We've spent the whole day at the hospital 'cos I've broken my foot. Chloe has been wonderful.' She said that last bit accusingly, as she started to climb the stairs, moving extra slowly like a very old, very injured person.

'Darling! How awful! I'm so sorry I didn't get your

225

message! I've been all *day* with the twins, they're just want, want, want…so I just thought I deserved a little lie-down. So how awful! Not getting your message.'

For a moment I thought Liv was wearing an unusually pungent scent. Then I recognised the scent and realised that she might have needed a lie-down after being up close and personal with her old friend Mr Pinot Grigio.

'Oh, Mum,' said Sally in the special world-weary voice that she sometimes saved for her mother. Now halfway up the stairs, she said to me, 'Will you bring the peas, Chloe?'

'Now, Sally,' said Liv, seeming to come to with a bit of an effort. 'I'm going to bring you your ice pack, darling. After all, what are mothers for if not to look after their injured children? Mmm?' And she gave what she must have thought was a comforting smile as she headed off in the direction of the fridge.

I was now so behind schedule – get Ralph's money/ to give to Charlie/to give to Mr U – that I left them to it. A little mother-daughter bonding could only be a good thing, in the circs.

I got back to find Ralph and Mum sitting at the kitchen table – he with a can of his extra strong stupid juice/lager, she with a large cup of milky tea.

Mum looked up with a smile. 'There you are, love,' she said with her usual unerring way of pointing out something that didn't need pointing out. 'Is Sally all right? Poor thing.'

I took a moment to feel pleased that I had the sort of mother who read her messages.

'She'll be fine, Mum,' I said. 'I'm sure it won't be long until she's just very glad she's got a brilliant excuse for not having to do any kind of sport for weeks and weeks.'

'You'd better look sharp, missy,' said Ralph and he took a long swig of his brightly coloured extra-strength can. 'Your friend Charlie rang to see if you were back. He says he's supposed to be seeing the Underwood fellow in the next hour.'

He reached into his trouser pocket – no mean feat as there wasn't much extra material for a pocket, most of it being used to encompass the ample Ralph Bottom – and pulled out a huge wad of notes.

'Goodness, Ralph,' said Mum sounding as surprised as I felt. '*What* a lot of money.'

I couldn't have put it better myself.

'Yes,' said Ralph, sounding exceptionally pleased with himself. 'This is what comes of having a successful business idea.' I supposed that the rolls of notes were

Merv's investment money. And rather thought that they ought really to be being invested somewhere. Rather than be lining the pocket of Ralph's trousers. But now wasn't the time to criticise.

'Thank you, Ralph!' I said, meaning it as he counted out £150. 'I WILL pay you back.'

I hurtled out of the door and down the stairs, dialling Charlie's number as I went. He was in Papa Pietro's pizzeria. Apparently it was the Dad Who's birthday, and Charlie, being the kind of all-round good guy that I would expect Mark's best friend to be, was spending that last of his earnings on Birthday Pizza for Amy and her parents.

The place was buzzing and humming and as hot as ever as I breathlessly made my way over to their table.

'Hi, Chloe,' said Charlie. 'I've just finished, so, good timing. Let's go!'

'Happy birthday,' I said to the Dad Who. 'Sorry to take Charlie away but this won't take long. He's been so brilliant. He's saved Albert's life.'

Amy and her lovely parents smiled tolerantly at me, which was exactly as nice of them as I had come to expect.

As Charlie was getting ready to leave I looked around at Papa P's emporium. The smells of many different pizzas wafted over to me, and made me suddenly feel ravenously hungry. I looked around at various people's pizzas and wondered idly which one I'd have if I didn't have to be somewhere else and didn't have another use for all the money in my bag.

I had just spotted the perfect pizza – it looked just the right balance of cheesiness and greenness – when I noticed the person about to eat it. He had slightly outsize ears and a serious rictus-like grin as he sliced away at the crust of the pizza. Rob.

He was sitting at the same big table by the window that I'd seen him at when we first laid eyes on Oscar, the Silent Swede. It was a noisy table – about ten people, more boys than girls – and I just had time to notice that one of those people was the QB herself when Rob looked up and caught my eye.

True to form I felt an enormous blush coming on. Especially when I realised that sitting next to the QB was the boy with properly big ears who was so good at laughing at people as long as he was safely surrounded by his gang.

Charlie was now ready to leave, and we had to walk past the big table on our way out. I steeled myself, and tried to look everywhere except at the QB. But I couldn't ignore Rob.

'Hi, Chloe,' he said casually when I got near enough to their table. 'Wassup? Sally all right?' He put a large forkful of pizza into his mouth, and seemed to swallow it almost immediately. For a horrible moment I thought I was going to ask him whether he always ate his food like that, and why his mother had never taught him that on the whole most people chewed stuff before they swallowed it.

'Yes, she's fine,' I said, fortunately not dwelling on the chewing issue. 'We're fine.'

'She been away or something?' said Rob, putting another huge piece of pizza in his mouth. 'Tell her hi.'

'Yes,' I said, fascinated to watch another lump of crust go straight down Rob. 'Sorry, gotta go,' I said. Out of the corner of my eye I could see the QB looking at me, and I could swear that she was forming a new plan to humiliate me in public.

'Come on,' said Charlie. 'Getting late.' With relief I turned and followed Charlie out of the hot pizzeria and the reach of the Queen Beeyatch.

As for Rob, well, I'd think about that later.

'This shouldn't take long, Chloe,' said Charlie as he walked beside me. 'You give me the money and go upstairs to your flat. I'll nip up when the deed is done, but best if he doesn't see us together.'

At the main front door, I handed over the notes, and slipped quietly upstairs. 'Good luck,' I whispered. Because I was glad it was Charlie and not me going into the lion's (aka Mr Underwood's) den. Mr U was a scary individual at the best of times, and I didn't like the thought of being on my own with him, in his lair, with the front door locked behind me, where no one could hear me scream...

When I got upstairs, I closed our front door behind me with relief. My imagination was running away with me, as it sometimes has a way of doing. And it made me almost happy to smell the smell of sausage and to hear Ralph and Gran talking to Mum in the kitchen.

They all looked up when I came in, Ralph with a frown, Gran with a purse of the lips – and Mum with a warm smile of welcome.

'Good news, love,' she said. 'We've got Steve coming home next weekend. We're going to have the whole of Saturday and Sunday with him. Won't that be lovely?'

She looked so happy that I could only agree that having my oily brother around would be a Good Thing, and I smiled back at her.

'Only he'll have to have his room back, so I know you won't mind if Gran shares your room just for

Saturday night,' Mum went on. 'She can have your bed, and we can blow up the spare for you.'

It was the work of a yoctosecond (a new favourite word; a yoctosecond being one septillionth of a second) for me to determine that Saturday night would be a sleepover night. Somewhere. Somehow. There was no *way* I was going to spend a whole night listening to Gran grind her dentures.

'Sure,' I said with my best false smile. 'I might not be—' I was about to explain that I had a pressing engagement with a different bed, any bed, when the doorbell rang. Charlie.

I rushed to the door. Charlie was standing there, looking a bit pale and holding a piece of paper and a dog lead in his hand.

'OK, Chloe,' he said. 'Here's Albert's spare lead. And this – apparently – is the guarantee that he's not going to give us all rabies or anything. Though it looks a bit dodge to me. Also. Chloe. You owe me big time! That man's flat is so revolting. Smells like there's a dead body in there. Plus, he was only wearing a vest and pants, which seemed to require constant scratching. I expect the dead body's given him fleas.'

Great, I thought. That's just what I want to go to bed

thinking about. A dead body downstairs, and numerous nameless fleas.

Charlie must have noticed my look of horror. 'Oh, don't worry, Chloe,' he said giving me a hug. 'He's going off somewhere. He still wouldn't say where, but I wouldn't be surprised if it's prison, and I wouldn't be surprised if it's for a while. You'll have a new neighbour soon, I'm sure.'

I hugged Charlie back hard. He was one of nature's good guys, for sure. Which made me think...

That night I went to bed determined to try to have a proper conversation with Mark, so I could tell him how much of a good guy *he* was.

»→ 10 ←«

Saturday Night Fever

What a week that was, I thought as I emerged slowly and carefully from a deep sleep on Saturday morning.

For a start, Sally had managed to avoid a considerable proportion of it. It was amazing how serious having a broken toe had turned out to be. Not only did it save her from gym, netball and swimming, but apparently it also rendered her incapable of Maths, English and pretty well every other academic subject. By the time she'd queued to have her toe realigned, queued for a plaster-cast for her foot, and rested and elevated the result there hadn't been much time for school.

Which meant that, what with one thing and another, I hadn't got round to telling Sally that Rob had said 'say hi to Sally'. But anyway, I thought, if he wanted to say a hello to her then he should do it himself. All the more reason, I said to myself, for Project Sally & Oscar.

Happily, by the time we got to Saturday, Sally was going to be back on her feet/foot, and was going to meet the rest of us in the skating rink café.

Extracting myself from my duvet, which had entwined itself extraordinarily cleverly around my left leg – probably not wanting me to leave it to the attentions of Gran – I headed towards the bathroom. If my inspections of last night were anything to go by, there was a lot of work to be done. The greasy hair, the new spot on the chin and the straggly left eyebrow...all made for a long list of Things to Do in The Bathroom.

Alarmingly, after about thirty minutes of in-depth attention most of these problems were as acute as ever. Hair just as lank even after washing, spots just as spotty, and eyebrow just as straggly – only now it was a straggly right one, not a straggly left one.

I sighed. A deep existential sigh.

I picked up my make-up brush to try to cover up the explosions on my chin and now another new one on my forehead, and I noticed that the brush had a rather stiff quality to it. Trying to flick the dirt out of it, I had a sudden flashback to a lesson Sally had shown me on YouTube. 'How I deep clean my make-up brushes – and save my skin from bacteria', it was called. The person telling us how to clean make-up brushes seemed to have so many hundreds of them that it was hard to believe that cleaning them was ever an issue.

I piled on the concealer with a brush that was almost certainly better at concealing bacteria then spots, until I realised that I had put so much concealer on that there was now a large dark pink mound on my chin.

Plus, I was now late.

Clutching my bag of overnight stuff – concealer, dirty brush, that sort of thing – I rushed into the kitchen.

'Bye then!' I said to Gran, who pursed her lips at me in a dismissive, disapproving way.

'Bye, Ralph!' I said to Ralph in a cheery way, because after all I was happy with him even if he wasn't happy with me.

'See you, Mum,' I said, now feeling guilty that I wouldn't be there for her happy reunion with my oily brother. 'Hi to Steve. Tell him I'll see him tomorrow.'

After I'd had a grunt from Ralph and a hug from Mum I fled the kitchen and raced to the bus stop, starting to panic about being late. The Global International Skating Arena (you would have thought that it could probably manage with just being either global or international) – was much grander than 'Slide 'n' Glide', and was over an hour's drive away. So we had agreed we'd all meet at the Andersons', or Albert's House as I liked to think of it, and go there together.

I caught the bus by the very skin of my teeth, and settled in a seat at the back, ready to relax and enjoy the ride knowing I wasn't going to be late.

It was a fatal thought to have.

Because we were instantly stuck in an almighty traffic jam, surrounded on all sides by totally stationary traffic. After about ten minutes, the bus just about managed to edge forward to the next bus stop where about fifty-six million people immediately pushed their way on.

Most of them were boys of about seventeen, many of them dressed in football kit, and all shouting at each other. It took me back to the beginning of our Boy Watching days, when we were in the early stages of trying to work out how The Boy worked, both in packs and alone. These particular specimens seemed to be proving beyond doubt our simple rule that The More the Shoutier.

Yelling at each other over everyone else's heads, they had an air of a rebellious army with no leader. The more one yelled, the more the others yelled. And it had got so I ceased to be able to understand what they were actually saying...although the kinds of four-letter words that came so naturally to Ralph featured a lot.

They were annoyed, as I was, that the bus didn't seem to be going anywhere, and the shoutiness got worse and worse. And then they started to make rude comments about some of the people in the bus that weren't them. I reckoned that if you were a middle-aged male or a young woman you were on the Boy Radar, and quite likely to have some aspect of your appearance pointed out to the entire bus. And generally not an aspect you really wanted to be pointed out to the entire bus.

As the atmosphere got more and more heated, I bent further and further down over my phone. Perhaps if I could somehow morph myself into being an integral part of its small screen, I could manage to disappear altogether so I couldn't be a target of these boys, who by now were very loud indeed, and getting closer to the back of the bus. And it didn't help that I recognised the tall one from our trip to the shop and, yes, sure enough, the boy with big ears.

The more I looked at The Boy In Its Pack, the more I became convinced that the best boys were boys on their own. Perhaps coming from another country (like, say, Sweden) or perhaps living in another country (France, for instance...).

And then I thought that it's all very well having these theories about the perfect boy, but they were hardly any help to me right now on this bus. By now I was nearly surrounded by very noisy and very imperfect boys – many of whom were deliberately nudging and shoving anyone who was sitting down, anyone who wasn't one of them.

And then I heard a thump from the upper deck. And then a bit of shouting. And then down the stairs came a huge bullet-headed figure, pulling a couple of the noisiest boys behind him.

Never would I have thought I could be so glad to see Chester Dubrovonich. Somehow he looked even huger close up, and especially standing next to the noisy boys – who now seemed so much smaller. Suddenly all of them ceased to fill up the bus, they just looked cowed and shame-faced.

'This lot,' roared Chester in the general direction of the bus driver, 'are getting off the bus right now. Open the doors.'

This'll never work, I thought. Bus drivers have very strict rules about when they can open the doors, and if you're not at a bus stop, there is absolutely no way they are going to—

The bus driver obediently opened the doors.

Obviously a huge American-Russian oligarch bellowing at him carried a lot more weight than Bus Regulation 225, 'Thou Shalt Not Open Doors in Unauthorised Places'.

'Out!' shouted Chester. 'Get out, every last one of you.' And he grabbed a passing schoolboy by the scruff of the neck and pushed him on his way.

So many rules broken, so many potential lawsuits! Not that that seemed to bother Chester, who allowed himself to look quietly self-satisfied as he shoved the last boy out of the bus, and then found himself being given a round of applause by everyone left behind.

As if to complete his demonstration of superhero powers, at that moment the traffic cleared a path ahead of the bus, and we ground into motion.

Looking at the time, I saw that all that drama had in fact only taken fifteen minutes. I settled back in my seat and watched Chester being patted on the arm by three elderly women.

I picked up my phone again. I needed to let the others know I'd be late, and Amy that her new coach was my hero.

I walked up Mark's road feeling a bit less nervous than the last time I'd been there. After all, the reports of Albert were encouraging. He was playing nicely with the puppies, hadn't disgraced himself in the eating or pooing department, and had enjoyed his walks with Oscar. (At least that was what Oscar told me. He had begun to text me on an almost daily basis – just with short reports on Albert's well-being. It was nice to hear that all was going well, but I was beginning to think that the sooner he started texting Sally rather than me on a regular basis the sooner we could all move on to the happy ending.)

Gabriel the angel/shepherd opened the front door to me.

'Good morning, Chloe,' he said in his rather patrician accent. (I think that's how you have to speak if you're a barrister.) 'We're going in two cars. Oscar in the first one, because the traffic's awful and we can't risk delivering him late. Come in for the moment, anyway.'

I followed him into the kitchen, which seemed to be very full of people – almost like a Saturday morning bus only not nearly so noisy.

There were Patricia and Georgie and Amy playing with the puppies and – I was pleased to see – a very happy-looking Albert. And there was Georgie's cool TV producer talking to James, who was holding a small crutch.

Next to him was the owner of the small crutch, sitting at the table with her plastered foot ostentatiously on a chair in front of her. She was talking to Charlie and Ethan. By the looks of it she was perfecting her delivery of the story of 'The Day I Broke Stuff and Nearly Drowned'.

And then over in the corner, clutching a mug and looking carefully at the floor, was Oscar. He was all dressed up in his ice hockey uniform. With enormous shoulders and a whole top half that tapered down into a narrower bottom half, he looked all out of proportion. And also over-the-top colourful. In fact, he looked so misshapen and fluorescent that some people might be tempted to giggle.

'Oscar!' I said, concentrating very hard on not being the sort of person who might giggle. 'Oscar!' And then I came to a full stop. The giggle was bubbling up inside, and any second now it would be bubbling up outside. There was only one thing to be done. I had a coughing fit.

Spluttering and choking in between the giggles, I was vaguely aware that Gabriel was looking slightly shocked and slightly disapproving, and that Oscar had taken a step forward and was coming towards me.

Two seconds later and I wasn't laughing so hard. Oscar had given me another of his mighty wallops on the back – he obviously considered it one of his core strengths after the success of the last one – and I was choked and walloped into silence.

'I am sorry,' said Oscar, frowning in concern. 'But this hysterical coughing is serious.'

'You all right, Chloe? OK, Oscar,' said Gabriel, turning to Oscar in a particularly patrician and commanding way. 'It's time for us to get going. We can't have our star performer arriving late. Come on, I'll take you, and – who else shall we take? Room for three more.'

'Sally,' I said instantly. Because obviously there were loads of possibilities of intimacies, even with a small crutch between them, in the back seat of a car. 'And Charlie and Amy wanted to get there early, I think.'

'Very well,' said Gabriel. 'Round them up and let's get into the car.'

I turned to make sure Sally was ready to get herself and her foot into the car. She was in the middle of the hilarious bit about when she had to go back to the hospital for the second time to have her cast put on, but was pretty amenable about being told what to do.

(One of her strengths, I've always thought.)

Moments later the kitchen felt much emptier. And then I realised that I was with all the people I knew least well – Patricia, James, Georgie, Mr TV Producer – and had a moment of shyness and worry about who I'd sit next to in the car.

One day, I thought to myself, I won't worry about this sort of thing, I will simply take everything in my stride, I won't giggle inappropriately, and I won't say the wrong thing and I won't blush.

And pigs will fly all over the International (and Global) Skating Arena.

'Chloe,' said Patricia, putting down one of the puppies. 'I don't think you've met Donald properly, have you? He's Georgie's producer, and he's just been telling us how well it's all going. Which I'm sure is a testament to his skills.'

And she smiled at him warmly but teasingly, which had the effect of making him look suddenly unsure of himself. I had a fleeting moment of thinking that I must never, ever, be tempted to show off in front of Patricia.

Georgie, looking extra glam in skinny jeans and super-high heels that made her tower over her mother, and pretty well everyone else, smiled at Donald too.

'He knows it's only going well because the cast is beyond brilliant at improvising – which is just as well given the script!' And she took the edge off the comment by smiling exactly the same smile as her mother had smiled.

All of which made me feel almost sorry for Donald, who was now grinning nervously and disguising his awkwardness by bending down to make a huge fuss of Albert.

'Hey, everyone,' came a voice from the kitchen doorway. It was Ethan, looking agreeably gentle and spindly. I'd forgotten about Ethan. Somehow he looked reassuringly unsure of himself too.

'Got the van all ready outside,' he said. 'Are we off now?'

'Yes, off you go,' said Patricia. 'I've got to stay and look after the dogs, but I know you'll give me a blow-by-blow. Tell Oscar good luck if you see him again before the match.'

And she turned to me and said, 'Bye, Chloe. Give Mark a ring when you can. I know he wants you to know how he's getting on.'

And she turned away to fill up the water-bowl of Puppy Number One. They were still known as Puppy Number One and Puppy Number Two. Apparently the family had only managed to whittle down the list of possible names to thirty-four. At this rate they would still be Number One and Number Two when they were breathing their last. A bit hard to spend your whole life being named after a lavatory function, I couldn't help thinking.

And then I started thinking about why Patricia had made a point of telling me to call Mark. It was code! Something was up! There was something – definitely something – going on between Mark and the dreaded Cecile! (What sort of a name was Cecile anyway?) And she was advising me to ring him, so he could put me out of my misery. I looked at her as she confidently and efficiently dug out some more dog biscuits for Number Two. Yes. Definitely a code.

I tried to stop my brain going into its usual feverish overdrive as we followed Ethan out to the Dad Who's purple van.

Georgie went straight to sit in the front, so I found myself clambering into the back of the van between all the Dad Who's camera gear and two men who were, in their different ways, rather scarily grown-up.

I needn't have worried about Donald, who immediately started examining all the boxes of equipment. I guess if you're in TV you know about camera stuff, and all camera stuff is kind of interesting.

Which left me squeezed up between James, a huge flashlamp and a very pointy tripod.

'So, Chloe,' said James, sounding almost as awkward as I felt – I always think people who start their sentences with the word 'so' for no reason at all only do so because they're playing for time while their brain comes up with something more interesting. 'How's it all going? Working hard? Liking school?'

I looked at his handsome profile as he stared fixedly ahead at a camera bag. He looked more outdoorsy than ever, as if he'd be more comfortable scaling up the side of the mountain carrying nothing but a knife and a loaded gun.

'Weeeell,' I said, thinking that for someone who'd been a spy and lived all over the world his conversational skills were a bit limited. 'I s'pose it's going sort of OK, but—'

I didn't have time to tell James about all the things that worried me and that he might be interested to hear about. Because he almost instantly interrupted me. 'How do you think Sally's getting on?' he said in a serious voice. 'Sometimes it worries me that I've come back into the family so suddenly, and I feel none of them know me and I don't really know them. But I'm working on it, and I'm sure once the twins get better we'll all feel more relaxed and I can spend some proper time with Sally and her friends.'

Then he looked at me as if he suddenly realised that maybe this was a rather adult stream-of-consciousness he was addressing to me. So he turned to Donald, now engrossed in his smartphone as people so often are, and started to ask him something safe about cameras and TV studios.

By the time we arrived at the international, global arena I knew a lot about studio management, and perhaps just a little more about Sally's newly returned real dad.

I think I'd learnt that a tough outside doesn't necessarily mean a tough inside.

Plus, if things were a little difficult at home for my hopalong friend, the sooner she was happily in lurve the better.

♥ ♥

An hour later the question of making conversation had become utterly irrelevant. As we watched something we couldn't see be hit from one end of the rink to the other by seemingly enormous padded men in bright colours, the noise level was literally unspeakable. Especially when everyone took a break to have a fight – which the umpires seemed to encourage.

As a spectacle the whole thing was rather impressive, but none of us really knew the rules, or what was at stake, so we just watched the red number 3 (Oscar) as he sped from one side of the rink to the other swiping away with his stick, and cheering if ever he seemed to do something clever when he swiped away at the thing we couldn't see.

We had somehow managed to get ourselves in the front row, on account of having a Disabled Person with us. (Some kind steward clearly having been moved by my hopalong friend's tragic hopping.) So we were well visible to all the players, and to the rest of the crowd.

Which probably explained how as soon as the match ended (Oscar's team triumphant by two goals) we became aware of someone pushing his way towards us.

It was Merv, looking determined in his trademark black denim, and strangely small compared to the giant coloured figures we'd just been watching. He was with some people carrying cameras and sound booms. He seemed out of place, but I imagined he must have been something to do with investing in the film rights to international (and global) ice hockey matches.

'Oh no!' said Sally in a loud voice that Merv could almost certainly hear. 'Look who's coming this way. Is it too late to hide?' We were standing around our seats in the front row and, yes, it was too late to hide.

'Chloe,' said Merv looking at me and not taking any notice of my rude Disabled friend. 'I'm glad to find you here. Gemma's been trying to get hold of you. I think she wants to talk about something. And I gather you sent her a message asking if you could stay tonight?'

I'd completely forgotten the distress call I'd sent out to Gemma in the morning. I'd had a thought that if Sally's not very reliable family couldn't have me over – and with the twins' rare rashes still taking over their lives I thought that was highly likely – then I was going to have to rely on her or Amy to rescue me from a night of Gran's Grinding Dentures.

'That would be great,' I said with my best strained but polite smile. 'Thank you.' I wondered what the 'something' was. I hoped it wasn't 'something' serious or horrible. But there was time to grill him about that later as Merv was going to drive me home.

But first, we all had to join Team Oscar in the glass-windowed burger bar at the top of the sports centre.

Obviously my work that day would not be done until I saw Sally enthusiastically chatting to Oscar about his triumph on the rink, and him looking down on her with a fond, if silent smile.

Things only worked out a little bit according to plan.

Gabriel commandeered a big table overlooking the now empty rink, and we all stood and sat about talking to the team as they emerged – now happily dressed in normal clothes – from the dressing rooms.

Seeing Oscar head towards us, looking more and more like Tom Hiddleston than ever in tight jeans and a white shirt, I suddenly had a brainwave. Oscar seemed positively elated, and generally happy and handsome. We must be doing a good job of looking after him, I thought, if he looks so well on it. And wouldn't it be good to reassure his second cousin, worrying over there in France, that all was good in Oscar World?

'Hey, Sally,' I said to my BFF, who seemed to be regaling Gabriel with some lively tale. Probably still to do with the day she broke-stuff-and-nearly-drowned. 'Here's Oscar! Let's take a photo of the champion!'

What could be more endearing to Mark, I thought, than a photo of his previously shy and silent cousin looking all upbeat and happy?

I went over to Oscar and stood next to him, put Sally

in front of us with her phone, looked up at our Swedish friend and said to Sally, 'OK, Sal, take a picture of our very own champion.'

Sally held her phone out in front of her, turned her back on us, gave an inane grin and took a picture.

I groaned. Inwardly and outwardly. Sally's obsession with the selfie is something that I try not to dwell on too much. But if there's a situation that normal people would photograph you can be sure that such a photograph in Sally's hands would have a picture of Sally in the middle of it.

I sometimes wonder what her children will make of it all. When they're looking at family photos of Sally's early life there'll be very little to see but a succession of shots of Sally grinning in front of something unidentifiable.

On this occasion I explained to Sally that what was required was a photograph of me and Oscar, taken by her but not with her. I think she got the message, and I was pleased when she seemed to take her duties very seriously; she must have taken about twenty photos of Oscar looking winning and Tom Hiddleston-like. This was all going very, very well, I thought. Here was a happy, handsome Oscar, and here was Sally taking endless photos just like a groupie or a girlfriend.

Out of the corner of my eye I saw Donald and Georgie looking over at us. Even more excellent, I thought to myself as I looked at Donald looking at Oscar looking handsome. 'Famous TV Producer Finds New Film Star Talent at Hockey Match' would make a perfect headline, and would show Mark how I'd played a part in setting up a whole new career for his cousin.

They both came over towards us just as Sally finished taking her twentieth photo.

'Well done, Oscar,' said Georgie, flashing a brilliant smile at him. 'That was amazing. Don't know how you manage to skate all over the place so fast AND hit that tiny thing with your stick.' And she blinked, quickly, three or four times. She had amazing eyelashes, I suddenly noticed, and, now that she was sucking in her cheeks a bit, I could see that she also had amazing cheekbones.

'Oscar!' Thankfully my clever BFF was still waving her phone. 'Hey, look over here. You look amazing against that black background!'

Even silent Oscar seemed to quite like a bit of old-fashioned flattery. He gave a gentle smile and looked into Sally's phone with what can only be described as a winning smile.

I gave one of those myself as I watched them both.

Surely it was only a matter of time before they realised how well they went together.

'Let's sit down, everyone,' said Gabriel in his commandeering tone of voice. 'Sooner we order, sooner we get some food.'

Oscar followed me to the table, so I took the opportunity to push Sally into the seat next to him. Job nearly done, I thought as they sat down next to each other.

Sitting down the other side of Oscar – that way if I didn't talk to him he'd HAVE to talk to Sally – I found myself with Donald on the other side of me and Merv opposite me.

'So, Chloe,' Donald began, unoriginally and irritatingly, as soon as we sat down. 'You known the Andersons long?'

Oh dear, this was going to be awkward, I thought. But still, my job was to be pointing towards him so that Oscar could get to know his other neighbour better.

'Not really,' I said truthfully. 'But they're great, aren't they? I mean they're all so good at what they do. Obviously. But you'd never know. I mean, they don't show off or anything.'

I was putting all this terribly badly, but I somehow wanted Mr TV Producer to know that I could spot people who showed off and who were pleased with themselves.

He didn't seem to notice, though. 'And Georgie?' he said. 'She a friend of yours, is she?'

I looked at him looking at Georgie, who was on the other side of the table looking rather bored by something Merv was saying. Donald seemed to be gazing at her rather intently, even though he was supposed to be talking to me.

'Well, sort of,' I said. 'I mean, I know her a little bit, and I'd like us to be friends. Yes.' I found myself answering his question completely honestly.

'I think if this show works out,' said Donald, still looking over at Georgie, 'that she's going to have a lot of fans.' He glanced sideways at me. 'I mean, you know, like blokes who might fancy their chances.'

I suddenly realised that I was looking at a bloke who fancied his chances.

At that moment a flurry of waiters (or whatever the collective noun for waiters is, perhaps a 'serving', or an 'order') arrived carrying lots of plates of burgers and salads.

My conversation with the TV producer got lost in a slew of 'who's having the Mediterranean with a twist?' and 'didn't you order the sweet chilli onion?' (who knew a beef burger could be so complicated?) and 'why would you fry something *three* times?' (a perfectly good question from Sally).

Donald had now gone completely silent. He seemed to be utterly preoccupied with his Rosemary and Feta Lamb Burger (obviously TV producers can't just have a beef burger like the rest of us) and – I strongly suspected – his attempts to listen to what Georgie was saying to Merv.

Which was just as well because I was trying to listen to what was happening between Sally and Oscar. Sally seemed to be doing most of the talking (good/only to be expected) and Oscar was nodding with a small smile on his face.

Everything seemed to be going according to plan, so I was able to focus on my own burger – which I'd rather imaginatively ordered with a bun and some chips. In between smothering it with some ketchup I assessed our table out of the corner of my eye to make sure no one was looking like they'd interrupt the putative (I think I mean 'putative') lovebirds: Charlie and Amy, fondly feeding each other chips – check; Ethan watching them – check; Gabriel saying something patrician to James – also check.

'… Chloe?' It was Merv, leaning over the table and

waving a chip to attract my attention. 'Gotta go, OK? Need to pick up Gemma on the way.'

He put the chip in his mouth, swallowed it immediately and got up from his chair. If it hadn't been Merv, I might have asked him what it was with the male of the species that meant they didn't see the need for chewing, but in the flurry of thankyous and goodbyes it wasn't really the moment.

'Send me those pics, Sal,' I said to my photographer friend. 'Talk later, bye.' I turned quickly away as I wanted her to concentrate on her handsome neighbour.

But not quickly enough. 'You go, Chloe?' said Oscar, looking up at me with a concerned expression on his face. Perhaps he was worried that I might have a fatal coughing fit if he wasn't there to whack me on the back. 'You come see Albert soon? We can go yogging in the park.'

And have just a jar of jam and jelly in the Jacuzzi with the judge and the jockey. Is fortunately what I didn't say.

But before I had another coughing fit, I managed a quick 'yes, sure', thanked Gabriel for a lovely day (tea-party manners never being far away in my world, it would seem) and started to follow Merv out of the restaurant.

As I climbed into Merv's ridiculously enormous car, I felt rather exhausted, but I reckoned that all I had to do was to make sure Gemma was all right and show Mark what a reliable girlfriend I was, and my day's work would be done.

⇻ 11 ↢↞

Steve's Curve Ball

It turned out that picking up Gemma was a rather more complicated process than I'd imagined. After her day's photo-shoot – and it seemed that a 'day' in photo-shoot-speak was from 9 am till 8 pm – Marianne had scooped up her daughter and taken her to a new tapas bar that had somehow omitted to enter itself into Merv's satnav machine.

This meant that I had to spend an extra half an hour in Merv's car with only my phone for company, Merv being too preoccupied with swearing at his electronics to make small talk.

But before he went into meltdown, I had managed to satisfy my curiosity on three important facts: firstly, he really had invested in Ghastly Ralph's virtual wheat (good, because it meant that at least Ralph wouldn't go bankrupt, or not yet anyway), secondly, that Gemma was all right but she wanted to talk to me about something 'to do with a party' he thought (which might also be good if it meant that Gemma had a plan to get us through the nightmare that was Maggie's Valentine's Day party), and thirdly, that not chewing food is exactly as bad for you as I thought it was. 'Acid,' said Merv as he swallowed two white tablets, quickly followed by two more. 'I'm a martyr to acid.' And he gave the kind of burp that a Ralph would be proud of.

Eventually we arrived in a part of town that I didn't know at all, and wouldn't have done even if I did. Apparently if you are opening a new cutting-edge tapas bar it's best to have it where all the rich people are. And the rich people tend to knock down landmarks that Merv and his satnav used to recognise and replace them with cranes and building sites advertising luxury flats.

'Rich blighters,' said Merv completely illogically, since he was almost certainly one of those himself. 'Always knocking things down, and digging things out. And who for? I ask you?'

There was a pause. I knew he wasn't actually asking me so I didn't actually answer.

'Not for the likes of you and me, that's for sure,' said Merv, continuing on his illogical and inaccurate summary of the Way of the World.

He then started to tell me all about how no one ever paid any taxes, and that everything was 'off shore' and 'off plan', and the country would go to the dogs if we weren't very careful.

I wasn't at all sure what I could do about any of this, but did know enough to know that Merv coming over all self-righteous was a bit – rich, I suppose would be the word. He had, after all, nearly gone to prison for tax evasion only six months ago.

But once he realised that his satnav was as lost as he was, he had to concentrate on finding the way and I was able to check my phone. Which was good because Sally (photographer to the stars) had dutifully sent through the photos she'd taken of Oscar.

They were very good photos, or at least two or three of them were. Oscar was looking very happy and handsome in all of them, but much more importantly there were one or two of me where I looked all right.

That is, none of the deformities of complexion or hair were showing, and with half my face in shadow as I looked up at Oscar it even seemed as if I had great cheekbones.

Perfect.

'Hiya! Had great day Oscar's team won! Look, here's a

happy champ! Talk later!' And I attached the picture of me where my cheekbones were at their absolute best.

Too late I realised that every sentence ended with an exclamation mark. Someone once said you should never use exclamation marks; it was like laughing at your own joke. But there was nothing to be done about it now, and anyway I hoped Mark would be so pleased his cousin was so happy that he'd forgive.

'Hoo-bloody-ray,' Merv almost shouted with relief. We turned into a street next to some scaffolding, and parked near a skip that was overflowing with rubbish. I guess the Land of Rich Blighters has to get worse before it gets better.

'Here it is,' he said. And I looked up at a sign that said *La Mesa con Hambre** and followed him into a small dark almost empty room – I supposed it was empty on account of it being too late for the English to eat and too early for the Spanish.

In the corner were Gemma and her elegant, glamorous, scary mother, Marianne. They were both looking at us as we came in. Not for the first time I thought how beautiful they both were, especially when viewed side by side.

* Which means 'The Hungry Table'. Although why a table should be hungry, or how you'd know if it was, I have no idea

No wonder my friend had been stopped in the street. Her cheekbones were the real thing, her hair was always perfect, she wore clothes in a way that made them look even more chic than they were...it really is a wonder I like her so much.

'Hi, Chloe,' said Gemma, as Marianne got up to get chairs for us. 'How was the ice hockey?' She asked the question in the way people do when they sort of have to but are really, really not interested in the answer.

'Hello, Chloe,' Marianne said before I could say anything. 'It's nice to see you.' And she gave me a kiss on the cheek. Which immediately made me worry whether some of my bacteria-filled concealer might come off me and on to her. I looked carefully, but surreptitiously, at her face, but she seemed to have survived.

'Nice to see you, too,' I said with my usual conversational aplomb.

'The hockey was great,' I said, turning to Gemma. 'Or at least I think it was. None of us really knew what was going on, but Oscar's team won, so everyone was very happy and we all had complicated burgers in this glass-plated restaurant thing. But how was your first day as a supermodel?'

'Unreal,' said Gemma, helping herself to the last of

some little bits of sausage from the plate in front of her. 'I mean, like, literally unreal. It was all outdoor clothes, so they're going to photoshop me on to a mountain, or on to a beach, or in a boat on a lake or something. So they kept blowing at me with wind machines to make it look outdoor and then they were surprised when my hair got in a mess.' She rolled her eyes with an expression of supermodel scorn.

'Don't they tell you not to eat?' I said as I watched Gemma wolf down a huge piece of bread dipped in olive oil.

'No, didn't come up,' she said tearing up another piece of bread and putting cheese on it. 'In fact, there was one outfit where they had to clip it together at the back because it was too loose on me.'

All that needed to happen next was for Gemma to meet and fall mutually in love with a multi-millionaire Mr Darcy figure, and life will officially be Not Fair.

'So unreal,' said Gemma again.

'Well, that's because it's not really real life, is it, darling?' said Marianne smiling at her daughter. 'You wouldn't want to be doing it every day, would you?'

'I don't want to stop yet, Mum,' said Gemma. 'I want to get to the stage where they know my name and don't just shout, "Model, look at me," or, "Model, look happy."'

'Well, I need to take this model home,' said Merv, fiddling loudly with his car keys. 'I've got a conference call with the Russians in half an hour and I can't be late.' He looked rather stressed as he said this.

Merv's business partners seemed to come from the parts of the world where all the film baddies came from. And indeed it was unlikely that this lot were the sort who'd tuck you up in bed if you were feeling poorly – insisting on a conference call at nearly midnight on a Saturday night was borderline sadistic.

I watched Gemma say goodbye to her mother (which she did very fondly) and then follow her father out of the restaurant (which she did quite bad-temperedly – Gemma was the mistress of the bad-tempered walk).

'Bye, Marianne,' I said. 'Hope to see you again soon.' There. It just gets better and better, I thought. How is it that the more I want to impress someone the more I come out with the sort of awkward conversation that wouldn't be out of place at a vicar's tea party?

Gemma and I got into the back of the ridiculous car, leaving Merv to swear at the electronics in the front.

'OK, Chloe,' said Gemma as the car jerked into gear

(Merv was the only driver I knew who could stall any car, even ones with so many electrics that they practically drove for you). 'Here's the thing. I got this message this morning from Jezza asking me to go and see him in Scotland at half term, and then – it's almost like a weird plot – five minutes later Jack asks me to go to Cornwall. Isn't that crazy? I don't know what to do. You go to boring school day after day and nothing much happens and then stuff happens suddenly and at exactly the same time.'

'You can't go anywhere at half term,' I said immediately. 'You've got to come with us to Maggie's horrible party.' Which was proof of course that we're all the same even if we think we're not. We're all wired to be selfish.

'Ever thought it might not be all about you, Chloe?' said my supermodel friend rather coldly. 'I mean,' she went on a bit less coldly, 'I don't think I'll be going to see either of them, but that's not the point. The point is, what do I say to them? Jezza hasn't suddenly changed from being selfish and rude and demanding, and I can't *believe* he thinks I'll go all that way just 'cos he says so. And Jack, well, I know Jack's going to be more interested in the sea however freezing cold it is. It's not my idea of a great day out to stand on the beach watching someone in a rubber suit splash around in sub-zero temperatures.' She paused. 'Even if they do look rather good in their rubber suit. On the other hand—'

'All right, girls,' said Merv suddenly as the car slowed down. 'Nearly there. Sooner the supermodel gets her beauty sleep the better, eh?' And he chuckled at what I could only suppose he thought was a joke.

I was annoyed to have our conversation interrupted, just when Gemma was getting to an interesting bit. She didn't often talk about what she actually thought about all the boys who seemed to jostle for her attention, and I was just getting ready to do some subtle psychological probing. Or, anyway, at least ask her who she really fancied most.

We made our way through the electric gates and then through the electric garage doors, and then through the huge wooden door into the house itself. Such amazing security made me feel safe; any Russian/Chinese/SPECTRE villains would have a serious problem getting into the house and bumping us off.

And then I thought if Merv needed this level of security, then he probably had very powerful enemies.

So I was relieved when Merv directed me to a bedroom at the top of the house. That way I'd at least have some warning when the mafia started bashing in the doors below.

The bed was unbelievably big and comfortable, and I was tired. I decided not to worry about the mafia.

The richer the blighter the softer the sheets, I thought, as I drifted off to sleep.

I woke up to a wintry sun lighting up my luxury attic bedroom. In the cold light of day, I could see how new and smart everything was, and how expensive the paintings looked with their thick gold frames.

I suddenly felt a longing for my scruffy old bedroom with its battered cupboards bursting with clothes and books, and its plastic bedside furniture and its walls covered in dog-eared posters featuring Bart and Lisa Simpson.

When I'd gathered up my stuff, I allowed myself to check my phone. No message from Mark. He would have got my photo and message at nearly midnight French time, but surely he would have sent me a 'well done' by now.

Feeling a little uneasy, I went down to the gold-plated kitchen, where Gemma and Merv were sitting at the table two large bowls of cereal in front of them.

The room felt like nothing had been said in it for some minutes.

'Hi, Chloe,' said Gemma. 'Want some breakfast?'

'Sorry,' I said, 'Gotta go. Steve's home this weekend, and I promised I wouldn't be late.' I turned to Merv and said in my best tea-party voice, 'Thank you very much for having me.'

'That's all right, Chloe,' said Merv. 'Always a pleasure.' And he gave me one of his special ingratiating smiles.

Happily, the buses were much better behaved than they had been the previous day. Perhaps they were refreshed after a comfortable night in soft sheets, too. I was soon home and unlocking our front door.

I passed Mr Underwood's door half expecting a cheery welcoming bark from Albert before I remembered that of course he was now in a far, far better place. Instead there were some mysterious bangings coming from inside the flat, which I decided to pretend not to hear, just in case they were the noise of a dead body being chopped up.

As soon as I put my key in the lock of our front door, I heard some familiar noises. First there was the sound of excited commentary coming from the sitting room

(Ralph in front of the football), then there was the sound of a piercing whistle coming from the kitchen (Mum making a cup of tea), and then there was a series of pinging noises (Steve. Playing whatever electronic game was currently obsessing him).

All was right with the world.

I went into the kitchen. There was Gran, sitting in Mum's favourite chair with one of her revolting creatures on her lap. From the brief moment I could bear to look at it, she seemed to be sewing hair on to the back of its head.

Mum was looking as pale as ever and pouring boiling water into her Mother's Day mug, the one that Steve had given her. I knew she never normally used it because she found it too big, but mothers – the best ones anyway – are notoriously tactful.

This tactfulness was probably lost on my oily only brother, who was sitting at the table utterly focused on an enormous smartphone, which seemed to have the sound turned up to max. He was wearing the kind of khaki camouflage uniform that I have always had rather a soft spot for.

Despite his fantastically irritating concentration on his phone (he should have been looking up at me with a warm, welcoming smile), I couldn't help thinking that he somehow seemed a bit more like a young man and a bit less like the spotty monosyllabic dork that I remembered.

'So what's new in Chloe World, then?' said Steve, without looking up. 'Been staying at Gemma's, have you? She OK?'

Ah. The older-brother-with-the-hopeless-crush syndrome. I'd forgotten about that.

'She very OK,' I said, helping myself to two sausages and a tomato that had somehow escaped the attentions of Ralph and Steve. 'She's modelling now. And juggling lots of glamorous boyfriends.' My policy has always been to nip hopeless hope in the bud.

'Steve's got a couple of army friends coming for tea, Chloe,' said Mum, gripping her enormous Mother's Day mug with both hands. 'That's nice, isn't it?' She looked rather crestfallen as she said this. I suppose mothers who don't see their sons very often tend to want to have them to themselves. I was sorry for that, but a small part of me, in fact quite a big part, couldn't help wondering if one of the 'army friends' might not turn into my date for the dreaded QB party.

'Yeah,' said Steve, finally putting down his phone. 'Nick and Alex. You'll like them, Chloe. They read books and stuff, just your kind of thing.'

Since Steve's idea of a book was a magazine or a graphic novel, I wasn't holding out much hope for an in-depth conversation about Dickens or Jane Austen. But, still, I hoped that if Steve thought I'd like them then maybe I would, and anyway I thought, looking at Mum, so long as they were nice and don't spoil her precious Sunday with her son.

I was distracted from any further speculation about Nick and Alex's reading matter by a sudden enormous clap of thunder. The sky had turned almost dark as night, and then was suddenly lit up by lightning. Seconds later the noise of rain firing horizontally against the window was so loud that it almost drowned out the noise of football commentary coming from the next room.

'Listen to that rain,' instructed Gran, completely unnecessarily. 'They didn't say anything about this on the weather forecast, did they?' She said this in an aggrieved tone of voice, as if the forecasters had deliberately insulted her intelligence by not warning her of the upcoming storm.

'Well, I guess it's the time of year for weather like this,' said Mum. 'But I suppose that puts paid to our walk in the park, doesn't it?'

'Yes, Mum,' said Steve quickly. 'I could do without

a walk anyway. Not as if I don't get plenty of exercise hefting backpacks all over the hills.' And he looked down again at his phone, which immediately started making the pinging noises that meant that we were unlikely to get any more conversation from Steve for a while.

I thought this the best moment to leave my happy family to enjoy each other's company.

I wanted to reclaim my room after its Gran occupancy, and besides I was way behind with my prize-winning creative writing essay.

Four hours later, the rain had stopped and so had my brain. My latest idea for my creative writing essay, all about a supermodel being killed by lightning, had ground to a halt. After I'd buried her in a basement being dug out by a Russian/American multi-millionaire, I realised that I'd rather lost the plot in the search for symbolism.

I tried to turn my attention to my essay about savannah grasslands and tropical rainforests, which was already overdue to the horse-faced boa constrictor that was Miss Bartlett. But I found the more I tried to concentrate on rainy seasons and animal migration, the more I wondered what Nick and Alex were like and why Mark hadn't answered my message.

So I gave up, switched off and headed to the kitchen.

Perhaps I'd been more engrossed in African scrubland than I'd thought, but there were unfamiliar voices coming from behind the closed kitchen door. Strangers…and I hadn't heard them arrive.

I turned quickly round and rushed to the bathroom and the only big mirror which would tell me what was wrong, where and whether there was anything I could do about it. Perhaps normal people would just walk straight into a room containing people they'd never met before; perhaps, then, I wasn't normal.

A close inspection revealed that things were as good as one could expect – not too much grease on the hair, blemish on the complexion or straggliness in the eyebrow department. I took a deep breath and went back towards the kitchen.

Opening the door without breaking step, I found myself looking at a room full of old people (Gran, and Ralph and Mum) sitting down, and Steve and two young people standing up. Dressed in the same combat fatigues (I think that's what they call my favourite form of camouflage uniform), were a tall dark man with glasses, and a short fair girl.

Why I hadn't computed that perhaps Alex was a girl, I don't know, but I hadn't. I tried not to look surprised – or disappointed that my chances of an escort to the dreaded party had suddenly reduced by fifty per cent.

'Hi, Chloe,' said Steve. 'This is Nick' – and he pointed rather unnecessarily to the tall guy with glasses, and 'this is Alex.' And as he pointed he gave 'Alex' a smile that I'm pretty sure I'd never seen Steve give to anyone before.

Ah HA, I thought, as I looked much more carefully at the short, fair girl. Maybe Steve was working through his disappointment about Gemma after all.

'Hello,' said Alex, giving me a slight smile. She didn't say anything more, but, so far as you could tell from someone saying just two syllables, she seemed nice.

'You've been working then, Chloe?' said the one called Nick, looking down on me from a great height. 'You got exams soon, have you?'

'I've always got exams,' I said in a world-weary voice as I realised this was almost literally true. 'If they're not proper exams, they're test exams, and if they're not test exams then they'll just put you in a room with a list of questions for the sheer fun of it.'

'Had enough of the education thing, have you, sis?'

said Steve. 'Why don't you join the army? See the world. Get some fresh air. Meet interesting people...'

'Certainly get all sorts of *them*.' Ralph scraped back his chair as he got up to put cake and biscuits on the table.

There was an uncomfortable silence. Looking at Ralph as he turned his back on us so that he could pop one of Mum's special biscuits into his mouth without us seeing, I thought that Steve's army friends had probably been a disappointment to the ghastly one.

After all, first there was spindly Ethan, who was much more interested in talking about books and who had then left the army to go off and be an actor, and now there was Alex (a girl!) and Nick, who was as dark as Mum was pale.

'That's certainly true,' said Nick smiling at me. Perhaps he could see I was internally rigid with embarrassment. 'I think that's a good thing on the whole. I mean, better that we're all fighting together than fighting each other.'

'Yeah, yeah,' said Steve. 'Nick's thought for the day.' He turned to Mum, 'Nick's our pet philosopher. If you want some great saying to carve in stone over your bed, then Nick's your man.'

I wondered why you might risk having something

over your bed that was made of stone, but I decided not to question Steve on the matter, since we seemed to have successfully moved on from Ralph's Neolithic prejudices and that really was the main thing.

'Can I help you with the tea?' said Alex at that moment, looking at Mum. She seemed to be a) tactful and b) aware that Ralph was busier checking out the cake and biscuits than actually putting anything on the table.

'Yes, thank you, dear,' said Mum getting slowly to her feet. I hated seeing her getting up from the table. It seemed to be such an effort for her, to drain her of all strength. But I knew she wasn't due another 'treatment' for ten days, so perhaps she'd get a bit better soon.

Alex and I rushed over to help with the cups and saucers, and soon the table was groaning (metaphorically speaking; I've never actually heard a table groan any more than I've heard it say it was hungry) with plates and cups and food.

Mum had got out her extra special teapot, which my father had given her the year before he died. It was white with little gold bits round the edges, and was apparently quite valuable as well as very big. I only half liked it, because whenever Mum got it out, it always seemed to make her sad. I suppose it just reminded her of Dad, and whenever she was reminded of Dad she went very sad and silent.

But this time, there was so much going on in the kitchen that she didn't really have a chance to be sad or silent.

'What a beautiful teapot, Mrs Bennet,' said Nick as we shuffled chairs around ready to sit down.

Perfect. Not only an advocate for world peace and the end of racial prejudice, but almost as good at tea-party conversation as I was.

'Isn't it?' said Mum. 'People tell me it's rather special china.'

'Just like,' interrupted Gran in a rasping voice, 'my china doll collection.' She looked around at the assembled company, seeming to expect a chorus of fascinated *ah*s and *ooh*s. Instead everyone just looked at her in slightly startled silence.

'Gosh,' said Alex. 'Are they here, or in a museum or something?'

'They're here,' I said quickly. 'But under lock and key and way, way too precious to get out.' The thought of Steve's friends being exposed to the revolting creatures was almost too much to imagine.

'Do you get lots of holiday?' I said brightly to Nick. A pretty random conversational subject one might think, but I thought it might be interesting to check out how much holiday soldiers in general got. Just in case some of them might have some spare time over the St Valentine's Day week. I did rather like the idea of me, and maybe Gemma, walking in to the dreaded party with a handsome soldier or two on our arm.

'Don't get a lot of leave, no,' said Nick. 'We've only just started really, and for the first forty-five weeks, you have to be pretty full on.'

This wasn't looking too hopeful, but I was still keen to carry on the research.

'So what do you do, when you ARE allowed out? Do you all go off and ski and practise shooting and all those outdoor things that soldiers do?' I asked.

'Mostly we just go home to see the folks,' said Nick. 'Like Steve's doing. But mine have just moved to France, so I'm a bit of an orphan sort of thing in England at the moment. Steve took pity on me, and that's why it's so nice of your mum to have us here.'

Mum looked up at this and gave Nick one of her best smiles. 'It's a pleasure to have you here, Nick,' she said. 'Always room here for Steve's friends.'

I, meanwhile, had another very important question. 'What part of France do your parents live in, Nick?'

I was thinking what an amazing coincidence it would

be if they lived somewhere near Dijon. I mean, I KNOW France is a big country, but if this were a novel I'm sure that it would turn out that Nick's parents knew Cecile, and he could tell me that actually she was either a completely horrible person who nobody could possibly like, or completely in love with some handsome farmer who owned the big house next door. A farmer who was totally French (like she was), lived in the countryside (like she did) and who was therefore the perfect Mr Right/M. Droit for her, and therefore she would have no need of the English boy from the middle of England who was the object of my affections.

'Just outside Calais,' said Nick.

Ah. Even though I try not to pay too much attention in Geography, I did know that Calais was somewhere up the top and near the coast, and therefore a very long way away from Dijon.

'We've got three hours left, folks,' said Steve, putting one of Mum's special-biscuits-for-guests into his mouth (and chewing it a bit, I was pleased to see). 'What are we going to do with our last moments of freedom?'

'What about going for a walk?' said Alex in her quiet voice.

'Brilliant idea,' said Steve, without a trace of

sarcasm. He truly looked as if the one thing he'd wanted to do all day was go for a walk. 'What do you say, Nick? We could check out the skateboarders, there are sometimes some ace ones doing their stuff in the park at the weekends.'

'Let's do it,' said Nick, grinning. 'You coming, Chloe?'

I thought about the Geography essay that was waiting for me and my endless failed attempts at creative writing, not to mention the puzzling Maths puzzles and the Biology and Chemistry. I had a great deal to do before school on Monday morning.

'Yes, great,' I said. 'Let's go.'

Half an hour later I think we were all beginning to question our enthusiasm for the outdoor life. It was colder than ever and, not surprisingly, there weren't any skateboarders doing their 'stuff' in the park.

But happily the café by the park gate was open and was serving hot tea. The fact that some of us (me) hated tea, and the rest of us had already had several bucketfuls of it, didn't stop us going into the hot steamy café.

The door made one of those jolly tinkling noises that make everyone look up as soon as you come in. I realised that I was the only one of the four of us not wearing uniform. But still if I'd ever fancied being escorted by men in uniform, here I was being escorted by men in uniform. The fact that one of them was a girl and another was my brother was just a detail, I decided, as I looked around at everyone looking at us, and thought how interesting we must all look.

In fact, I was so pleased with how interesting we must all look, I rather hoped there was someone I knew in the café who could see me looking interesting. I'd just come to the sad conclusion that there wasn't anyone when I saw a figure in the corner on his own. It was Donald, Mr Cool of TV. He was sucking away on an e-cigarette and staring morosely at his phone.

It looked very like he was having a deliberately miserable Alone Moment. So I turned quickly away from him and followed the others to a table on the other side of the café.

After we had four Cokes (tea seemed to be completely out of the question for everyone) and four pieces of cake (the same rules that applied to tea didn't seem to apply to cake), I looked over again at Donald's table. He was still on his own, still engrossed by his phone.

He looked up and caught my eye.

I immediately blushed. Of course.

He gave a slight smile and got up from the table. I could see he was heading our way, and just about had time to say to my soldier friends, 'TV producer alert at four o'clock'. I congratulated myself on my quick-wittedness in using the clock-face system to locate the enemy. As soldiers, it would of course have been familiar to them.

'What do you mean, Chloe? It's half past six,' said my brilliant brother just as Donald reached our table.

'Hi, Chloe,' he said as he came near our table. He waved his arm in a sort-of cheery salute, and went out of the café.

Right. So much for my introducing my soldier friends to my TV producer friend.

'Is he really a TV producer?' said Nick. 'How do you know him?'

I settled down to explaining how Georgie was a friend, and how she was going to be a star, exaggerating only a little bit because after all none of them knew that I only knew Georgie a little bit, and anyway only because of who her brother was.

'Is that the Georgie who's the sister of Mark?' said Steve suddenly.

'Yes,' I said, a blush never being far away. 'Yes, that's right, Mark's sister.'

'Is Mark your boyfriend?' said Alex, not knowing what a huge and loaded question she asked.

Out of the corner of my eye, I noticed Nick looking at me with concentration.

'Yes,' I said boldly. 'Yes, he is.' I left it at that.

'So where is he now?' said Nick. 'Is he away, or working or something?'

'Both, I think,' I said. 'That is, he's on this French exchange thing. So he's in France. Learning French.' I realised I was sounding like an Early Learning textbook. So I tried to elaborate.

'He's in a place just south of Dijon. It sounds very nice; they make wine there. I think it's quite a famous wine-growing area actually.'

'It certainly is!' said Nick. 'I know that part of France. It's where my girlfriend comes from.'

So we *were* in a novel! It *was* a small world. Plus, if Nick had a girlfriend in France just like I had a boyfriend in France…then I thought how perfect it would be if he could come to the dreaded party with me and Sally and Oscar and we'd look cool and all coupled-up but there'd be no pressure. Brilliant.

'In fact,' he said, 'I can't wait to go over there next month to surprise her on Valentine's Day.'

Right. So that was that then. At that moment

there was a sudden clap of thunder and it started pouring with rain again. How incredibly appropriate, I thought. It's raining on my parade, or whatever the expression is.

As we were running out of time, we headed out into the rain and back home. I immediately turned into a drowned and bedraggled rat.

But that didn't matter. I wasn't trying to impress anyone.

12

Say Cheese

By the time I had survived another week at school, my list of Reasons to be Cheerful had got even shorter. Lying in bed on the Friday morning, already late and likely to be later if my unlovely stepfather took any longer in the bathroom, I made my mental list of good news items:

1. Mum got through chemo.

It made her very tired but she seemed OK about it all. Perhaps she had been all buoyed up by seeing Steve. Also, I thought she'd already chosen her hat ready for Steve's wedding to Alex. (Amazing how quickly the older generation jump to conclusions. But as soon as we'd got back and everyone got dry and headed off back to boot camp/the Army, Mum couldn't stop talking about how nice Nick and Alex were. Especially Alex.)

2. There was a faint chance that I might actually be able to start trying to pay off The Albert Debt.

Georgie's TV pilot show was going to have a grand preview. Which meant that lots of Very Important People in the TV world were going to watch it in a theatre and then – because obviously doing something like that is very thirsty work – there was going to be a big drinks reception, so that everyone could talk about the show and tell each other how important they were.

I'm absolutely not knocking it. Sally, and Gemma, and Amy and I were all super grateful to Patricia – because she had suggested that we all be asked/ allowed to help serve the drinks. And we were actually going to get paid for it.

What a result was that? Not only being part of a glamorous Anderson family outing, but being paid for it too.

3. Project Oscar was going to forge ahead soon because he and Sally (and me and Albert) were going to go for a 'yog' in the park

Amy and Charlie were going to come too. Obviously if there was any running to be done Amy had to be somewhere near, and anyway it was always nice to watch Amy run because she was so much better at it than we were (and we were so much better at watching than running). Also, I might have to get Oscar just to watch too, what with his soon-to-be-beloved being a cripple and all.

4. Mark had finally answered my message.

Which was something. 'That's great,' he'd said. 'Well done, Oscar,' he'd said. Which wasn't nearly as good as 'Well done, Chloe'. Or 'Miss you lots and love you, Chloe'. Or 'Can't wait to see you again, Chloe xxxxxxxxxxxxxxxxxx'. All he said as well was 'Got exams so head down but Skype next week'. And he'd said 'Take care'. And there had been five Xs.

Not that I was over-analysing every last word and letter, of course.

5. The twins' skin diseases had finally been diagnosed, so they were being covered in some lotion or other and were now slightly happier (and back to happily beating each other up).

Which meant that Liv was slightly happier, and so was James and so was Sally.

I was struggling to come up with a number 6, but at that moment I heard Ghastly Ralph emerge from the bathroom, and I knew I had exactly three minutes to do all the fifty-seven things that needed to be done before I could show myself to the world.

I didn't want to miss a minute of our English lesson

that morning. It was going to be taken over by a talk from a famous author. And as I was going to be one of those myself, I wanted to hear everything she had to say and I didn't want to be late.

Luckily, it was a Good Eyebrow Morning, and a Not Too Bad Hair Day, which meant I didn't have to use precious seconds tidying up. I put my head round the kitchen door. Seeing that Gran was sitting at the kitchen table with her lips already pursed in disapproval, I decided that breakfast was less important than making a hasty exit. I could always have something incredibly sugary and unhealthy on the bus.

I arrived at the school gates just as the first bell went for registration.

'You're late,' said Sally, suddenly appearing at the side of the main entrance. She was looking cross and leaning heavily on her crutch. 'I need to talk to you because I don't know what to do about being a waitress.'

I raised a perfectly plucked eyebrow at her. Having spent so much time on eyebrow inspection, I'd accidently managed to perfect the art of raising one eyebrow. I'd decided that it made me look wise and quizzical. A bit like when grown-ups look over the tops of their glasses at you.

'I mean,' said Sally, not seeming to notice the incredibly clever thing I'd just done with my face, 'that I want to go to Georgie's preview thing, obvs, and I want to earn some money. Also obvs. But do you think they'll let me serve drinks and things with one hand? I mean, just between you and me, Chloe, I don't really *need* a crutch, but the longer I've got it the less likely it is that they'll ever tell me to do Games. Do you see what I mean?'

'I see exactly what you mean,' I said as we got to our classroom just as the second bell went. 'But I bet they'll let you cut stuff up in the background. After all, there'll be masses to do. There'll be loads of people there; it's going to be a huge party.'

'What's this, what's this?' came a voice from behind us. Lord. The QB herself. You'd think that by now we'd have developed a sixth sense and been able to detect her malign presence a mile off. 'A party? Don't tell me you're having a party without telling me, Chloe. I mean, haven't I asked you to *my* party? Where's this party then?'

Her cohorts had started to line themselves up behind Maggie, and were even starting to snigger. Even though Maggie hadn't yet told them to.

'It's not mine,' I said hurriedly. 'In fact it's nothing to

do with me, we just might be working there. Or we might not be. I don't know. It's really nothing, just some small gathering thing.'

'Well, I *think* I heard you say it was going to be huge. I *think* I heard you say there were going to be *loads* of people there. So all I want to know, Chloe, as someone who's actually invited *you* to a party, is for you to tell me what this party is. Not a lot to ask, is it?' She folded her arms. Which seemed to act as a signal to the cohorts to start their sniggering in earnest.

'It's not really a party,' I said, increasingly desperately, as I had sudden awful visions of Maggie and her horrible friends crashing into the reception and telling Patricia and Donald and all the smart TV directors and producers that somehow they were something to do with us, and then – it didn't bear thinking about. 'Really it's not. Ask Gemma!' I had suddenly caught sight of Gemma, who was leaning in the doorway. I knew I was being a coward to deflect attention on to her, but then I *was* desperate.

Gemma lounged forwards into the room, her supermodel walk now perfected so that it seemed to ooze scorn and superior beauty. If I hadn't been so terrified of Maggie at that moment I might almost have given her a round of applause.

'It's not a party,' Gemma said once she was standing in front of Maggie and able to look down on her in every sense. 'It's a Private Preview. The clue is in the word "private". So, Maggie, nothing to see here. Nothing for you and your friends to get all knotted up about.' She paused. 'OK?' she said with a brilliant smile. Really. It was a masterpiece of the Put-Down school of acting.

For a nanosecond (longer than a yoctosecond but not quite as long as a second) the QB looked distinctly put out. And then she started sniggering, and said, 'Yeah. Whatevs.' And turned round to her cohorts and carried on sniggering. Which was also brilliant in its own way. Maggie had been sneered at by someone tall and beautiful, but by pretending to have got the better of Gemma she somehow saved face in front of her cohorts.

Fascinating. Brilliant theatre, but really not the sort of theatre I wanted to see too often.

Two bells later and we were all safely in the English department's biggest classroom sitting in serried ranks (do you ever 'serry' anything other than a rank?) waiting for V Hillary Twohy to come and tell us all about being a bestselling author.

With only a week to go till the deadline for handing

in our creative writing prize essays, I was definitely starting to get in a panic. So when this small dark woman in a small dark trouser suit walked into the room I must have looked tense and hopeful. Here would be the inspiration and wisdom that would get me out of my writer's block, I felt sure.

'Hey, Chloe.' My BFF nudged me in the ribs with her crutch. (I was starting to get a bit fed up with having to accommodate that crutch in our lives.) 'Perhaps she'll be able to give you some tips so you can win the English Prize thing you want to win.' She looked at me expectantly, obviously imagining she'd get some reward for her great insight.

I raised a perfectly plucked eyebrow at her, something I was starting to get really good at. 'Yes,' I said. 'Brilliant. I hadn't thought of that.' My sarcasm was drowned out with the sound of applause.

VHT, as she called herself, turned out to have a lilting Irish accent. It had a bit of a lullaby quality to it, which I could tell was making a lot of my classmates drift off. I could just tell that by the way so many of them were gazing slightly sleepily into the middle distance. If they weren't doing that, they were pretending they weren't fiddling with their phones, or they were picking intently at the seams of their uniforms.

I tried to make up for their inattention by listening hard to the small bestselling author who'd been so kind as to come all the way to see us and talk to us.

'I disobeyed the rules,' she was saying, 'and I discovered rules don't mean anything, and even if they did they wouldn't necessarily help you. For a start, they said I should change my name. Apparently, it sounds too like an American politician, comes too near the end of the alphabet – so all my books will be on the bottom shelf – and it is incredibly difficult to spell.'

This piece of information made Chloe Bennet feel quite smug.

'...and then, if you get stuck, you get stuck; no matter how much you try to teach yourself tricks to unblock a writer's block there's very often nothing you can do about it.'

And this piece of information plunged me straight back into my Year 10 creative writing despair.

VHT told us plenty of interesting things about being a bestselling writer, like how she dealt with her fans...briefed her jacket designs...cut down her too-long sentences. But nothing about writing the sentences in the first place. None of it was of any help to my dilemma.

So my essay was still right up there on my list of

Things to Worry About. Just ahead of Money, but still way behind Mum, Mark and the Dreaded Party.

I needed distraction, inspiration and cheering up.

For many days, though, distraction was the only one of those things on offer. The powers that be, the Angry God of School Timetabling, and the business of trying to keep everyone at home sort of happy – or at least not actually shouting at each other – was turning into a full-time job.

Every time I sat down to try to write some deathless prose, I'd be told that something needed to be done – usually something dull connected with full dishwashers, clearing the table or even cleaning the bath. What with Mum being ill, Gran having a bad back and Ralph being Ralph and therefore ghastly, I was getting a lot of housework practice.

In between all this I had conceived an abiding hatred of whoever it was who was in charge of the French internet. They were obviously really, really bad at their job. Because every time Mark and I had a plan to speak on Skype, the system had crashed and I was left dressed in my best and smiling inanely at a blank screen.

I had the distinct impression, though, that Mark was having a very nice time. He didn't say much about what he was up to, which I reckon is a sure sign that someone's feeling guilty because they're having a nicer time than you are. Words like 'skiing' and 'wine' appeared in his messages, but in a roundabout, casual sort of way. Whereas mine were full of words like 'essays' and 'rain', but in an obsessed, completely uncasual sort of way.

He seemed to ask me more about Oscar than about me. I mean, I knew he was concerned that his cousin should be having a nice time. But hadn't I assured him I was looking after him? And wasn't it his job to worry about *me*?

It was all very frustrating and sad, and it made me even more miserable to think that it would be so long before I saw him again. And that in the meantime I was going to have to get through the DREADED Maggie party without him.

Somehow my misery seemed to be infecting the others. Sally would clutch her crutch in a soulful, sorrowful sort of way, and she'd mention Rob as if somehow he could make her feel better. Amy was her usual cheerful self most of the time, but she'd sometimes be all tense after her training sessions if she hadn't beaten whatever lap record she wanted to beat that day. And then Gemma seemed to be all over the place. She hadn't said much more about her (Poor Her) dilemma of having two invitations from two boys to two holidays, and there wasn't any sign of more modelling work. But apparently Marianne was coming to Georgie's preview – Marianne was quite a famous TV producer, as it happened, not that she'd ever tell you that herself – so perhaps, I thought, that would make Gemma a bit happier.

I found myself giving huge existential sighs at least four times a day. In fact, it might have been a bit more than that because Gemma had recently instituted a fining system. 'Every time we get another of those great big sighs from Chloe,' she had said at the beginning of the week, 'she is going to put 50p in the sigh box. And once we get to £25, which at this rate will be very soon, she is going to buy us all pizza.' This was actually something else to worry about. I hardly wanted to forfeit my Albert money before I'd even earned it.

But at last it was Saturday, the day of the preview party.

Annoyingly, from the point of view of Project Oscar & Sally, I wasn't sure if Oscar was going to be there.

Apparently, in a hockey match that morning, he'd had a bit of a fight with a Dane. According to the Dad Who, the Danes and the Swedes have a sort of friendly rivalry. Except in this case, I think the friendliness had got forgotten in the heat of the moment. But anyway, it had resulted in both Scandinavians lying prone on the ice with slightly serious leg injuries.

Which meant that Albert was probably going to have to miss out on a lot of his usual exercise, Oscar would be even more silent than usual, and the delays to Project Oscar & Sally would be a real problem. After all, this was the weekend before the weekend before the Tuesday of the Party To Be Dreaded Above All Others, so there were only ten days to hope for the miracle that would somehow make everything all right on Valentine's Day.

There was much to think about as I headed off to Sally's to pick her up for our tour of duty as waitresses.

'*There* you are,' said Sally when she opened the front door. I couldn't deny it, so I didn't.

In the distance I could hear some bangings and crashings. Either the terrible twins, Harris and Jock, were back to full-on fighting, or James and Liv were having one of their passionate arguments. (This is, apparently, how they described the noises they sometimes made. James had told Sally that he and Liv weren't arguing. But even if they were, it was a *passionate* argument. And apparently, passion was a good thing. I found the whole thing a little too grown-up.)

As if to clear up any misunderstanding, at that moment Liv appeared from the kitchen. 'Excuse the noise, Chloe,' she said as she wiped a small wine glass with a drying-up cloth. 'Harris and Jock are feeling much better. Which is both a good thing and a bad thing.' And she gave us a watery smile.

We followed her into the kitchen, and I watched as she reached into the fridge for a bottle of her friend Mr Pinot Grigio. She filled up the wine glass, raised it to us in mock salute and took a careful sip.

'Why d'you wash up a wine glass if you're only going to make it dirty again?' Sally asked.

'Rations, darling, rations,' said Liv, putting the glass down. 'James says I sometimes overdo it in the wine department, so I'm sticking to just the one glass.'

I wasn't sure that using one glass several times was quite what James had meant, but thought it definitely a good thing that Liv was at least counting.

'Right,' said Sally in an unusually commanding voice. 'We're off. Will you pick us up, Mum?' And then, looking thoughtfully at her mother as she took another sip, 'Or perhaps James will?'

'Of course, darling,' said Liv. 'Have a lovely time.'

Half an hour later we were at the theatre. It was all dressed up for its TV premiere, with big posters featuring all the cast standing in a garden looking like they were all having an incredibly hilarious time. Donald's name was in huge letters over everything.

There was an excited babble of voices as people queued to go into the auditorium.

Everywhere I looked people seemed to be approximately thirty two years old, dressed in torn jeans and leather jackets (the men) or torn jeans and sparkly tops and loads of make-up (the women. And some men).

Everyone was looking at everyone else and hardly ever at the people they were talking to.

As we were the paid workers we weren't going to get to see Georgie's TV debut, or not this time anyway. Instead we were shepherded backstage and into a makeshift kitchen. This was where we were going to cut up the canapes and put glasses on trays, and generally prepare for other people's pleasure.

A tall and rather scary lady dressed all in black showed us where the fridge was and where all the ingredients for making up the canapes were.

She looked furious. Not just at us, but at life, the world and, especially, everyone within spitting distance. A rather nice-looking girl with red hair, older than us and obviously well used to this sort of work, took us to one side and said, 'Don't worry about Florence. She's not cross with you, she's just cross she's out here and not with all the cool people inside watching the show.'

'Florence' looked over in our direction, and for a horrible moment I thought she'd heard. But all she said was, 'Here are the pineapples, here is the cheese. Put them together and make them look nice.'

'They're ironic nibbles,' said our friend with the red hair. 'It's 'cos the show is set in the Eighties. It's all going to be vol-au-vents, cheesy footballs and pineapple and cheese on a stick.'

I had a bad feeling about a show set in the Eighties where everyone ate cheese and pineapple on a stick, but I supposed Donald and all who sponsored him knew what they were doing.

By the time we'd chopped, and washed and set out a million glasses, the bar and entrance to the theatre were looking very festive. We could hear some distant laughter coming from the theatre, so we hoped that –

for everyone's sake – the show was going to be a palpable hit.

And indeed everyone had a smile on their faces as they came out. I hoped that wasn't just the eager anticipation of bottles of white wine accompanied by prawns nestling on a bed of lettuce.

Sally had decided to abandon her crutch for the evening, on the grounds that members of our school Games staff were unlikely to be at this gathering, and anyway it was clear that Florence would take a dim view of a disabled waitress.

'Hey, Chloe!' it was the Star, Georgie herself. There were lots of people following her, including the great producer, Donald, who was looking surprisingly gloomy for someone who'd just had a successful premiere of a new TV show. 'Sorry you guys couldn't see the show. People are saying it's good. Really, it's amazing. There are some BBC people here, and they're being very nice about it. What do you think about that, eh, Chloe? Don't forget to tell my brother he's going to have a famous sister, so he'd better get used to the idea!'

I loved the thought that she imagined Mark and I spoke so often that this sort of comment would just come up in conversation. But thinking back on our most recent stilted Skypings, I wondered when on earth we would next have anything like a normal conversation.

'Crazy clothes I had to wear, though,' Georgie was saying as I offered drinks to everyone standing round her. 'Still. Not too unflattering, on the whole. What do you reckon, Oscar?'

I looked up from carefully balancing my tray of drinks. Of course Oscar would have been there; he lived in their house after all, he was family. But somehow I had him down as injured, out of action, and anyway waiting until I'd finished our plans for a yog in the park with Sally and everyone. But here he was, looking distinctly Tom Hiddleston-like as he looked at me looking at Georgie.

'I reckon everyone look good,' said Oscar seriously. 'I reckon that why they cast you.'

I had a slight double-take at that. If I didn't know better, I'd have said that Oscar was being a bit waspish. But Georgie didn't seem to mind, she just laughed and batted her eyelashes and sucked in her cheeks in that way I'd noticed the other day.

'We still on for a yog in the park tomorrow?' said Oscar to me. 'Albert needs good Sunday run I think.'

'Aren't you wounded?' I said. 'I thought they said you'd been run over on the skating rink?'

'Small fracture,' said Oscar. 'Physio and being careful. That all.'

What a stoic, I thought. What a Swedish stiff upper lip. He's going to fit right into the English life at this rate; he and Sally will complement each other so well. He'll tell her how to manage her physio, and she'll want to nurse him and carry his crutch.

My musings on the future success of my matchmakings were interrupted by the sight of another glamorous friend. Gemma. She was just coming out of the auditorium with her mother. I realised that as the daughter of a high-profile TV producer, she too had been in the theatre and seen the show. As she and Marianne came smiling towards me, I tried not to feel resentful; I tried to focus on the fact that I was being paid £10 an hour to smile and hold trays of warm white wine. Why, only another fourteen hours to go, and I'd have paid my debt.

'Hi, Chloe,' said Gemma. 'Did you cut up all that pineapple with your own fair hand? That's a skill that's not often required these days. Still. I expect it'll come in useful for all those retro parties we're going to have to have when their series goes huge.'

'Now, Gemma,' said Marianne. 'Don't sneer. It's got a good chance of doing well. And your friend

Georgie is really good in it.' She looked at me with a warm smile.

I've always liked Marianne.

'We don't want to interrupt your work, Chloe,' said Gemma. 'But Mum's got something to say to you.'

For a moment I thought I'd done something wrong, and then I told myself to stop being silly. Not everything's about me having done something wrong.

'Do you remember Sue Baroo?' said Marianne. I did. I certainly did. The dog who'd been given to Marianne and Juliet by a Japanese friend. Sue Baroo, so named after the make of car because she had so much four-by-four energy.

'Well, she's dead,' said Gemma brutally. So. Not so much energy now.

'That's right,' said Marianne. 'Comes to us all in the end, so why we were quite so devastated when it came to Sue Baroo I have no idea. So Juliet and I have discussed it, and we wondered if your friend Albert might like to come and live with us. I think he'd like the Cornish fresh air. He could scamper about in the sea, and you could come and see him in the school holidays.'

I immediately thought that this was the most completely perfect idea I'd ever heard. A happy Albert.

AND I could go to Cornwall to see him.

'And Mum would give you the money for him,' said Gemma. 'So you can throw away your pineapple-chopping knife.'

It just got better and better. Suddenly it didn't matter that I hadn't seen the show, or that everyone, apart from my friends, was looking right through me as they grabbed a glass from my tray. All was right with a world where badly treated border terriers could end up in a beautiful house by the sea.

'That's so wonderful,' I said, meaning every syllable. 'I'm sure Albert would love that. We all would. I mean, that would be great. To come and see him, I mean. How wonderful.' I was starting to repeat myself, but perhaps that's just what being pleased about something does to you.

The rest of the evening was slightly blurry. Despite the happy news, I couldn't suddenly put down my serving tray. And anyway, earning £30 in an evening was a great result now that the Albert Debt had disappeared.

By the time James arrived to pick us up, the cool people were mostly saying goodbye to each other, and gulping a last beaker of wine. (Most of them had been very rude about the white wine. 'Warm' and 'disgusting' were two of the commonest adjectives. So it was strange that so many of them kept on having refills.)

'How did you get on?' said James to us as we climbed into the back of his car – a normal car, with lots of rubbish in it, not like Merv's shiny huge new-smelling monstrosity.

'It was great,' I said. 'We didn't see the show, nearly everyone ignored us, and we're exhausted. But I've found someone a new home, and I've got three ten-pound notes that I can do what I like with. I call that a result.'

But I was keen to get home, go to my room and shut the door on the world. There was still a long list of things to worry about, and the sooner I got on with that the better.

⇾ 13 ⇽

A Yog in the Park

It hadn't been a very constructive Worry Night. But I'd stayed awake long enough to decide that if the worst came to the worst I could always acquire a terrible injury just before Valentine's Day. Not something that required long-term hospitalisation, but definitely something that involved plaster, bandages and hospital appointments. Perhaps I could throw myself down some stairs, or be run over by a skateboarder.

And if I couldn't bring that off then I thought I could always eat a lot of something way past its sell-by date. With Gran in the house there was no shortage of things that were Put Back in the Fridge For Later. Generally, they soon came to have a thin film of green mould over the top of them, or large white lumps that you only saw if you stirred up whatever 'it' was. It was a measure of how poorly Mum was feeling these days that she didn't keep her usual eagle eye on the bowls and dishes that filled her fridge.

But my strategic injury plans had to wait for now, because it was Sunday and time to meet the others at the Andersons', and sit back and watch Oscar and Sally realise that they were destined to be together.

The previous evening, in between shredding lettuce and pouring out something called Thousand Island dressing, I'd told Sally that seeing as she was a cripple, like Oscar was, she was going to have to entertain him. As they were both wounded, I said to her, they could sit on a bench somewhere while me and Amy and Charlie, and Gemma if she came, took Albert for a 'yog'. (I was pretty sure there was a suitable bench near the park bandstand. It was the bit of the park where couples showed off their coupliness, so if Oscar and Sally needed some inspiration it would be right there in front of them.)

And this (I told Sally) would be the perfect time for her to tell him that she needed someone to look after her at the Valentine's party. And from then on everything, I told her, would be all about what a nice time they were going to have together. She would go to the dreaded party with Tom Hiddleston, I said, just to remind her how handsome Oscar was.

So when our dog-walking team left the Andersons' house later that morning, I was feeling slightly pleased with myself and quietly confident.

Oscar was limping a little bit, and was clearly in pain, but obviously nothing his stiff upper lip couldn't sort out. He and Sally – who was now reunited with her crutch and leaning heavily on it – were trailing behind us in a very satisfactory way.

I was marching on ahead with Amy and Charlie and Albert.

Amy and Charlie were in their yogging clothes, so I knew it was only a matter of time before the lure of the running track became irresistible and they'd be off. But I knew I would be quite happy to be left alone with Albert. After all, he was soon going to become a proper west-country dog, and I wouldn't see him nearly so often, so we needed to make the most of each other.

Almost as if he knew that our time together was limited, he seemed to be keeping near me as we walked. Normally he'd be bouncing off in search of small children to terrify or piles of dog messes to eat, but maybe some subconscious knowledge of our imminent separation was keeping his revolting habits in check.

As we turned the bend to go down the hill towards

the bandstand and the Lovers' Bench (which I noticed from a distance was empty and all ready for the lovebirds) I could see the familiar figure of Gemma in the distance.

Walking in the park was not one of Gemma's chosen forms of self-expression (so she used to say, and I'm sure she meant it) so I was surprised she'd decided to join us.

Then as we got closer I realised why it might have been that Gemma was taking some unaccustomed exercise in the fresh air. Walking just behind her, and taking pictures of her as they went, was Jack, the tall blond Cornish surfer, the original outdoor boy.

Watching the two of them stroll across the park, looking at each other looking at each other (they went well together and they knew it), I began to have a sneaking suspicion that Gemma might have decided on a strategy for the dreaded Valentine's Day. After all, if Jack had come up from Cornwall this Sunday, then maybe he could come up from Cornwall again.

We all arrived at the bandstand at pretty much the same time.

'Hey, Chloe,' said Gemma. 'Look who I found lurking behind a park gate.'

Jack winked at me and gave a knowing smile at

this. I looked at his suntanned (even in February) face and his thick blond hair and leather jacket, and thought I had to hand it to Gemma. If this were her chosen one, then she'd chosen well.

'Yup,' said Jack, still smiling. 'Came all the way from Cornwall, just on the off-chance that Gemma would be taking her usual walk in the park. You know what a one she is for going for walks, eh, Chloe?'

'He just happens to be in town to see his aunt,' said Gemma coolly, as if Jack's habits were nothing to do with her. 'Aren't you, Jack?'

'Sure,' said Jack. 'I'm really fond of my aunt.' Then there were more knowing glances between the two of them. I was starting to think they might be going to get nearly as bad as Amy and Charlie, but fortunately there then started to be a lot of general chat and jabber. But I had my agenda, and was careful to make sure that Oscar and Sally sat down on the Lovers' Bench as soon as possible.

Once I'd achieved that – with quite a bit of nudging and shoving I may say, amazing how people just don't get the hint sometimes – I led Albert and the others off for a walk back up the hill.

But Gemma and Jack had their own ideas of the direction they wanted to go in (I suspect in Gemma's case it didn't involve a steep upward incline), and then Amy and Charlie announced they were off for a run.

So I had my wish. Albert, 'the most reliable male in my life except I've got to get used to not having him around any more', and I were left alone together.

I set off up the hill at a fast pace. The sooner Oscar and Sally were properly on their own, the better.

Half an hour later, and I was bright red in the face, and not for the usual reasons. I was quite wrong about Albert wanting to stay by my side. Five times I had had to race after him. Uphill, and shouting. It was more exercise than I'd had all year.

He had managed two altercations with lady dogs, one fight with a boy dog for control of a ball, one total immersion in a pile of fox poo, and one prolonged bark at a small girl with pigtails.

'Honestly, Albert,' I said as I eventually put him on his lead. 'You can't be trusted for a moment, can you?' We walked down the hill, connected by the lead and my lectures on his bad behaviour.

I looked at my watch as Albert and I got nearer the L Bench. Three quarters of an hour. Which equalled a lot of exercise and plenty of time for Project Oscar & Sally to come good.

'Hi there,' I called out to them cheerily as I approached. 'Albert's been a very bad hound, so I'm afraid that's the end of his run in the park.' I glanced down at the hound, who by now was of course presenting the picture of innocence.

Oscar was looking at the ground. Sally was looking at her phone. Not a great sign, but then not necessarily a bad sign, I told myself.

'How's it all going?' I said in as relaxed a tone as I could manage. Really, they'd had nearly an *hour* to talk properly on their own.

Oscar looked up. 'Sally tell me there's a terrible party you have to go to,' he said, frowning as he spoke.

Sally got up from the bench. She looked down at Albert. 'Hey, Albert,' she said in that tone of voice that people have when they think they're meant to make nice noises to a child or small animal but don't really want to. 'Let's go off for another little walk, shall we?' And she took his lead and headed off to the edge of the bandstand.

Extraordinary. But maybe she just wanted to make her peace with Albert before he disappeared to Cornwall. I could understand that.

But I couldn't understand why she'd just leave Oscar sitting on the bench.

I looked down at our ice hockey hero. He was still looking up at me with a rather deep expression, as if he were trying to read the subtitles of a rather difficult movie.

'Is that right, Chloe?' he said, shielding his eyes against the low winter sun. 'Sally says you need looking after because there's some bad girl who's making difficulties for you?'

I went and sat down on the bench so he wasn't dazzled by looking directly at the sun. 'Well, yes,' I said, not quite knowing where this was going. 'Yes, I mean it's true that the person giving the party would do anything to make me uncomfortable, or to show me up in public or humiliate me, or any of that sort of stuff. She IS horrible. But we do have to go to this party. It's a pride thing.'

'Well, Chloe,' he said, now looking earnestly at me. 'I will look after you. You can rely on Oscar. You can, you know. For all things.' He took a deep breath, and seemed to be going slightly pink in the sun. 'I think you know how it is for me. I'm lucky to be here in England. Because this is where you are.'

I suddenly felt sick.

I looked at Oscar looking at me, and I realised that in all this time I'd got hold of completely and totally the wrong end of the stick. It wasn't Sally at all who Oscar wanted to be with. It was me. In that split second I thought back to all the talk of dog walks, of me gazing up at him admiringly after the match, and, and...

'Oh no!' I said, stupidly. Really very stupidly. 'I'm sorry!' More stupid. 'It isn't... I mean... I'm not...and I didn't...'

I looked down at the ground because I couldn't actually bear to see the expression in his eyes.

'I'm very sorry,' I said, a bit more calmly. 'I am really. But this wasn't what I thought would happen. You see, I thought you liked Sally.'

I looked hopefully at him – maybe there was another explanation for all this.

'No, Chloe,' said Oscar very solemnly. 'It isn't Sally that I like. It's you.' And he pulled his cap over his face and, so that I couldn't see the expression on his face.

'Oh, Oscar,' I said. 'I'm so sorry. But it's always been Mark for me. Always.' And I realised as I said it how true this was.

'OK,' he said in a quiet voice. 'OK, I go now.' And he got to his feet and headed off in the direction of the nearest park gate.

Oh, how dreadful to the power of awful was this. Poor Oscar. What a mess. And when I'd promised Mark I'd look after him, and all I'd done was mislead him, mess him about and make him unhappy.

I gazed at his limping figure as it disappeared towards the park exit, and then at the frozen blades of grass beneath the bench. Oh, stupid, stupid me.

I heard a rustle in front of me.

'Well, that went well, didn't it?' said my BFF. She came and sat next to me. 'I mean so much for Tom Hiddleston and the solution to all my problems. Can't *believe* you didn't see what was really going on.'

'I really didn't,' I said in a quiet voice. 'I'm such a fool. This is all awful.'

'Yup,' said Sally. 'And here's another thing. I've just texted Rob and said does he want to come to a Valentine's Day party, and you know what? He said yes. He's coming to the party with me. So how about *that*, Miss Know It All?'

I knew I deserved all the sarcasm and fury that Sally had at her disposal. I deserved it all. But there was some actual good news here, some actual, real, good and happy news.

'But, Sally,' I said, 'that's fantastic! How brilliant! Good for Rob, that's great.'

'Yes,' went on Sally. 'And I've just talked to him, and he said he'd seen you in the pizza place and had said to say hi to me and he'd thought I was away or something.'

Horror upon agony. I'd forgotten all about that, and in my stupidity had anyway thought it wasn't part of my Oscar plan.

'Oh, Sal,' I said. 'I'm sorry about that, I forgot. But he said he'd call you anyway, so I...' It sounded lame even to me.

I was a rotten, rotten person. Official.

Sally and I walked back to the Andersons' in total silence. Which would have been worse and a lot more noticeable and painful if it wasn't for the fact that Sally was entirely focused on her phone, and I was entirely focused on Albert.

As Albert snuffled and barked and pulled on his lead, I thought how effectively you could completely avoid human interaction so long as you had an animal or an electronic device. And if you were lucky enough to have both, why, you need never have a conversation ever again.

When we arrived at Mark's house, everything seemed completely silent and locked up. I had visions of having to tie Albert to a shrub in the garden with a note round his neck when the front door opened and, thank goodness, it was the patrician Gabriel standing there.

'Hello, you two,' he said, holding the door open for us to go in. 'Brought back our house guest in one piece, have you?'

Albert, released from his lead, immediately trotted off towards the kitchen. I guess he knew well by now that that was where the food was kept.

'Yes, but I'm afraid he's been quite naughty in the park,' I said as Mr Anderson followed him into the kitchen, and got bottles of cold water out of the fridge for us. 'I hope he's going to be better behaved on the beach.'

'I'm sure you don't have to worry,' said Gabriel, 'but we'll miss the little chap. He's fitted in very well.'

I looked at Albert having a good slurp from his water bowl, and felt very proud of him. As if he'd heard what I was thinking, Albert suddenly turned round and trotted up to Gabriel and started jumping up at his left trouser pocket.

'Extraordinary,' said Gabriel, putting his hand in the

pocket. 'He must be able to smell this tiny bit of dog treat. All the way from the other side of the room. With a sense of smell like that perhaps he'll be able to find my missing client when he gets to Cornwall.'

'So how did you lose a client then?' asked Sally, as if he'd somehow been careless with a piece of luggage.

'We had this case against a forger who'd impersonated a duke,' said Gabriel, pouring himself a glass of wine. 'He was rather good at it, and somehow managed to sign himself a few cheques for hundreds of thousands before he got caught. He was meant to be on remand, but it turned out he had an identical twin, who deliberately confused the courts when they were setting bail. So we had the wrong one at the police station and the forger one disappeared. Last seen near a beach not that far from where Albert's going to live.'

'Gosh,' said Sally. 'Wouldn't it be amazing if Albert found him?'

'I've a feeling it would take more than a good nose to catch hold of this fellow,' said Gabriel. 'Still, it's quite a story.'

It was time to go, I decided. Without being rude I said goodbye and thank you as quickly as I could. I left Sally at the bus stop moments later. I needed to get home quickly, because I had a creative writing essay to write. It was going to be a story of psychodrama, damaged egos and twisted motivations. Twins and dukes, forged cheques and mysterious disappearances came into it...

It was a long week. I suppose technically it was exactly seven days long, and the usual number of hours and minutes, but this one had had a slow, sticky feel to it all the way through. I think this was mostly because quite a lot of education had to happen during it. The exam season was nearly upon us, which meant lots of practice in silent rooms when we weren't being taught stuff.

I decided it was probably a good thing for my nose to be pushed quite so firmly to the grindstone. After all, there was no real happiness to be enjoyed even if I could take my nose away. Mark had gone even more silent – the French internet system had let me down again on the one occasion when we were going to talk properly – and I was starting to dread the QB party with a dread approaching sheer, naked terror.

None of which was helped by the fact that my BFF

was obviously feeling much more cheerful. As she crawled around school on her trusty crutch, there were often the beginnings of a grin on her face. Obviously I was nothing but very, very happy for her, because obviously her renewed relationship (because I thought it probably *was* a relationship) with Rob was making her very happy.

But there were definitely moments when I noticed I was feeling sorry for myself.

Still, and as the old saying goes, all bad things come to an end, and eventually we were all released into the freedom that was half term. That didn't mean we could go off and be happy or anything, because every single teacher had made sure that in those few short days (nine to be precise) we had a major project to do for them. So that first weekend of the half term, the one that was only four short days away from Tuesday's Party From Hell, none of us were being particularly social. I spent most of Saturday writing essays and messages to Mark. It wasn't a *brilliant* use of my time, because I never actually finished or actually sent any of the messages to Mark, and writing them pretty much stopped me writing my essays.

Then suddenly, at approximately 5.42pm, I got a message from Mark, just when I was thinking I might actually click Send on the one I'd just written him.

'So Chloe,' it said (strange how you can sometimes forgive someone for starting a sentence with 'So'). 'Just one more sleep then Im off on holiday.' (Ditto how you can forgive the lack of apostrophe.) 'Hoping for fun, snow and parties. Skyping Mum 3.00 Sunday afternoon. Talk then? You could go there and put Albert in front of screen for me to say Big Goodbye to him? Take care. Love M xxxxxxxx'

Hardly even pausing to work out that Mark's kisses added up to 80, I abandoned all hope of schoolwork, and focused all my energies on deciding what to wear for Sunday's Skype. I knew that Patricia had some incredibly super-fast reliable extra something-or-other broadband, and that – however incompetent Monsieur Internet was over there in France – she always seemed to keep her connection.

I reckoned that time spent on deciding what to wear wouldn't, for once, be time wasted.

'I don't know why you think it's such a big deal for me to come and say goodbye to Albert,' said Sally a little bit sulkily as we got on the bus. 'After all, he's never said anything *really* friendly to me in all the time I've known him. And now he's going away to live by the seaside he's got even less reason to be nice to me.'

I've always thought that Sally and logic have a rather arm's-length relationship. And on this particular Sunday afternoon the arm seemed to be very long indeed.

I steered us towards the back of the bus where I could see two elderly ladies were smiling at and making space for us. I like old people, or most of them anyway. And anyway, I think you have to be nice to them because they've got less life left in them than we have.

'About Mark,' Sally continued, not seeming to notice the old people at all. (I made a note to myself to remind her that one day she was going to be old too, and then she'd be grateful for young people like us being nice to her.) 'Have you asked him yet if he's got a friend who could take you to the party? You could ask him when you Skype with him today.'

Sally looked at me with a complicated expression. Obviously she didn't want me to be unhappy. Obviously. But there was a small part of the complicated expression that someone who didn't know her better might think was gloating a tiny bit.

'Also,' she went on, 'you're going to have to decide

soon what you're going to wear, aren't you?'

I groaned. That was another terrible thing. The previous day I'd had the Queen B's text to say what the dress code was for her party. 'Girls – Be Pretty in Pink! Boys – Be Brilliant in Blue!' said her message.

Ghastly to the power of a zillion yocto-units.

'I have no idea,' I said. 'I suppose I'll have to wear something pink.' Hideous, hideous.

'What?' said Sally. 'Why would you wear pink? You look awful in pink. It's your absolutely most worst colour. You're always saying so.'

I looked at her as she sat innocently opposite the nicer-looking of the old ladies.

'What's glamorous about being dressed in pink?' she asked.

I was beginning to have a nasty sneaking suspicion that all was not quite what it seemed.

'Can you just tell me, Sally,' I said, 'exactly what the dress code is for Maggie's party? I mean as in what did the message you got about it actually say? Word for word?'

'There weren't really many words,' said Sally. 'It just said "Dress Glamorous".'

Horrible, horrible Maggie. Supposing I hadn't talked to the others about what they were wearing? There was an outside chance, and it was one I could hardly bear to think about, that I could have gone to her party dressed in my least favourite colour, the one that made me look terrible.

I had dressed very carefully that morning and had been feeling quite self-confident: my favourite black top, tight white trousers (not that Mark was going to see them, but I always felt better if I was wearing them, and I was sure that would show in my face) and my favourite black boots (ditto, see above). But now I was starting to feel a bit wobbly. Perhaps it was imagining the expression of triumph on Maggie's face if she'd seen me walk into her party dressed uniquely, and unflatteringly, in pink.

As if it wasn't horrible enough that her party was also definitely and certainly going to have karaoke (**'Sing your ♥ out!'**); the prospect of noisy public humiliation was already sick-making enough.

'Right,' I said quietly. 'Glamorous, eh? OK. I will think about that...' Because right then and there we'd arrived at the bus stop near the Andersons' house, so I was going to have to get my happy face on ready for my Skype with Mark.

I walked up the path with Sally lagging behind.

Patricia opened the door and smiled at us. She

looking her usual elegant self; a long grey cashmere cardigan seemed to set off her grey hair (memo to self when old: grey can look really cool) and her huge hoop earrings bounced around in a way that made her look slightly less grown-up and scary.

'Hello, Chloe; hello, Sally,' she said. 'Come on in. Sally, come and help me get some tea, and Chloe, go into the sitting room. The Skype's all set up for you there.'

As Sally turned right, I turned left and went into the big sitting room at the back of the house that looked out over the garden. It was quite dark and full of books, just the same as I remembered from last time. Except now there was someone standing by the armchair in the window.

He was tall and slim and dressed in jeans and a black V-neck jersey. His hair dangled over his forehead and his adorable dimple was at its most pronounced.

'Mark!' I almost shouted in happiness and astonishment. 'It's you!' (Truly my mother's daughter at that moment.) 'I can't believe it... Aren't you skiing in the Alps?'

'No,' he said, smiling even more. 'Not skiing. I reckoned I could ski another time. I was missing home. Hey, I was missing *you*.' And he came towards me and enveloped me in the most wonderful, woolly, warm hug.

For a few seconds I couldn't say anything, it was just so very lovely to be so close to him. Now that he was actually here in the room, I couldn't believe how much I'd missed him, and everything about him.

He drew back, put his hands on my shoulders, looked down at me and kissed me. Moments later and I know I was looking up at him with my best top-notch goofy smile. But then he seemed to go a bit serious.

'So, Chloe,' he said (for which he was instantly forgiven, of course), 'what's going on with Oscar? Is there anything you want to tell me? I did say look after him, but you never stopped talking about him. And those photos of the two of you…'

'Oh, Mark,' I said. 'I am such an idiot. I only did it to please you. And to make him happy. But I was quite sure that he and Sally were going to fall in love. I was sure that he was just a perfect boyfriend for her, and she was all on her own, and they looked so good together. But then…' I came to a halt. This next bit was so awful to have to tell Mark.

He looked down at me looking very serious now, and frowning a little bit.

'But then what, Chloe?' he said.

'Well, it turned out... It turned out that actually he liked *me*. Not Sally at all,' I said haltingly. 'And it was awful, and I'm very much afraid he's all unhappy. And it was such a misunderstanding. Now I don't know what to do. It's awful,' I said again.

The sight of Oscar limping off into the winter sunset suddenly flashed before me. He had looked so broken and sad, and it HAD been all my fault. And now I was having to confess all this to Mark, who I realised might have thought I'd led Oscar on.

'Yes, Chloe, you're right. It's a bit of a mess,' said Mark, looking me in the eye. 'I'm sure you didn't mean to, but you've managed to upset someone very much. I expect Oscar will bounce back before too long, though. I don't think Sally was ever right for him, but I bet there's someone who is.' He paused. 'And as for me, Chloe, well, for a moment there I really thought you might have changed your mind about me. You were always mentioning Oscar, and you never seemed to say much about missing me.'

'Oh, Mark,' I said, hardly able to breathe because I so wanted to say the right thing. 'It was never like that. I've missed you so, so much. But I didn't want to say it too much because you were having a nice time, and I didn't want you to think I was boring or clingy.'

'I've never thought you either of those things, you fully paid-up dingbat,' said Mark. At last there was a tiny trace of the beloved dimple again. 'But that's why I had to come back. I had to be with you and see for myself.'

'And what,' I said, still having trouble breathing, 'do you think now you've seen for yourself?'

'I think,' said Mark slowly, starting to smile properly, 'I think we can make things better. Come here.' And he put his arms round me and gave me an extra specially wonderful hug.

'Come on, you two,' Patricia's voice came from the hall. 'Time to say hello and goodbye to that dog of yours.'

Mark and I came out of the sitting room. He had his arm round me – wonderful feeling – and we went into the kitchen.

Patricia, Sally and Gabriel were all hovering over the corner of the kitchen with Puppies One to Two and Albert.

Sitting at the kitchen table was one of the most beautiful girls I had ever seen not on a cinema screen.

Blonde, exceptionally well cheekboned, and wearing a white off-the-shoulder jersey that showed off her tan, she truly looked like a supermodel.

'Hello, Chloe,' she said in a slight accent. 'It's nice to meet you. I'm Celine.'

I stood stock still in the doorway, almost entirely unable to speak to Mark's French 'exchange', who looked so very much more glamorous even than in the one photo I'd seen of her.

'Hello,' I said. 'I'm Chloe.' (Brilliant. She knew that already.) 'Nice to meet you.' (Also brilliant. And also untrue.)

'I came over with Mark on the train,' she said. 'But I've got to go in a minute. Meeting my parents in London. Such a shame I have to rush. It would have been nice to get to know you. I have heard a lot about you.'

Lots of things about this were better outcomes than I could have hoped. She was going! Any minute now! She'd heard a lot about me! Plus, she also seemed quite nice.

Still. I was very glad she had to rush off to London. But I tried not to show it too much. 'Oh, I'm sorry about that,' I said. 'Maybe next time…' I couldn't really finish that sentence. Maybe next time – what?

'Come on, Chloe,' said Mark. 'Come and make a fuss of Albert. It's your last chance to talk to him before he emigrates to Cornwall.'

'Yes,' said Sally, giving Albert a tentative pat. 'Next time you see him he'll be talking in Cornish.'

I buried my nose in Albert fur. It smelt of dog and felt prickly and familiar. Which, after the turbulence of the last hour, was incredibly comforting.

After Celine had gone, it was time for Sally and me to disappear too. Mark had to go with his parents to see his grandmother, who apparently wasn't very well, and I had to get back home. I had promised Mum that we would watch her favourite programme together. Although I wasn't remotely interested in how well various people could stitch together a leather jacket, or cut out a kilt, or adjust the hem on a tutu...it was my job to pretend I was.

And a very tough job it was too...after nearly an hour, I found I had made Mum three cups of tea. Anything to get away from the near hysteria of watching three people stitch up the hem of a corset.

'Thanks, love,' said Mum for the third time. 'But really I think that's enough tea. They'll be testing for blood in my tea-stream at the hospital at this rate.'

It was a sweet joke. If only it hadn't reminded me of

her treatments coming up that week...

'Don't look so worried, love,' said Mum. 'They're really quite pleased with me at the hospital. I've just got to get on with it all. But they say it's doing the job, so I'm just grateful for that.'

I tried to make myself less worried, and then found that I actually *was* less worried.

'Now, love,' said Mum as the credits rolled on a picture of a triumphant woman holding up a pair of beautifully stitched Edwardian knickers. 'You should be all happy this half term. What with your lovely Mark being back, Albert in a new happy home, your prize essay being all finished, and a nice party to go to.'

Some of that was true. But I hadn't told Mum that my short story had been disqualified for being too long (I had got rather carried away with the cast of characters and had accidentally written a short novel).

Nor that 'nice' was hardly how I'd describe the prospect of the QB's evening of Valentine's hell.

'Quite right, Mum,' I said. 'Only trouble is that Mark's grandmother is ill, so he may not be able to come with me to that "nice" party. He may have to stay with her for an extra day.'

That's the downside of being kind to old people, I thought.

14

Party Time

All too soon it was Tuesday February 14th and the social media ether was awash with all those ghastly messages and toe-curlingly kitsch gifts that single people – and some coupley people – hate.

Mark was still a hundred miles away with his ill grandmother. Apparently, she was now much better, so I did feel it was time for Mark to stop being kind to an old person and start being kind to a young person who desperately needed him. Not that I said that in so many words, of course.

I was going to meet Sally, Rob, Amy and Charlie at Gemma's. Where I knew we would also find the beautiful surfing Jack, fresh from yet another visit to his beloved aunt. (All these boys being nice to old people…) If Mark was still by his grandmother's sickbed, then at least there would be safety in numbers. I could just hide behind all the others. And no one would notice I was on my own. Would they?

It took all morning to decide on the choice of outfits I was going to take to Gemma's. (Obviously what to wear was too big a decision to take on my own, but even I realised it wasn't reasonable to take my entire wardrobe.) Eventually I'd whittled it down to a dress (black, short), two pairs of trousers and six different tops. All in every possible shade of every possible colour. Except pink.

Squashing everything into my bag, I headed to the kitchen to make sure Mum was all right. James had offered to drive us all home after the party, so I needed to say goodnight – just in case I didn't leave the party after half an hour (my emergency position if things got too lonely and humiliating).

Mum and Ralph and Gran were sitting round the kitchen table. Mum had filled in nearly half of her Sudoku puzzle (good, maybe she really was feeling a bit better). Ghastly Ralph had his 'Keep Calm and Love Football' mug in front of him (good. Because the mug was a present from Mum, and he was drinking tea not extra strong lager). And Gran was frowning in concentration as she sewed the hem of a tiny old-fashioned skirt (also good, because no one had to look at the china doll that went with it).

'Bye then,' I said much more cheerily than I felt. 'May see you in an hour if it's all as horrible as I think it might be.'

Mum looked up. 'It'll be fine, love,' she said in that way that mothers have of looking on the bright side. 'I expect you'll be late, so I'll say goodnight and see you in the morning.'

'That's right,' said Ralph. 'Have a nice time.' He didn't look up as he said this, but it was still a surprisingly positive instruction from the ghastly one. Perhaps he was just happy at having his £150 back.

'Don't do anything I'd do, young lady,' said Gran, still focused on her tiny sewing. I decided that on the whole she meant well too, despite the hilarious (not) joke and calling me by my least favourite name (apart from 'missy').

I walked down the stairs past Albert's flat. The main door was open and I could see people putting things into boxes and moving furniture around. One of the men looked up as I passed.

'Afternoon,' he said with quite a nice smile.

Encouraged by the smile, I said, 'Afternoon. Is Mr Underwood moving out then?'

'Oh, yes,' said the man. 'Gone already. Gone to

work in a prison apparently. Some sort of warder. Got a flat that goes with the job, they say.'

Ah HA, I thought to myself. So Sally was half right. Mr U *was* going to prison. But only to work there, and I supposed prison warders aren't allowed dogs.

Then I thought that perhaps Sally might be wholly right, and the warder thing was just to cover up the fact that he'd been convicted of triple murder or something.

And then I thought, It's all right. He's gone, and Albert's safe, and those are the only things that matter.

Two hours later, and I realised that they definitely weren't the only things that mattered. Everyone else had arrived at Gemma's not only with a boyfriend but also already dressed up and looking brilliant. Sally was in a bright green top that was just right for her. As I looked at her sitting on the leather sofa with her crutch on one side and Rob on the other I did have to admit that she looked very happy.

Rob had tied some heart-shaped tinsel round the handle of her crutch. Which I actually thought was one of the most singly sweet Valentine's Day gestures I'd ever heard of.

Almost on a par with the mutual goofiness of our friends Amy and Charlie sitting on a small stool in front of them. There were plenty of chairs dotted around the room; it was entirely unnecessary for them to share a small stool, but apparently you can't ever get close enough to the one you love...

Meanwhile, in the kitchen Gemma and Jack were getting many tins and bottles of dangerously sugary drinks out of the enormous fridge.

As I watched them out-cooling each other as they draped themselves over the bar stools (of course Merv had bar stools) I thought what a perfect match they made. They would probably never tire of admiring each other, and would live happily ever after with their four ridiculously beautiful children.

But I was getting ahead of myself. I headed off to one of the master bedrooms, where I eventually decided on The Outfit: favourite tight white trousers, and a slightly off-the-shoulder (well, it *was* a good look...) black top.

Finally, we were all ready. The karaoke bar where the Event to be Dreaded Beyond All Others was happening was only ten minutes' walk away. I felt almost as sick as I had done at the school dance two years before – nervous, alone, and with a sure sense that somewhere along the line I would be publicly humiliated, just as I had been at that dance. Only this time I had no friends to suffer with. This time they were all happily paired up with the boys of their dreams.

I gave a huge sigh as we set off for the karaoke bar.

Twenty minutes later (walking can be quite slow if your heels are way too high and some of you have to stop to adjust your crutch) we arrived at the entrance.

There was a bouncer on the door holding a clipboard with a list of names.

For a horrible moment I felt sick again. How easy it would be for the QB to simply not put my name on the list. There I'd be, all dressed up with nowhere to go – my friends being allowed in and me bounced out into the street.

But before I could cry with pity at this image of myself, the bouncer was nodding at all our names, and we were all allowed to go in.

The first thing we saw was the horrible, horrible karaoke bar all ready, like an instrument of torture, to humiliate anyone who held its microphone. (I know not everyone feels like this about karaoke. But I think you have to be with good friends and/or be on a high – whether it be of an artificial or natural nature – to enjoy such a thing.)

And then right in front of us was a line of cohorts. All Maggie's favourite ghastly hangers-on. And all looking super made-up with extra-long nails and shiny hair that had clearly come straight out from under the smartest blow dryers.

'Hey, Chloe,' said one of the tallest, nastiest, shiniest cohorts. 'Where were you this afternoon? We were all at the spa. Wasn't it great of Maggie to treat us? What a great party!'

The other cohorts crowded round. All waving their extra-long nails, flicking back their shiny hair and smiling false smiles under their three inches of foundation and two shades of lip gloss.

Ugh. But fortunately at that moment I became surrounded by my lovely friends. All so nice, and so real; it made me think again how the un-nice and the unreal simply don't matter.

But moments later I felt miserable again. How I longed for Mark. Everyone had gone straight into dancing, and even though I knew they were sort of looking after me, Amy and Sally and Gemma were obviously dying to join in. Then suddenly, in a blur of action, each must have thought the other was staying with me, and I was standing on my own in the corner of the dance floor completely and utterly wishing I were anywhere in the world but there.

I set off towards the place where they were serving drinks. I pushed past people as if I had a purpose and was getting something for someone else. But then when I had a glass in my hand, what should I do next? No one to talk to now, everyone was 'throwing shapes' on the dance floor or snuggling up to a boy or a girl depending on which one they weren't.

Everywhere I looked people were having a great time, or looking as if they were having a great time. I wanted to run for the door. And I started to think about which bus would be the quickest to get me home, or whether it might be faster to take a train.

'Why, if it isn't Chloe, the winner of the English prize. Not,' came a voice from behind me. The QB herself. She was wearing the shortest skirt, the heaviest eyeliner, the brightest lip gloss, the thickest foundation I had ever seen in my life. She also looked so maliciously pleased with herself it made me feel ill all over again.

'Thank you for coming to my party,' she said with a hideous sly smile. 'Got a special treat for you. You're going to start the karaoke. I thought you could do a duet thing with your boyfriend.' Then she made a point of looking around. 'You *did* remember to bring a boyfriend didn't you, Chloe? It *is* a Valentine's party after all.'

I couldn't think of a thing to say. Nothing at all. The only crumb of comfort I could think of was that since everything was so noisy, not many people could hear what she was saying. But then I heard some titters from behind me. I looked round and saw four more of the cohorts, and I realised I was wrong about that too.

'Come on then, Chloe,' the Queen Beeyatch was saying. 'Over here. Come on, come on. We can find something you can do just on your own.'

And she started to fiddle with the karaoke equipment.

'Hey, what's going on?' It was my BFF. She'd abandoned her tinselly crutch and had just emerged from the throng of people on the dance floor. She ignored the QB, and said to me, 'Guess who I've just seen come in through the door.'

Maggie was pulling on my sleeve now with one hand and grabbing a microphone with the other.

'Come on, Chloe,' she said in a steely, bossy voice.

'Come on, Chloe what?' came a voice behind me. I looked round. Never, never in the history of handsome boys has any boy looked so indescribably beautiful as Mark did at that moment. He was dressed in the same jeans and black V-neck that he had been wearing in all my fantasies and dreams in the last two days. He looked kind and brave and strong.

And at that moment quite angry as he turned to Maggie. 'Hey, Maggie,' he said. 'It may be your party, but not everyone wants to make a fool of themselves with a microphone.'

He turned to me and put his arm round me, 'Come on, Chloe,' he said. 'Let's make a move.'

He looked at Maggie, now standing stock still with the microphone still in her hand looking absolutely furious. 'Thanks for the invite, Maggie,' said Mark. 'See you around.'

And with that he gathered me up, with Sally and Rob following closely behind. Then we saw Charlie and Amy whirling round in front of us. Mark grabbed Charlie's arm. 'Come on,' he said, 'Georgie's having a party at the club round the corner. Better music there. Better company.'

As Amy went and scooped up Gemma and Jack, I turned to Mark and put my arms round him. I buried my head in his V-necked jumper. I didn't want anyone, not even Mark, to see how close I was to tears. Only now they were tears of relief and happiness.

Georgie's party was, as I rather thought it would be, a very different affair from the Dreaded Maggie's. It was on the top floor of a wine bar that had a private members' club on the roof. The chimneys of the original building poked through between the tables and chairs, and were a part of the bar at one end of the room.

As we all walked in, the DJ was playing one of the few pieces of music that make me want to take to the dance floor. It seemed to have the same effect on everyone else. Because soon we were all out there spending energy as if our lives depended on it.

I looked at Gemma and Jack – beautiful, moving beautifully, as you'd expect – and Sally and Rob – Sally moving a little less beautifully as she tried not to hop on her toe – looking very happy. And Amy and Charlie, always happy – Valentine's Days are made for Amys and Charlies.

And then I saw someone not so happy. A very morose Donald was leaning against the wall in the corner, nursing some dark drink. In between throwing myself about, I watched him look up. And I could see what he was seeing. There was Georgie, looking absolutely amazing and already like a famous TV star, dancing her heart out with her arms round a very handsome boy who looked just like Tom Hiddleston.

I looked at Georgie looking at Oscar, and then at him looking at her. They were gazing deep into each other's eyes and smiling. Of course! What a fool I am, I thought. But how great that Oscar saw the light so quickly. What a brilliant happy ending.

I looked up at Mark smiling down at me. 'Hey,' I said, looking over at Georgie and Oscar. 'How great is that?'

'It's pretty great,' he said as he leant down. 'Pretty great, but not quite as great as us. Nothing is as great as us.' And he kissed me.

And as I kissed him back, I thought, Yes, this is actually as great as it gets.

Acknowledgements

I am lucky to have the wise and wonderful Caroline Sheldon as my agent and friend. My thanks for all her help; she is both a rock and a star.

I am also lucky to be published by a company as utterly tremendous as Orchard Books. And I owe a particular debt of gratitude to my editor there, Anna Solemani, whose enthusiastic professionalism and editorial subtlety are without equal.

As ever, I am hugely and wholly indebted to all my lovely friends for their encouragement and support. Whether they are lending me their garrets to write in, their daughters to interview, or just plain entertaining me, they are the *sine qua non* of this writer's life.

About the author

Chloe Bennet is the pen name of Val Hudson, a former publisher and editor who has been responsible for a number of famous bestsellers over the years. Now a full-time writer, she has developed a great affection for Chloe, and has loved being her for her three *Boywatching* books.

Luna has a secret.
She is different
but no one must find out.

PBK: 978 1 40833 425 6
EBOOK: 978 1 40833 426 3

EBOOK: 978 1 40834294 7